TOWARDS YESTERDAY

JAMES KING

Towards Yesterday

© James King

Cover design: James & Pat King

First Edition published 2011

Published by:
Palores Publications,
11a Penryn Street, Redruth, Kernow, TR15 2SP, UK.

Designed & Printed by:
The St Ives Printing & Publishing Company,
High Street, St Ives, Cornwall TR26 1RS, UK.

ISBN 978-1-906845-22-3

TOWARDS YESTERDAY

JAMES KING

Britain circa AD 50

ON A LARGE SLAB of granite a young Roman soldier lay on his back, tightly held down by four men dressed in rough brown cloaks, their faces hidden from him by cowls. The young man still wore the uniform he had been wearing when he had been discovered, but, whereas then it had been shining and polished, now it was smeared with mud and excrement from the cowshed where he had been held prisoner during the night. The muscles of his limbs bulged as he strained to escape from the iron grip with which he was held, but there were too many of them, and even though he was strong and well used to fighting against many odds, their combined strength and determination were too much for him. After a while he became still, suddenly seized by a grip of fear so icy that all his body seemed to freeze solid and he became incapable of movement.

The sun hung low in the east casting long, deep shadows from the ring of roughly hewn grey stones and the tall trees that surrounded them so that most of the glade was still quite dark. Except for the marks caused by the men who had marched over it dragging the prisoners with them, the grass smoothly glistened with dew, bright with the promise of life and the wonder of another new day. The stones that surrounded the men in a huge circle had been standing there for longer than the memory of the tribe; some said from the dawn of time itself, built by the gods of old for reasons long forgotten. However, even though the origins of these stones were now lost in the mists surrounding their history, whoever had put them there must have been beings of awesome power and knowledge, for even now anyone who had any awareness of the secret powers of creation could feel and resonate to the strange forces which surrounded these ancient rocks. These days their use was reserved for special times of celebration, ceremonies of initiation and offerings to Gods. On rare occasions they were used for punishment on those who had committed the most grievous crimes.

Today was one of those rare and terrible days.

To one side of the slab a young girl was kneeling, sobbing, her face streaked with dirt and blood and tears, her head pulled back by two brown-robed priests so that she was forced to look up at the young soldier. Suddenly she cried out, "No!" as a tall hook-nosed priest walked slowly towards them carrying the ceremonial sword. He reached the slab, stopped and turned to look first at the Roman soldier and then at the girl. His face completely impassive, he showed no sign at all of the terrible thing he was about to do.

The girl shuddered and moaned, "No, father, no," but she knew what he had to do. She knew also that there was no escape for any of them from the horror that was about to happen. He looked at the girl, his eyes without any pity, his face as hard as the sacred pillars which surrounded them.

"You were warned," he said, "We told you what would happen if you continued with this liaison, with this," he hesitated, "this treachery." He shook his head and, staring directly into the girl's eyes, he lifted the long knife and plunged it into the soldier's stomach. It was a cruel, calculated blow designed to cause pain more than to kill. The boy screamed once, and his body arched in agony as the priest withdrew the knife. The girl knew what was coming next. She cried out in terror, struggling fiercely as the men holding her picked her up and dropped her face down on top of the young soldier. As she lay on him she raised her head and looked down at his face, now twisted in agony. It was a face she felt she had known forever, a face she had loved before the Gods had created the world, a face she would love till the end of eternity.

And she wept for his suffering, for her fear of the inevitable. Most of all, she wept for what could have been, the happiness that might have been theirs, but never would be, in this life.

His eyes opened slowly and looked past her as if he were blind, or perhaps staring at the billowing clouds, dark in the shadow of the sleepy dawning sun. Then, as if he were just waking from a terrible dream, his eyes focused on her. As he suddenly recognised her, the lines of pain in his face smoothed away, his eyes shone with his love for her and he smiled. And with his smile she felt her fear and her sadness drain away.

Very briefly, their lips met for the last time, and they sank deeply into a sweet, tender kiss. So soft, so deep was it that they hardly heard the cry of despair and fury that roared out of the priest as he struck once more.

The sword pierced both their hearts almost simultaneously.

Chapter One
Cornwall – 1990

DAVID HENDERSON WOKE EARLIER than he had expected to, driven up amid the sound of raindrops falling onto the roof of his cottage. It seemed to him that he had spent the night in the depths of a bottomless black pit, and now, as if gently pushed by an unseen force he was emerging from darkness into light, from nothing into something.

"Bloody hell," he muttered. "What the . . . ?" He opened his eyes and then immediately closed them. He felt strongly that there was an event that he should remember, a happening that had had great importance for him. A feeling also came to him that it had been the source of a terror he could not face, pain he could not bear. He tried to recall it, to understand what it was he had been experiencing, but nothing substantial appeared, only a faint trace of the echo of an evil shout of triumph.

He lay for some time on his back, not moving, trying to reassemble the scattered parts of his consciousness. The fear that had been his first waking experience for as long as he could remember stretched down from his shoulders to his buttocks and tingled along the backs of his legs. Normally his response to it would be to leap up through it, out of the bed, and into whatever the day was to bring, pushing it down, squashing it in a frenzy of nervous activity.

Until now he had never really even consciously acknowledged its existence, so much had it become a part of himself, his everyday life. Today, however, without knowing why, he found himself lying on his back with his eyes closed, inspecting the feeling.

Nervous tension had been so much a part of his life as a musician that he took it for granted, perhaps even welcomed it, for it gave him an edge, energised his performance and kept his mind concentrated on the job in hand, stopped him playing the cracks instead of the keys. For some people at work a mistake can be ignored or glossed over. A wrongly typed word can be changed without any repercussions, but when there is an excitable, demanding singer depending on a perfect accompaniment and there is an audience not famed for its generosity towards apparent incompetence, mistakes, even when they very rarely happen, are not received well at all.

He lay in the warmth of the bed listening to the branches of the hawthorn tree outside the bedroom window randomly swishing in the cold westerly wind that had been blowing fiercely for two days now. He curled sensuously into a ball, savouring the delicious contrast between the cosiness of his bed and the potential discomfort that awaited him on the other side of his front door. He was puzzled, for there appeared to be no reason at all for the dreadful feeling that seemed to surround him. He owed no money to anybody. There were no potentially demanding gigs on his immediate horizon. In fact, when he thought carefully about his life, he had no reason to be concerned about anything at all; he should have expected to be totally at ease. And yet he wasn't.

Charlie, a small, brown mongrel bitch, lay on the bed on the side which his wife, Tina, used to occupy until her death a little over two and a half years ago. The dog stirred, grunted as if slightly irritated at being woken and turned to look back at David over her shoulder.

"Okay, Charlie, you can go back to sleep. Sorry I woke you." He reached over and gently stroked her.

Her head dropped back heavily onto the bed and she started almost immediately to snore quietly.

David smiled at the dog, closed his eyes and returned to the darkness and his fear. He tried again to analyse the feeling, but again failed to understand what was at the root of it. He rolled over away from Charlie, but the darkness had the same emptiness on that side too.

Suddenly he had the impression in his mind of someone gently smiling at him.

God, what on earth was that?

He quickly turned over again onto his back and listened once more to the rain beating its irregular rhythm on the roof.

There was of course Beth.

But what the hell had she got to do with it?

He grimaced as the memory returned. He'd failed again last night. They'd been out together on a gig, which, as usual, had gone well. With her voice, a mixture of Barbara Streisand and Karen Carpenter, and his exciting yet sensitive playing, they couldn't help but be an overwhelming success wherever they went.

Afterwards they'd gone back to her house, on the cliffs overlooking the sea just outside St. Agnes, for a nightcap and to wind down. They'd kissed good night. This had happened more and more lately, the kisses had been lingering longer, more reluctant to end. He had an increasingly strong impression that she wanted him to go further, but each time he had found himself overcome by fear. No, that was an understatement. He had been terrified, for God's sake! He'd mumbled a nervous 'good night' and had run out into the damp night air.

On the way home, shouting curses into the darkness, he had driven faster than he should along the narrow, misty Cornish lanes, swerving dangerously to avoid the odd badger digging for worms on the roadside. At his cottage he'd let Charlie out and had stood motionless in the garden, shivering in the cold night air, trying to work out what was happening to him. The dog frantically ran about as if searching for something in the bushes, squatted down, looking at David as if to make sure he wasn't going to leave her before she had finished, and then excitedly continued her search.

The fear of sex had been a problem to him since his first real girl friend when he was sixteen. He had met her in the local park. She'd been feeding bread to some ducks and he'd made a silly joke that made her laugh. They'd talked and found they both liked the Beatles. That night he took her to the pictures and a week later they went dancing in a crowded, very noisy club in the centre of town. On the way home they passed through the park where they had first met and lay on the grass shuddering with excited anticipation. It was his first real sexual encounter. He found he delighted in the velvet smooth texture of her body, but when finally she said, "Alright, go on. But be careful, mind," he was suddenly so overcome by fear that he found himself unable to continue. She sat up and spat at him spitefully, "What's the matter? Aren't I good enough for you?" And when, in his embarrassed confusion, he wasn't able to answer, she stood up and shouted, "You're bloody useless. Call yourself a man! You must be queer!" She had flounced away waving her panties and shouting, "Bloody useless! What a ponce!"

David had remained on the ground, shrivelling.

He never saw her again.

But now, he was forty. He'd been a married man, for God's sake! It shouldn't still be happening, surely?

When he was seventeen he finally lost his virginity to a girl he'd known since he was six. He'd been terrified again and that plus his inexperience had made him clumsy and of course very quick, so he wasn't surprised when she said to him quite brazenly, "Was that your first time, then?" He'd shamefacedly admitted that it had been, but all she had done was smile and say, "Wow! I've had my first virgin!" She'd looked quite proud of the fact, too.

He hadn't seen her ever again, either.

This morning he lay for a long time trying hard to relax using techniques that Beth had taught him. Breathing deeply he first of all tensed up and then relaxed each muscle, starting with his toes and slowly working his way up to his head. As he did this he concentrated his attention on a spot just in front of the space between his eyebrows. To begin with all he could see was an impenetrable darkness, but as he gradually became more at ease, pictures started to appear before his eyes, as if someone had switched on a television set in the darkness. Faces, scenes, shapes in perfect clarity and brilliant colours came rapidly one after the other and disappeared into the blackness. He had experienced them for as long as he could remember, back into his childhood, but even so, they had never ceased to amaze him, the more so when he found out that none of his friends ever saw anything with their eyes closed. Except, that is, for Beth. It was one of the things that had helped to build a bond between them.

Of course there had been the music. They both enjoyed the same composers and performers, had the same approach to musical arrangements, but the secret of their successful partnership lay in something much deeper. They had only been together as a team for just over a year, so the bond between them was not the result of a long period of intimate growth. It had started to develop strongly almost immediately they had met.

A year and a bit ago, ten months after his wife's death, David had been at a loose end. The summer season was over. The mid-week gigs in the county had dried up and he was on the point of packing up and going back into the international circuit, when he'd gone to a party at a café in St. Agnes. It was his watering hole, and he frequented it practically every day, a neat, clean little place, serving the best food in the district. The owners were two gays, former entertainers and every year at the end of the summer season they would give a party for their friends and regular customers. Two years before, David had been there with his wife and thus dreaded returning to it this year alone. However, during the time he had been in Cornwall the friendship between him and the owners of the café, Anthony and Ben, had become something very special, so, not wanting to disappoint them, he had gone to the party.

For weeks leading up to it Anthony had been talking incessantly about his 'little get-together', constantly reminding David about it, insisting that he come. It was only a few moments after his arrival that David had had the distinct impression that he had been 'set up'.

He had arrived rather late so the room was already crowded and noisy with voices and music, but immediately he had opened the door and hesitantly walked in Anthony had pushed his way through the crowd, calling to him, "Dear boy! Welcome! Take off your coat and come with me. There's someone I want you to meet." Taking his arm Anthony had led him over to a rather large, mother earth figure, dressed in a bright, loose, colourful ankle-length dress. Her arms were covered in bangles and a heavy Celtic cross hung on a gold chain between ample breasts. Her hair was long and dark and tightly curled. David found himself looking down into a pair of brilliant brown eyes shining with laughter and energy.

"This is Beth, dear boy. She sings like an angel, and she's looking for someone to play with, Beth-David."

They had all laughed as the two of them had shaken hands. Anthony had immediately turned away leaving them looking at each other's blushing face.

"Oh, and by the way. She's got the gift," Anthony called out to them in a casual way as he disappeared into the crowd.

David looked at her. "The gift?"

"I'm psychic. Like he is."

She had a smooth, deep musical voice, and although she was definitely not the type of woman he would have normally looked at twice, David felt himself attracted to her. He then experienced a tingling down his spine.

"So you are," he said.

"I don't understand." She smiled and gently shook her head.

"Whenever I meet a psychic I get a wonderful tingling down my spine. It never fails."

"So you're psychic too." It wasn't a question.

"I wouldn't go as far as to say that. I've experienced psychic phenomena, off and on, all my life, but it's been too irregular for me to call myself a psychic."

"Well, you are, whether you like it or not." Her gaze was cool and very direct. She seemed to look right into him.

It was only then he realised that they were still holding hands. David hurriedly took his hand away from hers and, embarrassed, they both laughed.

There followed a few awkward moments until he said, "You're a medium, as well, aren't you?" he asked, unconsciously running a hand through his thick, black hair.

"Mmm." She absentmindedly nodded her head, and continued looking directly up at his thin, dark face, as if searching for an answer to an unspoken question.

At that moment, as they were looking at each other, wondering awkwardly what to say next, Anthony returned.

"Dear boy, you haven't got a drink. Come with me and I'll fix you up." He firmly took David's arm and began to steer him away. David turned to Beth to excuse himself, but saw by the amused expression on her face that there was no need to say anything, so he shrugged and allowed Anthony to drag him away to the bar. As they pushed through the crowd Anthony shouted to him over his shoulder, "Well, what do you think?"

"What about?"

"Don't be coy! Beth, of course."

They reached the bar.

"Interesting. There's something there. I don't know what yet, but there's something."

"Good. I'm glad you felt it. It means you're coming on fine."

Anthony handed him a large fruit juice. "You two are going to do a lot for each other."

He smiled as David screwed up his face and said, "No way. She's not my type."

"Oh yes, she is. You just haven't realised it yet."

He didn't see much of her at all for the rest of the evening, but all the next day he found his thoughts returning to her again and again. At six o'clock he'd just fed Charlie her evening meal when the phone rang.

It was Beth.

"Hello, Beth here. I hope you don't mind my calling you, but Anthony gave me your number. He said you wouldn't get too angry."

He felt the delightful tingling moving again down his spine. *I think I'll be having words with Anthony.*

"Oh, that's okay, Beth. I'm glad you rang. What can I do for you?"

She waited for a moment as if embarrassed and then said, "I've been hearing great things about the way you play." She spoke matter-of-factly, and David had the impression that no flattery was intended.

"That's good to know," he said. "From anyone in particular?"

"No. Just generally, you know. Everybody says so."

David remained silent and turned to watch Charlie eat her meal.

"Well," she hesitated, he heard her take a deep breath. "I've been looking for someone to work with, someone who doesn't just play notes, someone who knows what the spaces in between them mean as well."

"You mean, a musician," David said drily.

"Yeah. That's it, I guess." She laughed.

"And you want for us to have a get together to see if we can make music?"

"Yes." Emphatically.

He hesitated, torn between his inherent desire for independence and an increasing desire to get to know more about this intriguing woman. "Well, I normally work on my own these days. Not that I hate working with other musos, it's just that the money's better on my own. You understand?"

She laughed. "Sure, I understand, but when they hear how much better we are together, you'll be able to ask for more. Right?"

David hesitated. He'd never worked with a girl before. Sure, he'd accompanied many in cabaret, but this would be different.

"Well, I don't know," he said doubtfully, "musicians working together get to know each other more closely than most married people do. And look what problems they have! That's one of the main reasons that so many groups break up."

"I know you think it could be difficult, but it won't be. You'll see. I swear to you, you'll never ever regret it." She spoke very softly and David again felt the feeling run down his back.

"Is that a prediction?" he asked smiling.

"I just know it will be right," she answered with conviction.

"Okay," he said finally, "we'll give it a shot. Come round here tomorrow afternoon and you can sing me some songs. Will three o' clock suit you?"

"That'll be just fine. I'll have just about woken up by then," she answered smiling.

And now, as he lay on his bed watching the pictures dance before his eyes, he thought of how he had felt the first time she had sung for him, and how his delight at her voice had transferred itself to his fingers so that he had started to play with an even greater degree of excitement and delicate sensitivity than he normally did. The session had lasted until late in the evening, when, finally, they had both looked at each other and smiled, they had known without saying anything that what they had together was something very special.

Downstairs, in the small, untidy living room, the telephone rang demanding his attention. Hurriedly and with a growing excitement, for he had the feeling of who it would be, he rushed down the creaky old stairs, followed at a much slower rate by a sleepy, irate Charlie.

He was right. It was Beth.

"Hi, David. How are you feeling?"

"Hi, Beth. Okay, you know."

"The hell you are."

She chuckled, a low, friendly, I-know-exactly-how-shitty-you-really-feel-type-chuckle.

David said nothing.

"Look, I thought we could have a lovely walk along Perranporth beach. Charlie can stretch her legs and we can have a nice talk about this and that."

He looked out of the dining room window at the garden sodden with water. "It's raining," he said, disappointed, for the thought of a walk along the beach with Beth had immediately filled him with a surge of delight.

"I know it is. I've heard the rain banging on my roof for most of the night, but I can see down the coast from my window. In about twenty minutes it'll have stopped raining and the sun will come out. It's gorgeous already down St. Ives."

David felt himself, again, becoming excited. "Okay, then. Give me half an hour and I'll pick you up."

She hesitated for a moment, "Three-quarters."

"Okay."

Chapter Two

THERE WAS A BUSTLE of activity on the beach, even though it was only late March. A cold sou'westerly was blowing so briskly that it tossed the white horses on the waves into a jittery froth. At least a dozen dogs raced in a dozen directions eagerly searching for something to do, for the tide had washed away from the sand all the smells worth sniffing. Their owners hurried after them, vainly calling, but the sounds of their names were lost in the power of the wind. Four or five joggers joylessly bobbed their tedious way along the edge of the water, hopping away now and again as an over-ambitious wave threatened to swamp their trainers. About a dozen or so heads rode the waves waiting for that special wave that would carry the lucky ones on a ten second trip into the land of surfing bliss.

"Ever tried that, Beth?" David nodded in the direction of the surfers.

"Never felt the urge. And you?"

David shook his head. "No, thank you." He looked at the sea. "The last time I went into a pool of water that big the temperature in it was 85°. In the Caribbean. As far as the sea here is concerned I'd only go in there if I were seriously looking for a lethal dose of hypothermia."

They walked on in silence for a while enjoying the sight of the vast length of slightly off-golden sand that stretched away for three miles to Ligger Point.

As Beth had promised, the rain clouds had moved on and were, by now, damping down the uplands of Bodmin Moor. The sky was blue but any heat delivered by the miserly sun was lost in the breeze.

They walked briskly, both to get warm and to keep up with Charlie, who had dashed ahead to try to persuade a handsome retriever that she was going to play an important part in his life.

"I've been getting a bit concerned about you, David." Beth was being her usual direct self.

"Oh? Why's that?" David felt a sinking sensation in his abdomen.

"You've not been yourself lately."

"In what way?"

"Oh, you've been withdrawn, and your playing has been a bit erratic."

David's head quickly turned towards her.

"Erratic?" He frowned defensively.

"Oh it's nothing bad, you know. The punters won't have clocked anything, but I have. I know that there's something bothering you."

"I don't know what you're talking about. Erratic! I'm playing exactly how I always play. I'm not erratic!"

"Okay! Sorry I spoke. You're not erratic. You're perfect!"

David began to feel the anger rising within him.

"No, I'm bloody well not perfect. I never have been."

He stopped and glared at her. "What's all this about?"

"Look, I'm not attacking your musical abilities. I'm just saying that there's something not right. It's nothing to do with the music, but the music is suffering because of it."

Beth looked down at her feet and then took hold of his arm. "You must have felt it. You can't feel as bad as you so obviously have been feeling without knowing it!"

David pulled his arm away from her and turned to look out to sea, where a few would-be surfers were heroically attempting to swim away from the shore into the foaming waves.

After watching them for a few moments he sighed heavily and then shrugged his shoulders. Turning back to Beth he admitted reluctantly, "Well. It could be that I've not been sleeping well lately."

"Do you know why?"

He shook his head. "No idea."

"Have you had any bad dreams?"

"No, I can't remember a thing when I wake. But first thing in the morning I feel as though I've been on the rack, my body hurts so."

"Maybe you have," she whispered.

"What was that?" David asked, screwing up his face.

She shook her head. "Nothing. It's not important," she muttered.

They started to walk on again.

"Does it last?" Beth asked, frowning in thought.

"What, the pain? No. It only lasts a moment or two. But the fear goes on for a long time."

"Is this a new thing?"

"The fear? No, I've had fear as long as I can remember, but, you know, you just feel it and carry on with your life. At least, that's what I've always done. But the bad feeling on waking is quite new, and it's getting stronger."

"What kind of a bad feeling? What have you got to feel bad about?"

"I feel as though something really terrible has happened during the night, something that makes me feel quite guilty. And it's a feeling that there's some really serious pain involved with it somewhere. That, plus the fear, makes for a really unpleasant start to the day sometimes, I can tell you."

They watched as Charlie tried to entice the retriever by running in circles around him. The retriever, however, was not impressed and ignoring her ran back to his master. Charlie, completely unabashed by her failure to win him, decided that perhaps a small Jack Russell, happily playing ball with its mistress, would be a source of greater entertainment, and ran to join it.

"Listen," said Beth. "My psychic antennae have been probing around for a while now about this."

As he heard her, David, without knowing why, immediately felt awkward. Without thinking of the consequences he attempted to cover up his embarrassment by saying, "And have you picked up anything from the great broadcasting station in the astral belt?"

Beth smiled and shook her head. "You know, sometimes you're a bit of an arse-hole about this sort of thing."

"What do you mean?" David said, "I was only joking."

"The point is, this isn't a joke. It's bloody serious. I'm trying my best to help you and all you can do is act the fool."

She stopped and turned away from him to hide the tears that had sprung to her eyes.

The empty feeling that tugged at his stomach made David realise how thoughtless he had been. "Oh, I'm sorry Beth," he said putting his hand on her shoulder. "I really am."

They were silent and David acknowledged to himself, as he had several times before, the confusion he felt about psychic matters. It was a confusion he didn't quite understand, for he had, on many occasions during his life, personally experienced clairvoyance and clairaudience, so he knew that he was a psychic. And yet he still had a level of doubt in him, which caused him to feel awkward when confronted with talk about psychic awareness. He smiled as he remembered awakening one morning to find a tall figure standing by his bed. Later, looking back on the event, he was surprised not to have been frightened, but instead of fear he had found himself basking in a warm, totally peaceful glow. He had been lying on his front with his face turned towards the figure and had immediately thought, "If I close my eyes and then open them maybe he will have disappeared."

So he did just that, but the vision, still and peaceful, had remained standing there as he re-opened his eyes. The feeling of being utterly safe and secure was still with him. Again he shut his eyes and opened them. Still the figure stayed there, but now it was bending over as if to inspect him more closely. Again he closed his eyes and opened them. Whatever it was towered above him, about six feet tall, in an orange gown with a hood over what would have been its head. David had tried to make out a face but all he could see was a dark shadow where the face should have been.

Again he closed his eyes, but this time when he reopened them the figure was no longer there. The feeling of peace had remained with him for a minute or two and then faded.

He'd asked Anthony if he had any ideas about it.

"He was just checking on you," he'd said with an annoying, enigmatic smile.

"What do you mean, 'checking'," David exploded in frustration. "Who the hell's 'he'? And why was he dressed in that orange gown?"

"I don't know who he was. That's up to you to find out." Anthony was infuriating sometimes the way he by-passed questions. "And as for the orange gown, you provided that."

"I did?! How? Why?"

"Because you couldn't have accepted him as he really was. That's why." And with that Anthony had laughed and hurried back into the kitchen leaving David none the wiser and completely bemused as he sipped his coffee.

A cold gust of wind brought David's mind back to the beach at Perranporth. Beth was still facing away from him, her hair blowing freely in the wind, her usual long dress swept back against his legs. He took her elbow and gently turned her round to face him.

"Look, I'm deadly serious now, and I'm sorry I played the fool. What is it you were going to say?"

She sighed and wiped her face with the back of her hands.

Hesitantly, as if she expected him to ridicule her, she said, "I was going to say that I have the strong impression that you've got something on the way out."

"What do you mean, 'something on the way out'? The way out of where?" David was starting to sound irritated so Beth put her arm around his waist and gently squeezed him.

"Something happened in your past," she said. "Something you've buried away and didn't want to look at is trying to make its way up into your awareness."

David scratched his head, "But nothing bad's happened to me that I'm aware of," he said, frowning in concentration.

"Precisely." She stopped and turned him to face her. She smiled and went on, "'That you're aware of'."

"Oh, come off it," he snorted. "If anything as horrible as what I'm obviously experiencing at night had happened when I was a kid, I'd certainly remember it. Wouldn't I?"

"Not necessarily," she said, and they carried on walking. "If it was bad enough you'd definitely want to keep it hidden from yourself."

Still frowning David kicked at a pebble and stopped, perplexed. "Why the hell would I want to do that?"

"Because part of you doesn't want the terrible experience of going through it all again."

"But my childhood was quite uneventful."

She took his hand and they slowly walked on, followed now by a sadder and wiser Charlie, having uncovered the dark side of the Jack Russell.

"I didn't say it was necessarily to do with this life, David."

He stopped and turned to look at her.

"What do you mean?"

"I mean that whatever it is that is bothering you could be a memory of a nasty experience in another life."

He laughed. "Like, I was Napoleon, or something, and feeling bad about all the wicked things I did to Josephine."

"You're doing it again, David."

"What?"

"Being bloody stupid, David."

"Sorry." He gently squeezed her hand and gave her a rueful smile.

They followed Charlie as she ran over to a pile of rocks and sat in a pool of sea water left by the receding tide.

"The kind of problem I'm thinking of, when it occurs, is usually the result of a traumatic death in some life or other," Beth said. "When the memory of one of those starts to surface then all the difficulties surrounding the event may come into your conscious awareness." She bent down to pick up a piece of wood and threw it for Charlie to chase. "Unfortunately that can include the physical difficulties."

"I don't think I like the sound of that," he said screwing up his face.

"It can be unpleasant, believe me," Beth said in a quiet voice.

David turned his head and stared at her. "Have you had any happen to you?" he asked.

Beth raised her eyebrows and nodded. "I'm afraid so," she said.

She stopped and looked down at the curious patterns in the sand.

"Sorry, I shouldn't have said that. I shouldn't have said, 'I'm afraid so'," she said.

"Why not?"

"Because it implies that what happens when you have a release is a bad thing."

"And isn't it?" he asked.

"Well it may, or may not be."

"Oh, great!" David smiled at her. "Depending on what?"

"On how you look at it. Which means, very often, on whether you know what is happening." Beth sighed, thinking that perhaps she was going into this a bit deeper than she had intended. "You see, what comes out can be very unpleasant indeed. If you don't know what is going on the results can be quite shattering," she explained.

David chuckled. "That's nice to know."

"Fortunately the only people I've met who've undergone a spontaneous release and experienced a past-life memory have been people, like yourself, somewhat psychic and in possession of some knowledge. When it happens to those who know about it they usually welcome it, knowing that they'll be better off with it out."

"Are they better off with it out?"

"Oh, yes, definitely."

She bent down again and pulled the stick from Charlie's mouth. "Does she ever get tired of this game?"

"Never. You have a job for life."

"Oh, to be so simply satisfied and entertained. Last time, Charlie," and she hurled it into the distance.

"Well?"

"Well, what?"

"What happened to you?"

20

"Oh, I've had a lot of them come out." She smiled and then went on, "Once I experienced a time when I was a young woman in a tribe in the far North of America. I'd got myself pregnant, out of wedlock. It was against the rules of that particular society and they threw me out."

"Where did you go?"

"Unfortunately it was winter. I wandered for hours in a raging blizzard. Then I sheltered in a cave and quite expected to die there, but some hunters from another tribe found me and they took me in."

"So, all's well that ends well."

"No, I'm afraid not." She shook her head. "The journey had been too much for me and I died in great pain giving birth to the child. It too died. Far too premature."

"Did you suffer pain when you remembered it?"

"No, not really. The problem for me was the guilt about sex before marriage. That I did feel. That's been a real bummer for me most of my life."

David stopped and looked at her, his mouth wide open.

"What's the matter, David?"

"Nothing."

He turned and called Charlie who was on the point of chasing another object of her desire.

"When you remembered this event, did it make any difference to your guilt?" he asked as he bent down to put the dog on a lead.

"Sure. It went."

"Just like that. No pills, no electric shock treatment, no psychiatrists."

"Yes, just like that."

They turned and started to walk back the way they had come.

"Have you had any others? Have you had any other memories?" David found himself getting quite excited.

"Yes, quite a number, as a matter of fact."

"And did each of them result in you getting rid of a problem of some sort?"

"Almost always."

"Shit! This is amazing."

Beth smiled. "You may think so, but, believe me, it's nothing compared to what is going to come to you."

David again felt the sinking feeling in his stomach.

"What do you mean?" He walked away and turned back towards her. "You're getting me really worried now." He laughed nervously and turned away, not wanting to show just how concerned he was.

Beth reached forward and held his elbow.

"Listen. There's nothing to be afraid of. Even though it may be a little unpleasant, it'll be nothing you can't handle."

When he didn't turn round she put her arms around him and gave him a hug from behind. "Honest. You'll be fine. Besides, you'll get heaps of help."

He turned his head so that his lips were just an inch away from hers.

"From whom?"

"They're all around you, David. So close. And, my God but they're strong. I've felt them ever since I met you."

She gently turned him to face her. "And then, there'll be me. I'll be with you."

"So, I've nothing to fear, eh?"

"Nothing," and she pulled him to her in a tender hug.

But she lied, for she knew, having seen with her 'gift' that what lay before him would test him more thoroughly, more savagely than he could ever have imagined.

*   *   *

That night, he lay in his bed unable to sleep because of the noise of the storm crashing against the trees outside his window. Suddenly a bolt of lightning flashed across the sky filling the room with light, making Charlie shiver with fear. David remembered the magnificent storms he had witnessed in Switzerland and with that memory there came another.

Nineteen years earlier he had left the fast growing chaos that was Beirut and had gone to work the nightclubs and casinos of Northern Italy and Switzerland with an Italian band. The work was hard, the hours long, but he was young and still thirsty for experience and adventure.

One of the biggest problems they always had was the difficulty of finding digs, especially in Milan, where potential landladies seemed to be deeply suspicious of musicians. Whether it was their reputation for loose, loud living, or whether too many promises, and hearts, had been broken, he never did find out. But about a month after their arrival in the region, when it seemed to them that the difficulties were so great that they would have to concentrate solely on the Swiss, it suddenly occurred to all of them that the solution would be to live in Switzerland and commute each night to Milan.

The band had had no problems at all with accommodation in Switzerland and established a base in Melano, a small village nestling between the wooded sides of Monte Generoso and the shores of Lago di Lugano. It was an ideal location, not only beautiful, but just a short drive away from Lugano, Mendrisio and Chiasso on the Italian border. The people in the village were friendly, especially the landlady, as long as the rent was paid on time. From there they were able to commute into Milan and the outlying districts easily and swiftly, either by car or by train.

They had been working the area for a year, when they got a contract to play a club just over the border into Italy. The strange thing was, as far as David was concerned, that this was not the first time that they had commuted nightly to Italy for a month, nor was it their first appearance at this nightclub, where they were welcomed and very well liked. So there didn't appear to be any reason for what happened.

Each night as David approached the customs sheds to cross over the border into Italy he experienced a nervous reaction. At first he thought it was the normal apprehension he felt whenever he was faced with authority and paid no attention to it, for it was only slight. But as the days passed by he found the unease growing bit by bit until it had turned into fear. By the end of the second week he was so terrified as he approached Italy that he seriously considered not going to work. From that point on, however, the fear lessened gradually each night until, by the end of the month's contract he was back to normal.

The other strange occurrence, for which he had no explanation either, happened each night as he returned home to Melano. He found himself experiencing a feeling of relief the nearer he got to the Italian/Swiss border. It was as if he were escaping from something powerfully dreadful and its level seemed to match the intensity of the unease and fear he had felt when he had entered Italy eight long hours before. It too had grown in strength and depth so that, whilst he felt the terror on the journey in, he experienced a most wonderful relief, growing to an almost indescribable bliss, on the way out.

One particular, very special morning, travelling back on the train, at about five o'clock, along the edge of the lake, with the rays of the early morning sun cutting through a slight mist and glowing with ethereal light on the steep sides of the hills, he was filled with a joy that was so great that it appeared to extend beyond the limits of his body. It seemed to him that he swelled with relief and the wonder of life, so that the whole valley shone, not just with the light of the sun, but also with his delight.

At the time he could find no explanation for what he had experienced, and afterwards, perhaps because of the difficulties and insecurities of the life on the move, the memories of what had happened had been driven into the back roads of his mind where they had lain buried until now, brought back into his awareness by the sound of the storm, nineteen years later in Cornwall.

Or could it be that what happened so long ago were part of what Beth had spoken of? Were they to do with this awful memory she said could be on the way out? Did something dreadful happen some time in Italy?

David felt his hands start to perspire and the muscles over his stomach begin to form into a knot.

Why is it that I can remember so easily the fear, and feel it, but it's so damned difficult to experience again that wonderful feeling I had experienced coming back into Switzerland?

He breathed deeply, and with this question lying heavy in his mind, slipped into a troubled sleep.

Chapter Three
Windsor, England

ANNA TAVERNA STOOD AT the top of a broad staircase that swept in an imposing semi-circle down away from her into a richly decorated room full of expensively dressed, well-groomed people. She paused, deliberately, for effect, knowing that most of those present had already ceased their conversations when they had noticed her appearance on the brightly lit landing. Slowly, taking the utmost care not to look down at anyone in particular, she started to walk down the soft, thick carpet that covered the stairs, her beautiful face a mask of disinterested disdain, the product of years on the catwalks of the world of haute couture.

Well, at least the bastard won't be able to complain about this one. This is exactly what he married me for.

No sign of the pain she felt, nor the terrible fear that churned in her stomach showed through the mask she presented to those present. For, all she allowed them to see was the perfect form of the perfect woman, dressed in the perfect dress created by Gucci and bought especially for this evening.

At the foot of the stairs she stopped and turned her head slowly to look in the direction of her husband, so that her shiny sleek hair flowed in a gentle wave over her right shoulder.

"Ah! At last," he cried out, "my God, but you look wonderful!" For a moment she was fooled into thinking that he was truly pleased to see her as he quickly walked towards her, his handsome dark Italian face smiling as if in loving welcome. But as she looked deep into his eyes she could see that, behind the facade, what he was really saying was, "Where the hell have you been? We've been waiting for you, you bitch. Just wait till I get you alone."

He reached her, took her hand in a show of gentle familiarity and there began a long series of introductions that put enormous demands on her self-control and her extensive abilities as a hostess. For, Anna had an ability, one which some would call a gift, others, a curse, to feel, to sense the personality, the essence of the character of anyone with whom she shook hands. She had had it all her life and it had only failed her once, with, for her, tragic consequences. It had failed her when she met Antonio Taverna, the man who was to be her husband. Many times she had crawled into her bed, her body aching from the beating she had received from him, her ears ringing and her head reeling as a result of the verbal attacks she had suffered, and she had wondered why her senses had failed her that fateful day when he first entered her life.

They hadn't failed her tonight as she met the guests. Most of them had had very little effect on her, but with some she had touched a level of evil that had made her feel quite nauseous. These, she realised, had all been, without exception, 'associates' of her husband.

Later, as she sat at her dressing table preparing herself for bed, she stared at the face in the mirror. The flawless beauty remained, but she could see the signs of the strain of the last few years.

There was a time when you were able to laugh, when life was fun and you hadn't yet learned the meaning of real fear.

She wiped away the tears from under her eyes and slowly, ever so carefully peeled the dress away from her shoulders to expose the bruise beneath her ribs where Antonio had punched her. Of course he had waited until everybody had left before he had started screaming incoherently at her, his normally handsome face twisted by ugly hatred. In the end he had lashed out at her with a vicious, controlled blow in her side that flung her on to the bed where she lay in agony as he stood over her and laughed, revelling in the intoxicating feeling of power.

She had met bullies before, but had never had to endure the agonies of the helplessness she felt at the hands of Antonio. At her school in Switzerland there had been several of the nuns who had vented the frustrations that accompanied their calling on the girls, particularly on those who failed to show the respect they demanded for their religion.

Anna had been born into a Catholic family and had received the usual indoctrination from a variety of priests and nuns and schoolteachers. Most of them had found their senses of Christian compassion, tolerance and understanding tested to the limits by her refusal to accept even the basic teachings of the faith. No matter how hard they tried, their efforts were always met with a wall of incomprehension. For Anna it was as if they were speaking in a foreign language that she had never heard before. She just could not even begin to understand the concepts they were trying to hammer into her.

Sister Maria, a small, withered, middle-aged nun became her main tormentor. Taking Anna's failure to agree to her teachings as a personal insult she would beat her without mercy or pity, much as Antonio did now.

When Antonio left her, lying on her bed breathing as shallowly as she could to lessen the pain in her side, there flashed into her mind the memory of her lying on the floor in the school hall, also floating in a sea of pain. Sister Maria was standing over her shouting an incoherent babble about Jesus loving the world so much that he died for all her sins.

Anna had looked up at the ugly face of hatred and managed to gasp out, "What sins? There's no such thing as sin. Don't you know?"

Faced with such a level of blasphemy she had never met before, Sister Maria lost her self-control yet again and started to kick out at Anna, whilst screaming, "You devil! You wicked, sinful, evil devil! You'll suffer hell and damnation for all eternity!"

It was only the timely arrival of several other nuns, who, with difficulty managed to drag Sister Maria away, that saved Anna from serious damage.

Later that day, lying on the hardness of her bed, she had wondered just what it was that made certain individuals, like Sister Maria, lose all control and lash out at those they were supposed to support and help. She had had cause to ponder on this question many times throughout the long, painful days she spent at this school, but no answer had come to her.

Now, years later, the answer came to her in a flash of inspiration. *They hate themselves, that's why.* With that thought she managed, at last, to see Sister Maria as the poor sick, frightened woman that she had been.

But Antonio was not the same. Although she could see how much he hated himself, in no way could she think of him with the same understanding as she had done with that poor unfortunate nun.

Maria was a victim herself of her position, her upbringing, her indoctrination, her fear.

And so is he.

But he enjoys it!

Lying on the bed Anna felt herself drifting into unconsciousness, but before she fell into the darkness a terrible foreboding sprang into her mind.

I've got to get away, away from this maniac before he kills me. He will do, one day, I know.

That night she had the dream again. It was a dream she had had many times in her life, always during a time of crisis. As ever it left her feeling weak, helpless and overcome with a profound grief, as if she had lost the most precious thing she had ever known in her life.

In it she found herself in a meadow surrounded by tall, dark trees. She was being held down and then felt herself lifted onto a man's body. She looked into his beautiful face and felt a mixture of sadness and regret, which was then pushed aside by an overwhelming surge of love. He was obviously in pain but nevertheless smiled at her. They kissed, briefly, lovingly, without passion, but with the greatest tenderness. It was at this point that Anna always awoke, but just before she opened her eyes she could see in vivid detail a scene that seemed now very familiar to her. A young girl was lying on top of a man on a huge slab of granite. They were encircled by a ring of men dressed in dark robes. One of the men stood apart from the rest. His head hung down and in his right hand he held a large sword. They were all still, as if frozen in the horror of the moment.

Anna opened her eyes and felt the warm tears flowing down her cheeks and on to her neck. There was a pain in her side and the memory of the previous evening rushed into her head.

Slowly she eased herself out of the bed, showered, carefully sat before her mirror and applied her make-up. Then she dressed in a sweat shirt and jeans and went downstairs into the kitchen. Gerhard, one of her husband's 'associates', stood by the toaster. He was dressed in torn jeans and a vest designed to show off his heavily muscled, sunburned torso. His eyes were insolent, joyless and mean.

"Is my husband around?" Anna asked.

Gerhard's head moved very slightly. His mouth twisted in an ugly sneer.

"By that do you mean he's not in?" Anna felt herself becoming exasperated.

"He has gone to London, on business." Gerhard's English was good, but still thickly coated with a German accent. It made him seem so much more insolent, more menacing than the other members of staff.

28

"Have you finished here? I'd like to get some breakfast." Her anger and despair made her sound more positive than she felt.

Gerhard stared so hard at her, with such malevolence that she was forced to look away. Without saying another word he took his toast, slowly buttered it and walked out of the kitchen.

Christ, I can't stand any more of this atmosphere. I've got to get away!

Frantically she rushed through into the living room, breathed a sigh of relief when she found that none of her husband's men were in there, and hastily dialled her friend Sylvia.

Like all Anna's friends Sylvia had at first been delighted when Anna married Antonio. He was handsome, highly educated, well connected and apparently very rich and the couple were obviously deeply in love. Only later as she slowly got to know Antonio a little better did doubts come into Sylvia's mind about him. There were hints, stories, nothing substantial, but put together with what she noticed about him – such as expressions on his face when his guard was down, the change in the tone of his voice when, one day, visiting Anna, she overheard him, by accident, talking on the phone – all these things and more had made her become more and more concerned about him and the effect he was having on her friend Anna. Over the past three years she had seen the change that marriage to Antonio had brought about in Anna.

At one time she and Anna had been like very close sisters. Each knew the other's most intimate secrets. It was a closeness that had grown over the years they had spent together at school in Switzerland, and later, even though they had gone into different professions, Sylvia into journalism and Anna into modelling, they had always managed to keep in close touch. However, after Anna's marriage Sylvia slowly became aware of a subtle change in her friend. She noticed how Anna, normally exuberant and spontaneously joyful, outgoing and gregarious, became gradually more and more withdrawn, sad and unusually quiet.

"Sylvia! Anna here. How are you?" There was no hint in her voice of the despair and fear she was feeling.

"Darling! Fine! Just being chased around by the most hideous monsters in the sick Principality of Hackdom. You know how it is. Each thinks he's God's gift to the world of journalism and womankind. How are you? When can we meet? How are things at home?"

"Fine. I just wondered if I could take you up on that offer you made of the cottage in Cornwall? I'm feeling the need to get away from it all for a few days."

"Sure. Be my guest. I gave you a set of keys last time we met, didn't I?"

"Yes, you did."

"I'll let David know you're coming. He'll open up things for you."

"David?"

"Yeh, David. David Henderson. He lives opposite. Keeps an eye on the place for me. You'll like him. A great guy, tall, dark-haired, slim, quite good-looking, musician, travelled a lot. You'll have a lot in common, I know. Oh and by the way, remember I told you the keys I gave you don't include the garage key. You'll have to get it from him."

"Okay, thanks. But, if anyone wants to know where I am, don't say anything, will you?" She tried to sound nonchalant, but Sylvia felt her concern.

"Don't worry. I've no idea where you are."

Chapter Four
Cornwall

DAVID WAS STANDING BY the dining room window looking out at the daffodils in his flower beds when he caught a glimpse of an Audi saloon sweeping very positively into the drive of the cottage opposite. It was just about time for Charlie's afternoon walk so he called her, put on her lead and went out of the front door to see what he could see.

A woman was walking away from the car carrying a small suitcase. As she saw him she stopped and called out, "Hello, I've booked the cottage. I believe you have the garage keys for this place." She was extremely beautiful, tall, slim, expensively groomed, elegantly dressed and, seemingly, very self-assured. Later on he realised that he must have been standing for at least a full ten seconds just staring at her as if in a trance, before realising that she was still waiting for an answer. He blushed, for, as he suddenly became aware of the fact that she was waiting, he also realised that she was smiling, perhaps confident of the effect she was having on him.

"Hello. Er, yes, that's right," he called out. "Sylvia called me to let me know you were coming." He realised how flustered he was and went on a bit hesitantly, "I'm just taking the dog for a short walk. You can have them when I get back. Okay?"

At first she hesitated and frowned for a fraction of a second, as if she were wanting to insist on getting the key immediately, but after a moment she smiled, tilted her head to one side and called back, "Yes, sure, okay, when you get back," and walked into the house.

David was intrigued. Smitten by her beauty, a bit overwhelmed by the air of wealth that surrounded her, he found himself curiously disturbed by her. He quickly turned away and walked up the hill. Charlie, knowing the route, was already half way across the heath on the way to the beach by the time he reached the top of the lane. There had been times on this walk when he had been disturbed by the memories of the loss of his wife which would rise up, dark, like the storm clouds in the west, driving him to rush headlong into the rituals of doggie games on the beach, throwing stones, chasing seagulls, running till he was exhausted. However, since Beth had come into his life, he had changed and had taken to strolling more calmly along the stony path through the tough gorse, dodging the many puddles, content to let time drift past smoothly like the wisps of mist which often drifted in from the sea.

Today, he found himself once more driven by a nervous energy, an excited curiosity, in which was mingled a dark shaft of guilt. Hurrying along the path after Charlie he thought about the new arrival in the cottage opposite, wondering what an obviously sophisticated, wealthy person could be doing on her own in this part of Cornwall. Sylvia hadn't explained much. As usual she'd been in a frantic rush, had just said that her friend was coming to stay and would he open up the cottage? For some reason he'd thought that she'd meant a man friend and was surprised by his reaction to the sudden appearance of a woman of such beauty and presence.

He reached the end of the track where the gorse bushes gave way to a steep scree which led down onto the beach. There was a faint haze in the air, thrown up from the sea crashing against the dark rocks. Carefully, but swiftly, he followed Charlie down. At the bottom his feet sank immediately into the softness of the sand and he stopped and looked out at the beach. It was about fifty yards wide and on each side cliffs rose abruptly up, dark and wet, to a height of about three hundred feet. On his left, slightly away from the base of the cliff, like an afterthought, a large rock stood alone, pounded by the waves. Before him the sand was still solid with water left by the receding tide. There was just one other figure standing, alone, at the water's edge, watching his own dog splashing in the sea obviously looking for a stick or perhaps a stone that had been thrown in for it.

David found himself a soft place to sit on, shielded by a large rock from the keen south westerly that whipped across the surface of the sea, whilst Charlie amused herself chasing gulls and lying in rock pools to cool her hot stomach.

Momentarily David's thoughts dwelt on the new arrival, and then suddenly he became conscious of the faint feeling of guilt that had accompanied him across the heath.

What the hell is all that about? I distinctly remember feeling great this morning. Got the call from Sylvia. Did the cottage in time for the woman's arrival.

Then it came to him. The feeling had only come to him after the start of the walk when thinking about the woman.

Surely it wasn't her that had caused the guilt? I've only just met her!

His thoughts were interrupted by a loud bark. Charlie had brought him a piece of driftwood to play with so, leaving his thoughts about the guilt, he spent a few moments playing with the dog before his curiosity about the new arrival got the better of him and he decided to return home. Calling Charlie away from a particularly disgusting pile of seaweed, the smell of which had deflected her from chasing the driftwood, he scrambled up the scree more quickly than normal and crossed the heath.

Back at the cottage he had just put Charlie's dinner down for her when the doorbell rang. Charlie looked at him, uttered a half-hearted woof, and carried on swallowing her food as fast as she could. When he opened the front door, the woman was standing there, beautiful, poised, completely self-controlled. All his working life David had been used to dealing with beautiful women, so he was surprised, when he felt his face grow suddenly hot, at the effect this woman was having on him.

"Sorry to trouble you," she said, "I saw you come back, and I thought it wise to lock the car away as soon as possible."

"There's no problem." David was trying very hard to appear as normal as possible, "but you really shouldn't worry yourself. This is Cornwall, you know. You could leave it there for a month and no-one would bother with it."

"I really would like the keys." Her face had a determined set to it, but as she spoke, in spite of her apparently totally controlled exterior, he suddenly sensed that underneath she wasn't half as calm as she wanted to appear.

"Okay, come in." he stepped back and as she walked past him engulfing him in a cloud of very expensive perfume, he said, "But brace yourself. In about forty seconds you're going to get attacked and licked to death."

She stopped and turned, alarmed, unsure of what she'd walked into.

"Oh, I'm sorry," he said, quickly realising, as her eyes widened and her mouth dropped slightly open, that his silly joke had frightened her, "I didn't mean to scare you, I was just trying to warn you about Charlie, my dog. She's . . ."

At that moment Charlie burst in, a living whirlwind. She had waited as long as she could, her hunger overcoming her enormous desire to see who had invaded her territory, but finally, her curiosity had overcome her greed. David was lucky. He managed to get to the dog and grab her collar before she did irreparable damage to some very expensive clothing.

"Sorry about that," he said, as with difficulty he held Charlie away from her. "She's not dangerous, just excited at meeting someone new." He smiled to cover up how awkward he felt but, as she said nothing and just stood there, expressionless, he went on, "By the way, I'm David Henderson."

"Anna Taverna."

They shook hands a little awkwardly and also with a little difficulty as he was still struggling to keep Charlie from stripping her face of a few pounds worth of expertly applied make-up.

Firmly holding the dog, he looked up into her green eyes, smiling slightly now at his discomfort. "Taverna," he said, "is that Italian?"

"My husband is Italian but I'm English." She hesitated, and then, feeling that a little more explanation was called for, added, "He will be joining me in a few days." She told what she knew was a lie without any sign of embarrassment or of the fear that swelled up in her at her mention of her husband.

There was an awkward pause during which, in spite of her totally calm exterior, he again felt her unease, so he reached over Charlie, took the keys to her garage off a hook on the wall behind the door and handed them to her.

"Here you are. You'll find the garage lock sticks a bit. You just have to wiggle it." He realised immediately how inane he must have sounded and to his horror he again felt his face becoming very, uncomfortably hot. As she took the keys David expected some response, a 'thank you', at least, but instead she looked at him strangely, as if searching for an answer to something, a tiny frown almost creasing her flawless forehead. Then she turned, walked to the front door and opened it. For a moment it seemed to him that she would just walk out without saying anything further so he called after her, "Well, I hope you have a very pleasant holiday, and anything you need, just give me a call."

She turned towards him and said, "Thank you," but she was still frowning as she walked away from his door, down the steps on to the road and across to her cottage.

David let Charlie go and they both walked through to the kitchen. He cursed silently, and then out loud to Charlie, "What a supercilious, pompous, arrogant bitch!" Charlie hung her tongue out of the side of her mouth and tentatively wagged her tail.

"Christ! Who does she think she is?" Noisily he moved about the kitchen preparing his evening meal. His anger surprised him for normally he thought of himself as quite a placid, uncomplaining type of person. In fact, one of his late wife's main complaints was that he was so hard to rouse to anger. He stood for a few moments and then more calmly went on, "People like that don't come for holidays down here. Other coast, perhaps." He stood, silent for a moment, moved into the kitchen and reached into a cupboard for a plate. "No, there's something not quite right here. This is the wrong place for the likes of her. And what's all that nonsense about her car? Why the hurry to lock it away?" He lifted the lid off a large pan of cold chicken stew, spooned out a generous portion onto the plate and put it into the microwave. Four minutes later as the bell of the oven rang, he turned to Charlie and, quickly shaking his head said again, "No, definitely no. I bet she hasn't even got a pair of wellies." Charlie quickly padded round him as he moved to the table with a now steaming plate of chicken stew. Patiently she waited at his side and watched, uncomprehending as David drew up his chair and stared at the empty television screen, lost in deep thought. He was suddenly perplexed. Anna had had a profound effect on him. As a musical director he had worked with countless beautiful women without ever being returned into the bumbling awkwardness of adolescence that he had experienced this afternoon. So she was beautiful, so what? However, it wasn't the effect of her beauty that caused his confusion. It was the realisation that he was attracted to this woman. Oh, of course he was attracted to Beth, but in a completely different way. Going to Beth was like coming home after a long day's hard toil, sinking into a soft, warm bath and being surrounded by love and light, joy and gentle music.

But here he was, attracted to Anna, and yet he couldn't for the life of him understand why. He had always been wary of the extremely rich. They somehow frightened him. So many of them seemed to possess an innate arrogance. The way they appeared to him to exude a sense of their own superiority caused him to feel both anger and fear. However, this woman affected him in other ways too. The attraction he felt was akin to the feelings that arose when he thought of the good times he'd had in some of the beautiful, bright, colourful places of the world he had visited in his life. She brought out in him a yearning for something he couldn't quite put his finger on, as if it were something he had lost and desperately wanted to find again.

He was attracted to her, and yet it had suddenly hit him that he didn't like her!

There were two distinct levels of himself in conflict!

As usual it was Charlie who brought him back to reality. She had patiently waited, as she always did, knowing that at the end of his meal he always saved some titbit for her. Tired of waiting she brought him out of his trance with a gentle push with her nose against his leg. David looked down at her, smiled, patted her head and hungrily ate his stew, still turning over in his mind the inconsistencies of his feelings.

Later he took Charlie for her usual last trot around the garden. Across the road the Audi was gone. The cottage was in darkness, still wrapped in the gloomy, lonely, cold shroud of the holiday cottage out of season, as if no one had moved in at all.

* * *

In the bedroom of the cottage Anna lay on the unmade bed. Even though she had soaked herself in a scented hot bath and was dressed in a full-length dressing gown and wrapped in a thick blanket she was shivering, not so much with cold, for the night had not yet lost all the warmth of the first glorious sunny day of the Spring, but with a fear that gripped her more strongly than she had ever experienced before. She could feel all the muscles of her body tightening as her terror grew in intensity until finally she could stand it no longer and let out a piercing shriek. With it came a certain relief and she curled up into a ball and sobbed for a long time until mercifully she drifted off into a deep sleep.

An hour or so later she, very gradually, started to come out of her dream. With her eyes still closed and her mind only partly aware of the bed pressing up against her side, she lingered, looking back at the scene she had just left. Glorious bands of light from an early dawning sun were bursting through the trees illuminating the bodies of the girl and the soldier. Around them stood a circle of dark, hooded men, silent in their shame, their heads bowed.

Anna awoke with a start. She had had the dream again, and even though she had lost count of the number of times she had experienced the horror of that dreadful event, the intensity of the tragic sense of loss and futile waste still left her weak and shaking with grief. This time, however, there was a difference. This time she felt the start of a glimmer of understanding of why she had come to Cornwall, a feeling of familiarity with the soldier and the girl, that soon she would know who the young man in her dream was. With that thought came a picture in her mind of David Henderson when she first met him. There had been an instant recognition, a comfortable feeling of familiarity, a certain appreciation of the fact that she knew this man, had known him for a very long time. With this realisation came a certain relief. She felt herself slowly relax as the tension in her oozed away and very quickly she fell into a deep, dreamless sleep.

Chapter Five

THE NEXT MORNING DAWNED fresh and shining, one of those Spring mornings which, as if by magic, sweep away all the dark, wet, cold memories of the long, icy, dripping winter. David woke earlier than usual, feeling strangely buoyant and optimistic, as if something he couldn't put his finger on had changed for him. It was as if, during the night, someone had spring-cleaned his brain, pushing a magical duster into the dark corners of his mind. He lay for a while with his eyes closed, looking at the exquisite colours and shapes that rose out of the darkness. Charlie grunted and grumbled as David jumped out of bed and stood at the bedroom window feeling the joy and optimism bursting from the ground with the birth of the first daffodils and felt as if he were somehow joining in with them and starting anew. Quickly he ran downstairs to the bathroom, got himself ready for the day, fed Charlie and hastily ate his own cereal. He hadn't been into St. Agnes for a long time, but as he had some shopping to do and a letter to post off to his agent, he decided to walk the two miles into the village. The air was crisp and clean as he walked out into the garden, his sudden appearance driving away a crowd of sparrows, greenfinches and blackbirds, noisy in their warnings. Charlie, her nose full of the metallic smell of a scavenging fox, rushed, barking her challenge, up the rise of the garden to the gap in the hedge through which her enemy had slunk away in the night. Calling the dog to heel David set off on the walk, past the cottage opposite, which still had the deserted joyless look of the holiday cottage out-of-season, and down the hill towards the stream which crossed underneath the lane on its way down to Chapel Porth and the sea. They had been walking for about fifteen minutes when the Audi drew up alongside.

"Would you like a lift?" Anna called out.

*   *   *

That morning she had woken feeling curiously more confident and alive than she had for a long time, delighted by the bright rays of the morning sun streaming through her window. She lay relaxed, basking in the warmth of the bed and revelling in the unaccustomed feeling of safety. True, she still felt a certain level of fear, but the mindless, soul-freezing terror that had driven her to a panic flight down to Cornwall had quite subsided.

"Anna," she said to herself, "what you need is a good hot soak in the bath, then sort out clothes and clean this cottage." She thought of David, "He may or may not be a terrific musician, but he's got a lot to learn about keeping a cottage clean." Slowly she got out of bed and looked across the road at the cottage opposite where David lived. It was a small, white, two bed-roomed Cornish traditional cottage, surrounded by a large well-kept garden filled with budding daffodils. The land rose up away from her towards a small group of cottages and what looked like a farm house where a bulky man was just bending down to look under a tractor. To the left, in a field alongside David Henderson's cottage, a group of bullocks contentedly grazed. After a few moments of drinking in the idyllic country scene she turned and headed downstairs towards the bathroom. In days gone by the Cornish cottage rarely boasted of a luxury like a bathroom and any that had one had had to have it added on, very often downstairs. It was only when she got to the foot of the stairs that she realised that in her hurry to get down to Cornwall the day before she had completely forgotten to buy any groceries. She had been standing to one side of the kitchen window, a little unsure as to what to do next, when she saw David walk down the steps that led from his cottage down to the road. She saw him glance her way, so she waved, but, obviously not seeing her, he walked on down the lane. Quickly, she hurried into the bathroom, splashed and dried her face, ran back upstairs, expertly applied lipstick, put on a denim shirt, thick sweater and jeans, searched for, and found, her handbag and hurried down to the garage. She was out of breath but feeling for the first time for longer than she could remember a certain confidence and zest for life. She quickly backed the car out of the garage.

It was one of those glorious mornings that make living in Cornwall a most magical affair, so when Anna drew alongside him in her car, David felt a certain disappointment at having his walk interrupted. However, he was sufficiently intrigued, and even a little excited by the arrival of his new neighbour, to jump at the opportunity to perhaps find out a little more about her, so, in answer to her offer of a lift, he said, "Wonderful, thank you, but what about the dog? I'd hate to have her mess up your seats." To his surprise she shrugged and with a smile said, "That's okay. They clean easily," and in a voice so quiet that David only just managed to hear, she muttered, "That would be the least of my problems."

Again, as he looked at the smooth clear skin of her face David became aware of her unease, but at the same time, remembering his initial reaction to her the previous day, he was surprised to discover how comfortable he felt to be near her this morning.

"How was it in the cottage last night?" he asked as he helped Charlie into the back. "Not too damp, I hope. If Sylvia had let me know sooner that you were coming I'd have aired it through for you, but she only rang an hour or so before you arrived."

As the car smoothly picked up speed she smiled and said, "Don't worry, I slept like a log." She paused whilst she changed gear, and then continued, "I've got some shopping to do. Which is the nearest town?"

As she drove David felt her relax, as if she gained comfort and some strength from her swift decisive actions. "St.Agnes village is only a couple of miles further on. You'll be able to get all you need there," he said, nervous at the speed she was driving along the narrow road. To the uninitiated the lanes of Cornwall appear safe, there being so little traffic, but so often an empty road can be suddenly and very unexpectedly filled with a massive tractor, or half a ton of errant beef, ambling along totally unaware even of the existence of time.

"At the crossroads along here, just before the Beacon, you turn right and the road leads straight into the village."

"What's the Beacon?" she asked. "Is it a pub?"

"No, it's the hill there right in front of us."

"Why is it called the Beacon?" she asked as she bent forward to look up at it. "It looks to me like an ordinary hill."

"It used to be part of a chain of beacons, stretching right up country. In days gone by they were lit when there was danger of invasion. On a clear day there's a terrific view from the top, up to Perranporth and down to St. Ives, across to Truro and St. Austell." He hesitated, unsure. "If you like, after you've done your shopping we could drive round, park and walk up it."

She stopped at the crossroads, turned and gave him a long, penetrating look. It occurred to her that it would do no harm to have someone who knew the locality on her side, and, besides, she was becoming intrigued by the feeling of familiarity that accompanied this man. So, again to his surprise, she quietly said, "Why not? It could be fun. And it is a glorious day."

Chapter Six

AN HOUR LATER, SHOPPING done, they drove round to the far side of the Beacon, parked in the little parking area and started to walk up the stony pathway that leads up the hill. About half way up there was a bench and as they were both breathing rather heavily they decided to sit down, have a break and admire the view for a while. Before them the coast stretched away down to Godrevy Head and beyond to St Ives. The sea was a shining blue. Above it seagulls swooped and fought and screamed at each other. Below them, at the foot of the gorse-covered hill, lay a patchwork of fields and hedges and black and white cows idly nuzzling the ground. Here and there were scattered some of the remains of Cornwall's industrial heritage, engine houses and the grass-free spoil from mine workings. Everywhere daffodils nodded easily in the gentle breeze.

"Isn't this gorgeous," she said after a few moments of drinking in the view. "It's so peaceful. And there's absolutely no-one else around. I could really believe that we were the only people alive in the world." She sighed, "Do you come here often? If I lived here I'm sure I'd be up here every day."

"You don't come to Cornwall very often, do you?" he asked, smiling.

She turned to him, her perfect eyebrows slightly lifted. "Why do you say that?" she asked, puzzled.

"It's not every day that you'd want to come up here," he said. "I'm afraid we get more than our fair share of bad weather in the winter."

She turned to face him. "Chinese proverb: No such thing as bad weather, only inappropriate clothing."

They both laughed. "Whoever thought that one up has never been here," David said. "I've seen big, strong coast guards knocked flat by the wind along this coast."

"I don't care what you say, it's wonderful. I've travelled quite a bit and this compares well with most of the beauty spots I've seen anywhere in the world." As she said this David realised that she wasn't boasting. For her there was no need to try to impress. Her self-confidence in this respect was genuine.

"You're not an outdoor person then?" she asked, still gazing out along the rugged coastline.

"I'm a musician, not many blokes in my business are," he answered with a wry smile.

"Oh, and what kind of music do you play?" She turned to look at him.

"I'm lucky. I can manage pretty well any kind from rock to jazz to classics. Although I'm a pianist, these days I mainly play synthesizers."

Her eyes inspected his lean, handsome, rather Italian looking face intently as if looking for an answer to a problem she was having difficulty with.

"Who do you play with? Are you with a band?" she asked, turning her head away from him to stare out in the direction of the ruins of the old Wheal Charlotte mine, high above Chapel Porth.

"I'm one half of a duo. I work with a singer, Beth. She's terrific."

She looked at him again and noted the excited look in his eyes as he mentioned the name of his musical partner.

"I bet you're great," she said smiling. "Perhaps one day I'll be able to hear you?"

He realised immediately from the tone of her voice that she was merely being polite, so he just answered a little awkwardly, "Yes. Maybe."

They were silent for a moment as she looked over towards the cliffs on her right.

"What are all those ruins, those chimneys?" She waved her arm in a graceful semi-circle.

"Engine houses," he said.

"What do you mean, engine houses? What engines?" she was frowning, perplexed.

"This whole area, at one time was a centre of mining, mainly for tin and copper. It's been mined for perhaps thousands of years, but these engine houses were, for the most part, built in the nineteenth century." David was starting to warm to his subject. "They were given lovely names, nearly always beginning with 'Wheal'. There's Wheal Charlotte and Wheal Coates. The one just past it, on the edge of the cliff there, is an exception. It's called the Towanroath Engine House, but all along this coast there are Wheals. Wheal Kitty, Wheal Friendly, Wheal Music . . ."

He would have gone on to explain a bit more but he realised that she was no longer listening. The colour had drained from her face, her mouth was open slightly and her eyes were staring past him as if she were looking at something in the distance.

He turned to see if there was anything or anyone that could have caused her to look so vacant. Seeing nothing untoward he lightly touched her shoulder and asked, "Are you alright? Is there anything the matter?" As he touched her he felt her start, her eyes focused on his face and again, as she had done earlier at the crossroads on the way to St. Agnes, she gave him that long penetrating look. Then, shaking her head and turning away she said, "No, sorry, I'm fine. Come on. I'll race you to the top." With that she quickly stood up and strode up the path almost tripping over Charlie, who had been lying patiently at her feet. She was breathing hard, not with the effort of the climb, but from the effect of what she had been staring at. For, once again she had been transported back to the field of her dream, but this time she had been looking at it from above, as if she were a skylark, hovering, and then slowly rising higher. The hook-nosed man who had stabbed the young couple to death was standing at the foot of the slab gazing at the bodies, but now the hardness that had been like a mask on his face had gone, his shoulders were slumped, his face was wet with tears. The other men were slowly walking away, their heads bowed as if in sorrow or shame.

The surprise for Anna had been that this time there had been no fear for her. On the contrary what she had experienced had been a profound sense of peace that what had happened was now over. She hurried ahead lest David see the tears that flowed down her cheeks, tears of relief and joy as she felt herself becoming somehow lighter, and the burden of sadness and guilt was lifted from her.

She arrived at the top before David and to hide the tears from him cried out, "God, that wind is keen. It's brought tears to my eyes." Then, turning so that her back was towards him as he arrived, she closed her eyes tightly and quietly started to sob.

David arrived at the top and, as usual, felt himself relax in the delight of the scenery before him, so that he didn't immediately notice Anna's discomfort. It was only when he turned to her to draw her attention to the coast sweeping majestically away to the right toward Perranporth and Newquay that he saw her standing with her hands covering her face, her shoulders moving slightly as she sobbed.

Not knowing what was happening, he lightly touched her elbow. "Anna, are you okay? What's the matter? Did I . . . ?" He hesitated as she shrugged him off. Taking a handkerchief from her bag and gently dabbing her eyes, she said in a slightly husky voice, "It's alright. I'm okay," and with a decisive movement closing her bag, "I think I'd better go now, back to the cottage." With that she moved rapidly down the slope of the hill followed by a bewildered David and the ever-optimistic Charlie.

On the drive back he was silent, sweating and trying to appear calm as she hurled the car through the narrow lanes. Outside the cottage they sat for a moment in silence, before he turned to her. "Thanks for the lift," he said, "I'm sorry about what happened up there." She just turned, looked hard at him, then silently got out of the car, gathered up her shopping and went indoors.

David stayed in for the rest of the day trying to work on some arrangements for Beth. Normally he found them easy and a joy to do, but today he found his mind constantly wandering away to the events of the morning. He still had no idea what had happened to Anna to upset her so. Going over in detail in his mind everything that had happened brought him to the realisation that it had had nothing at all to do with anything that he had said or done. He also realised something else that took him a little by surprise: the dislike he had felt for her had disappeared. She was so beautiful, but he knew that it wasn't her beauty that was causing him to feel as he did. As a musician he had mixed and worked with singers and dancers of very great beauty, and, since the death of Tina, even though he had had no love interest in his life, he had been completely unmoved by any of them. Except, that is, for Beth. But with Anna it was different. There was something else, something very powerful that he couldn't put his finger on, an attraction that was coming from deep down within him. He sat for a long time trying unsuccessfully to make sense of what had happened, so that it was well past midnight before he was able to call it a day and finally give Charlie her last walk out around the garden. The night sky was clear and bright with countless stars, a sight he never tired of seeing. Normally he would have spent a long time drinking in the beautiful majesty of the sky, but tonight he was tired and he could feel the beginnings of a sharp frost starting to bite his nose and ears, so, calling Charlie back down from the end of the garden, he turned and went back into the warmth and comfort of the cottage. As he reached his front door he looked at the cottage opposite. Just like the night before there were no lights shining in its windows. In the darkness it looked empty, deserted and somehow very lonely.

Chapter Seven

NEXT MORNING HE WAS up bright and early, for him, at around ten thirty. After a quick breakfast he went out for a walk with Charlie up the lane onto the open land that stretched for about half a mile before dipping down sharply to a little bay. It was Charlie's favourite walk as there were always rabbits to be chased and very often other dogs to be sniffed at and if possible to be bullied into believing that she was a force to be reckoned with. David had to be careful, though, and watch her closely for there were still one or two uncapped mine shafts hidden in the gorse. Also in the summer months there was the added danger of disturbing one of the many adders sheltering in the shade of the open-cast mine spoil. At one time the locals used to throw all sorts of unwanted rubbish down the shafts, and he wouldn't have been at all surprised if they had in the past been the last resting-places of one or two undesirables.

Down on the beach David sat in the lee of a large rock. There, sheltered from the keen north easterly he gazed out at the majestic waves which burst with terrifying force onto the sand some twenty yards away. In spite of the awesome splendour of the cliffs towering above him and the magnificent deep roar of the sea he couldn't help but think about Anna, and wonder what had brought her down to Cornwall. "One thing's for sure," he thought, "she's not down here on holiday." He picked up a stone and hurled it along the beach for Charlie to chase. "And she's got problems. Biggies. To do with a bloke. Her husband?" David had always had this ability to read people. It was something he took for granted and would have been surprised to hear that not everybody had the ability.

He watched Charlie as she ran into the sea, dodged a wave and, not finding anything of interest, barked her disappointment and dashed across the sand to play with a plodding Labrador.

Suddenly, David found his thoughts turning to the time his wife had died. He remembered the shock, the disbelief, the denial and finally the realisation that he would never see her again. For month after month the grief had been almost too much to bear, but then, from deep within his anguish there had arisen a furious anger that such a thing could have happened. For a time he used up the energy created by the anger in his work and took every gig offered to him regardless of the type, or the money offered. Today, lying on the beach, looking back at those dreary days, he had the impression of himself rushing, without purpose or direction, like a chicken about to die, squawking its disbelief at the horror that fate had settled on it. And yet, in spite of the way it had seemed to him then, there had been some direction, and he could see how he had been led to a climax of painful, furious resentment at life itself. Then one night, as he was lying in his bed, trying to relax to a recording of the slow movement of Rachmaninov's second piano concerto, he had seen her, Tina, his wife, standing at the foot of his bed, as beautiful and alive as he remembered her. She was laughing and waving her arms in delight. She seemed to speak to him and say, "Look! I'm not sick any more, I'm alive, and happy! Don't be sad for me!"

Her face had shone with joy and love, and David suddenly felt all the pain and anger that had filled his life since her death disappear, melting away with the tears that flowed down his cheeks. The vision only remained for a few moments. When it had gone he had lain staring into the darkness, filled with wonder and joy, and then had fallen into a deep, dreamless sleep.

He was brought back to the present with a start by wet snuffling and sniffing in his ear and a sandy paw scratching at his leg. Charlie had tired of the Labrador, had returned and was demanding attention.

David resignedly stood up. "Okay, Charlie, my girl, let's play for a while, and then it's off to the pub."

He bent down, picked up a stick and threw it hard and high for Charlie to chase, but as he watched it sailing out over the beach he again was surprised to feel a sharp stab of guilt. It only lasted a couple of seconds and then his attention was again focused on the dog and her demands, so he once more forgot it.

For half an hour they played together on the beach. When they had both had enough of the biting wind and the heavy, soggy sand, they walked back up onto the road and called into the Green Man for a cool half pint of best bitter.

"Morning Tom," he said.

"Morning David. The usual?"

"Please, I'm gasping."

"There you are my 'andsome. Drink it nice and slow mind,"

and then after a short pause he went on, "See you've got a visitor opposite. Some posh she is too."

"I should have known. I suppose the whole village knows how many hairs she's got on her chest by now," he exclaimed as he turned and faced the few locals who by now were all looking expectantly at him.

"Nice chest," said Norman in the corner.

"I suppose you've got one o' they spy cameras in her bedroom, Norman," called out Alfred, surprising everyone because he didn't usually have much to say this early in the day.

Norman said nothing. He just gave a knowing wink as he lifted his glass to his thin cracked lips.

"I heard you been out showing her the sights," said Tom.

"I got some sights I'd like to show her," said Norman.

"Dream on, Norman," called out George, his big, round, weathered face creasing into a smile.

"Along with the rest of us," whispered Alfred, but nobody really heard him above the loud hoots of ribald laughter and the drumming of half a dozen pint glasses on the tables and the bar.

David was about to say something to Tom, when his eyes caught the reflection of her in the mirror behind the bar as she walked into the room, elegant and very beautiful. Her coat was loose and he could see the seductive shape of her body under her jeans and T-shirt. The rest of the bar went silent very suddenly.

"I appear to have interrupted something." Anna was smiling as she spoke, totally confident.

"You can interrupt me any time you care to, my dear," called out Norman with an embarrassed laugh. However the rest of the bar remained silent, straining to hear what she had to say next.

She gave Norman a quick, impersonal look and walked over to David, who was standing at the bar with his glass halfway raised to his lips.

"I thought I might find you here," she said to David. "I have a little problem."

Chapter Eight

THE PREVIOUS DAY ANNA had got out of the car feeling totally wrung out. She had just managed to close the door of the cottage behind her before she was again overcome by an uncontrollable fit of sobbing. Exhausted and still crying she lay on the bed and immediately sank into a deep sleep.

When she awoke she felt disorientated, not realising at first where she was. Then there came awareness and astonishment to find that she had slept through the night until well into the following morning. Bleary-eyed and stiff she managed to find her way downstairs to the bathroom, bursting for the loo.

"It may be a bit primitive," she thought, sitting there, "but I love it."

Then shortly afterwards as she lay in the bath allowing the gentle warmth of the water to ease away the stiffness from her muscles, the picture came to her again of the young couple lying in their tragic embrace on the granite slab. But now she was no longer overcome by the terror that used to accompany the vision. All she could feel was sadness at the waste of their young lives. She realised that she was now taking it for granted that the Roman soldier had been David.

"It just feels so right," she whispered to herself, "but I wonder what he'll say when I tell him." She hesitated, "If I tell him."

Slowly she dried herself, applied her make-up, dressed in a t-shirt and jeans and made herself a cup of coffee. She smiled as she savoured the bitterness of the drink. "I bet he'll think I'm bonkers."

She spent the rest of the morning tidying her clothes and dusting round the cottage, loving the bare, stone walls, the homeliness, the feeling of days gone by.

"It's lovely," she announced to no-one in particular, "but God, the place smells damp. What I need is a damned good fire."

When she had arrived at the cottage she had been so tired that she had hardly noticed that there had been a fire burning in the grate, and yesterday she hadn't had the time or the inclination to do anything about it. She looked at the sad, cold, dead ashes in the grate, poked at them and wondered what to do, for never in her life had she had to light a fire. At the side of the grate on the hearth, was a pile of logs and matches and even some newspaper, but she realised to her shame that she had no idea how to even start to put them all together to make a fire.

She sighed and put on her coat. "Just hope he's in a good mood," she said as she crossed the road to David's cottage. The echo of her knocking sounded hollow and, after a few moments, when no-one came to the door, Anna remembered David saying in passing that he sometimes went to the pub at the top of the lane when he and Charlie had had their walk. So, savouring the beauty of the Cornish hedges, which sheltered her from the cold north easterly, the sound of the birds chattering in the bushes and the mild warmth of the early Spring sun on her head, she walked up the steep lane. At the top she shivered as the cold wind caught her. Turning to her right she looked across the yellow gorse to where the sea glistened and the gulls screamed out their hunger. Opposite her stood the pub, where, she thought, David would by now be surrounded by his friends. She was surprised to discover how nervous she had suddenly become and hesitated for some time. Then, breathing deeply, her poise regained, she opened the door and coolly walked in. "Just like the cat-walk," she thought, pleased with herself for her control. She was aware immediately of the raucous laughter dying down, and felt the stares of the men in the pub, curious, lustful, slightly antagonistic. In front of her stood David at the bar, his glass lifted almost to his lips. Quietly and very calmly she walked over to him, her smooth, perfect curves raising blood pressure to dangerous levels in the bar, and explained her predicament to him.

She spoke quietly, hoping that the others in the bar wouldn't hear her shameful secret.

"I hate to have to admit this," she almost whispered, "but the fire's gone out, and I'm afraid I've absolutely no idea how to light it again."

She realised that she was stooping over the bar and standing with her head very close to David's.

She straightened and laughed nervously, for there was perfect silence in the bar.

"And I'm spitting feathers," she added more loudly.

"What'll you have? First visit, it's on the house." It was Tom trying to appear cool and unaffected.

"Thank you," she said, surprised. She paused and then astonished everybody with, "I'll have a pint of bitter, please."

To a man the whole bar fell in love.

* * *

Later as David walked with her back down the hill he said, "That was a good move in there, the pint of bitter. What do you normally drink, champagne?"

She stopped for a moment, looked at him and then walked on with a slight smile on her lips. "That's a lovely dog you have. What breed is she?" she asked.

David laughed and said, "I've no idea. She was given to me by a farmer down the road. He said her father was a pack of foxhounds. She may be lovely but I tell you this, if you were brown and furry and a few inches smaller than she is she'd have you for breakfast. Things of beauty are not always what they seem to be, are they?"

She turned her head quickly towards him. For an instant her eyes again had the look of fear that he had noticed when they first met. Then she looked away. He saw her take a deep breath and relax her shoulders.

"Would you mind?" she said. "Just come in and light me a fire. It's very damp and a bit smelly."

"Sorry about that. There's not much can be done until someone comes and lives in it permanently, but I'll be delighted to come in and light your fire." He turned and looked away as he realised he was blushing at what he had said, so that he missed entirely the smile that lit up her face.

Once inside the cottage he was able to cover his embarrassment as he busied himself with the newspaper and wood in the hearth.

"I'll put the kettle on," Anna said. "Tea or coffee?" and then, to his surprise, turning to the sink she said, "I'm starving. Care to join me? It won't be anything exciting, just some eggs, cheese and salad."

David grinned and said, "Sure, that would suit me fine. Can I do anything to help?"

"Thanks, but no. You just finish that fire and let me get on with it."

David soon had the fire started, washed his hands and sat at the small table, at first a little awkwardly, but then began to watch with delight as this beautiful elegant figure moved with unexpected confidence around the kitchen.

"You can talk to the kitchen staff, if you want," she said turning to him with a smile. "We're not proud."

"I'm sorry," David said quietly, "It's been a long time since I've been in a situation like this." He hesitated and then gently

53

laughed, embarrassed. "The only woman I've had any close contact with since my wife died has been Beth, the girl I work with."

Anna turned back to the worktop. "Beth," she said as if she were trying to remember something. "Have you mentioned her before?"

"I think I did. Yes, I did, up on the Beacon, but you wouldn't remember. When I did speak of her you had started to . . ." David hesitated wondering how to put it, "act a little strangely." He laughed nervously.

"Ah, yes." Rapidly she gathered together onto the worktop the food for lunch. "I'm so sorry. That messed up the whole visit up there."

"It doesn't matter. We can go again whenever you want." He looked at her and sensed her deep unease. Quickly he asked, "Did you enjoy what you did see up there?"

"It was really wonderful, thank you. I definitely will go up there again one day."

She had been quickly chopping lettuce, but as she finished speaking she turned to him. "I'm sorry about your wife. It must be devastating when that happens."

"Yes. It was," he said, "but life goes on, and I've just recently realised I'm almost over it. Oh, don't get me wrong. I've not forgotten her or lost any of the feelings I had for her. I think I've just stopped feeling sorry for myself, that's all. Just this morning for the first time for a long time I felt it was terrific just to be in existence." David laughed and looked up at Anna who was standing with her back to the window, her face in shadow so that a few moments passed before he saw the tear on her cheek.

"I'm sorry. I didn't mean to upset you. Here's me going on about how wonderful I feel and from what happened up on the Beacon you've obviously got a load of trouble yourself."

Anna turned away and looked out of the window. "I don't really know how to put this," she said, and then to his utter astonishment she asked, "Do you think we've lived before?"

Taken completely by surprise by the unexpected question David had no idea how to answer.

"What do you mean?" He stammered out. "I'm sorry I don't understand. What are you talking about?"

She turned to him, the kitchen knife loosely held in her hand. Her eyes were closed. "I'm sorry. I made a mistake. I shouldn't have asked you that. It was stupid of me." She sighed and turned back to the window. "I suppose you think I'm a real idiot."

"No," he exclaimed, "not at all. You just took me by surprise that's all. It's not every day that someone asks you a question like that. If you're talking about reincarnation, well, as a matter of fact the idea of it appeals to me very much. Is that what you were talking about?" When she nodded her head he went on, "My problem is that I just haven't thought about it very much, or rather, I hadn't thought about it very much until Beth . . ." She didn't say anything further so he went on, "You just said that it must be devastating when something like losing your wife happens. Well, it's true. It is. More than I hope you ever have to experience. It's something that affects you in many, many ways on many, many levels. And one of the ways is that it gives you what a friend of mine, whom I hope you'll meet very soon, calls a 'spiritual kick up the arse-part'."

She looked at him over her shoulder, laughed and turned back to the chopping board.

"Yes, I think I would enjoy meeting your friend, but I'm sorry, I didn't mean to upset you by dragging up unpleasant memories."

"No, as I said before, I'm over the worst of it now, but when it happened it turned my life upside down. I got that kick up the arse-part and it forced me to think about things I hadn't bothered with for years. You know - life, the universe and everything. So I started to read about it, about reincarnation, that is."

"I didn't know there was anything written about it."

"Oh yes, there is. There's an enormous amount of research about it, some of it very serious and academic, too."

"And do the professors come to any conclusions?"

David laughed. "Of course they don't. Nothing definite, that is. You wouldn't expect them to would you?"

"Why not? Either it exists or it doesn't."

"Yes, but the problem is that there's no way any of them could accept any of the evidence they've found as proof."

"Why not?"

"Just think about it. What would you be able to accept as proof?"

Anna stood quite still, her knife part-way through a tomato and gazed out through the window. After a few moments she continued slicing and quietly breathed, "Yes, I see what you mean. There's nothing, is there? I mean in an academic, or a scientific sense."

She rapidly finished cutting another tomato and then slammed the knife down on the bench.

"It's so bloody infuriating. When you know, when you've had it happen. When you've felt it happen, so real it's as real as today, this moment."

"Right. It all boils down to personal experience."

"Have you had any?"

"Not like some of the cases I've read about, and Beth has told me about some of her experiences."

He paused and watched as she carefully put two eggs into a pan of boiling water. "However, I've been to lots of countries, for instance, Egypt and Italy and Israel, where the first time I went was like coming home. I felt as if I really belonged there."

"I know what you mean," she said excitedly as she sliced thick slices of freshly baked granary bread. "I've felt the same in those countries too, especially Egypt. When I saw the temple at Karnak for the first time I just broke down, I felt so happy to be back home again. Everything was so familiar. There was nothing strange or foreign about it at all." She slowly, even absent-mindedly arranged tomatoes, cheese and lettuce on the plates and rolled up some slices of ham. "I suppose you think I'm really weird talking about this and we've only just met," she said and stared out of the window. "But I do believe that nothing in my life has been coincidental. I can see a reason, a purpose for everything that has happened. And that includes coming down here." She turned to look at him. "You're not going to believe this, but meeting you has helped me a very great deal with something that's been bothering me for some time now."

David laughed, a little embarrassed. "You really are full of surprises, you know. First reincarnation, then this. How on earth can I have helped you? I've done nothing."

She scooped an egg out of the boiling water with a spoon, ran it under the cold water tap 'til it had cooled, swiftly peeled away its shell and expertly sliced it. "Here's yours," she said as she handed him a plate full of food. "Help yourself to bread and butter." He waited until she had prepared her own plate before starting.

They ate silently for a few minutes, and then she said, "I've been having this dream for several months now. I say dream, but it's more than that. It's completely real, as real as it feels sitting here talking to you." She waited as if deciding whether to go on, and then said, "We're both in it."

"Me!" he cried, incredulous. "How the heck can I be in your dream? Two days ago we'd never met."

"I know it sounds unbelievable, but believe me I didn't know what was going on until I came down here. It was only yesterday that I realised who the soldier was."

"Soldier?" David laughed. "Christ! What soldier?"

56

"Okay. Here we go." Gently she brushed away some crumbs from the corners of her mouth with two fingers. "It takes place in what I suppose you'd call Roman Britain. But, to tell you the truth, I don't suppose you could call it Roman Britain, for they had only just arrived. I think your lot had only just conquered us, and for us, fraternising with the enemy was a huge no-no. I was the daughter of the chief of the tribe and you were a young Roman officer. By the way would you like coffee with your food? I know it's not supposed to be a good thing but I love it."

David, his mind in a whirl, his fork poised mid-way between plate and his open mouth, said nothing and just stared as she poured him a cup without waiting for his reply.

"Anyhow," she went on, "we apparently fraternised. Boy, did we fraternise." She let out a wicked chuckle. "That was the best part of the dream." Delicately, she sipped her coffee and smiled. "However, we got caught and they killed us." She stopped and looked at David, whose fork had finally found its way to his mouth, and was slowly chewing. "Is that good?" she asked him. Still not able to speak he nodded and then after they had looked at each other for a few moments he swallowed and managed to say, "Was that what you were seeing up on the Beacon yesterday?"

She nodded. "A part of it. The nasty bit, actually. I've been seeing just that bit for some time now. The executioner, who, by the way was my father then, stabbed you. The other men there held me and forced me to watch, and then they lifted me onto you and stabbed us both at once."

"Ouch, they really knew how to make a visitor feel at home in those days."

Anna smiled at him and then chewed for a few moments on a piece of bread.

"Normally that's as far as I get with the dream. We're killed and I wake up covered in sweat. But yesterday I saw a bit further. It was as if I was floating above the scene. I saw what happened immediately after we were killed."

"After?" David cried out, and Anna couldn't help but be aware of the scepticism in his voice.

"Yes, I know it sounds unbelievable," she said raising her hands, "but, honestly, there I was, above it all, looking down as my father walked away. We were still lying on the big stone and my father was crying as he left."

David looked across the table at her and saw that there were tears in her eyes. "Are you alright?" he asked, concerned. Anna crossed the kitchen and rummaged in her handbag. "God, where are the tissues when you need them?" she cried. After a few moments searching she triumphantly pulled one out and blew her nose. "Up 'til then he'd always seemed so damned cold and cruel." She sat down again at the table, dabbed at her eyes and stared at her plate.

David waited for a moment and then said, "You know, I think you might like to meet Beth. You know, the girl I work with. She's a terrific singer, and she's psychic."

"Psychic? In what way?"

"Well, she's clairvoyant, clairaudient, and a medium, and she's made a study of reincarnation. She's had a lot of things come back to her about her past lives. Some amazing stuff."

"She sounds fascinating. I think I'd like very much to meet her."

David looked down at his plate and frowned. "Have you . . . ?" he started to ask very tentatively, for he suddenly began to feel afraid of a rebuttal.

"Go on," Anna said, smiling her encouragement.

"I was wondering," he hesitated again and then went on, "Beth said that when she had a recall of a life in which she was a native American, she lost some of the problems that had bothered her all her life. Have you noticed that any of yours have disappeared?"

Anna thought for a moment and then said, shaking her head, "I don't really know. It's perhaps a little early yet."

"But can you see if anything unpleasant resulted from what happened to you and the Roman which has been a problem to you in your life now?" he persisted.

She stared at him and then looked away. "Well, I've always been terrified of losing someone I love, even when I've not had anyone to love. If you know what I mean," she added laughing.

"Yes, I think so," he said smiling.

"And then, I've always been troubled by a feeling of guilt that comes and goes, even when I've not got anything to feel guilty about." She laughed and covered her mouth with her handkerchief.

"The nuns at the school I went to said it was me feeling guilty about original sin," she said. "Can you believe that?"

"I believe you," David said absently, for he immediately thought of his own feelings of guilt for which he had no explanation.

Suddenly he felt a nudge at his knee and looking down saw Charlie, tongue hanging from the side of her mouth, eyes earnestly asking for her share.

"Okay, darling," he said, "it won't be long now."

"Pardon, what did you say?" Anna's face was flushed and her eye-liner had smudged. "Am I keeping you from something?"

"No. Sorry, no. I was talking to the dog. She's feeling a little left out."

"Oh, God, I'm sorry, I'd forgotten her. Here, she can have the rest of my plate. I've had enough."

She carefully placed the plate on the floor. Suspiciously, Charlie sniffed the food, delicately chose what was left of the ham, swallowed it and turned in disgust away from the rest.

Anna was at the sink, staring out of the window. "I'll just put the kettle on for some more coffee and then do a quick repair job on my face, if you don't mind."

"No, not at all, you go ahead. I'll finish up my salad."

Anna quickly climbed the narrow stairs leading to the bedroom and David sat down again at the table. Whilst he slowly ate the rest of his meal he thought about Anna's dream. His mind was buzzing with so many questions he found it difficult to settle on any one in particular. He didn't, for a moment, doubt her sincerity, or for that matter her sanity. Nor did he dismiss what she had said as a load of rubbish for he had learned and experienced enough to keep an open mind about what she had said.

His thoughts went back to one summer in Beirut in 1970. There had been a lovely, dark Lebanese girl, strikingly beautiful, and very mysterious in that she had gone out of his life as quickly as she entered it. They had had together just a few months of amazing passion, made more intense by the rapidly deteriorating situation out on the streets. Curfews were common and shots would be heard at regular intervals. Once, when he was just on the point of waking after a night of frantic love-making he saw in his mind's eye, with wonderful clarity, a couple standing before him. It was as if they were somehow posing for a picture. They were both Indian, obviously from another era, and in bright blue, richly decorated dresses. Later in the morning he had hesitantly mentioned his 'vision' to Laila, expecting her to perhaps laugh at him, but was surprised when she just stared at him for a moment and then said, "Oh, you saw them too. That's good. It is karmic, then. I thought it was." She then changed the subject and started to discuss the situation in her city. At the time David had thought that she was just over-wrought by the problems of her country and fears for her future, so he didn't pursue the subject and it rapidly went out of his mind as it became more and more difficult for him to carry on working. Very soon afterwards she suddenly disappeared. He tried his best to find her, without success, and then had to leave Lebanon in a hurry. He had often wondered what had become of her, whether she had managed to survive the horror that engulfed that wonderful country.

"It's alright for you," he said to Charlie, "all you have to worry about is where the next sniff is coming from." Charlie was still miffed about the food so didn't even look up at him. Her tail just slightly twitched.

"Did you say something?" asked Anna as she came slowly down the stairs, her face wiped clean of any make-up. David was totally captivated by the freshness of her beauty, but managed to stammer out, "Oh, er, I was just talking to Charlie. It's what I do when I'm alone and perplexed."

"I'll pour us some coffee and you can tell me what's worrying you."

"I just don't know where to begin. Let me think." He sighed, looked out of the window and then said, "Right, for a start, how has meeting me helped you?"

"Well, at least now I know who the soldier was. Just knowing that has helped me go on and see further." Delicately she sipped the hot coffee. "'Til I came down I seemed to be stuck with that awful scene."

"Tell me. How did you feel, after you had died, when you were looking down? Were you still frightened?"

"No, not at all. It's funny, but I have never before felt so at peace."

They sat for a while without speaking and drank their coffee, until suddenly Anna whispered, "I wish to God I could feel it again instead of . . ."

"Yes?" said David, "Instead of what?"

Anna sat bolt upright. "Forget I said that. I'm not going down that road." She took a deep breath and stood up. "And now I'm going to kick you out. It's the tub for me, some radio, and who knows perhaps a glass of wine."

"Okay," said David. "Come on Charlie we know when we're not wanted." He walked over to the door where Charlie was already waiting. "Thanks a million," he said as he opened the door. "There's a Russian toast which I think is very appropriate."

"What's that?"

"God grant it's not the last one."

She smiled and nodded, "I'll drink to that."

Chapter Nine

AN HOUR LATER ANNA lay in a comforting, delicious hot bath thinking about David. Slowly the healing power of the warm water worked its magic on her and gradually she became more and more relaxed. The terrible events that had brought her down to Cornwall seemed to become less and less frightening the more drowsy she became. As she drifted on the verge of sleep, she felt as if she were being drawn down a long tunnel. For a while all was black, but then she started to see the green slopes of a hill and heard the voices of children calling to each other. Then, slowly, the picture became clear. A boy and a girl were walking hand in hand down a hill towards the outer walls of a city. The sun blazed down out of a clear blue sky causing the air to shimmer above the orange tiles of the roofs of the villas in the town. The girl tossed her long braided hair, her hips innocently swinging her knee-length frock. Proudly she squeezed the hand of the boy who gazed at her adoringly. A rumbling sound behind them made them stop and turn to look at the mountain behind them from which a plume of white smoke belched into the clear blue sky. Nervously they laughed and then continued skipping and running down the hill.

Suddenly the scene changed. Anna found herself in a room dimly lit by the light of a single candle. On the wall immediately behind the candle she could just make out a large painting of a woman. On a low bed lay the young girl, her eyes closed, hardly breathing. The boy sat on the floor, his hands covering his face, softly crying. At the foot of the bed stood a group of people, their heads bowed.

As Anna strained to pick out the details of the scene through the smoke from the lamp, she felt herself being pulled backwards into a long black tunnel and it seemed as if all the breath was being sucked out of her body.

She awoke suddenly in the bath, overcome with an overwhelming sense of loss. The water was now quite cold and she found herself unable to move, so great was her grief. After what seemed a long time she dragged herself from the water. Still sobbing she dried herself completely, lay on the bed and, exhausted, fell into a deep sleep.

Much later, when she awoke, the sun was streaming in through the bedroom window. Shakily she dressed and slowly made her way down the stairs. Opening the front door she stepped out into the narrow front garden. Temporarily blinded by the light it was a few moments before she saw David waving from the end of his garden, which sloped away from her up the hill. He raised his hand to his mouth as if holding a cup, little finger exaggeratedly high, as an invitation in for a drink. She nodded, held out five fingers to indicate she would be over shortly and went back indoors to repair some of the damage done to her face.

David put away his spade and fork, walked down the sloping garden path and went inside the cool, dark cottage. He washed his hands and put the kettle on to make himself a cup of tea. He was surprised when, after only a few minutes, Charlie's barking told him Anna was on her way, for even from the end of the garden he had been able to see that something untoward had happened to upset her, and he hadn't expected to see her for at least a good half hour.

"She's going to need a major repair job," he had thought, so when she walked in he was not surprised to see that, although she had obviously tidied her hair, her face still bore the signs of some serious upset.

"You look as though you could do with a really strong hot coffee," he said as he went through to the kitchen for the kettle. "It's only instant. Do you mind?" When he got back he found her staring out of the window, gently stroking Charlie's head.

"Charlie says she'll give you twenty-four hours to stop doing that to her," he joked, not really knowing what to say as she looked so very sad. "Milk and sugar?" he asked and was relieved to see her nod. He waited for a few moments and then as he handed her the cup said, "Do you want to talk about it?"

Very slowly she turned towards him. "I've had another," she said very quietly.

"Another what?"

"Dream, vision, hallucination, whatever you like to call it."

David looked at her and felt a sinking sensation in his stomach.

"I know," she said, "you think I'm a bit crazy. But I'm not."

"No, of course I don't," he said.

He waited for a moment as she sipped the coffee. "Have you had many of these before?" he asked.

"No, not many. I've been seeing the scene I saw yesterday for a long time now, but the one I've just seen in the bath I haven't seen before. This has come on since I met you."

He frowned and shook his head. "Are you trying to tell me it's my fault?" he asked.

"No, of course it's not your fault," she said defensively, and then obviously finding it difficult to know how to go on she paused and frowned slightly. After a few moments during which she gently started to rub Charlie's ears she went on, "I know this is going to sound a bit ridiculous, but I feel we have known each other for a very long time, a very, very long time, several life-times in fact."

"I think I can live with that quite happily."

She looked out of the window and said, "You may like the idea now, but I'm beginning to think that perhaps we've had some very unpleasant times together."

David frowned, unsure of precisely what she meant and asked, "This last one, this afternoon, where did it take place?"

She looked up into the corner of the room noticing the cobwebs in spite of her concentration. "Naples, I think, before the mountain blew up. We were young. We'd grown up together, and we'd taken it for granted that we'd always stay together, so when my parents said I had to marry someone else I couldn't accept it and I took poison." She stared into the distance, tears slowly flowing down her cheeks. "It was so sad. I can still feel it. Such a waste."

They sat quietly for a few moments staring out into the garden before David broke the silence with, "Since I left you at lunch time I've been doing some really heavy work in the garden and I don't know about you but I'm absolutely famished. I suggest that we go out and find some food."

She turned her head to look at him and he was relieved to see her smile.

"There's a place in the village I go to, usually in the morning for a coffee, but they serve delicious grub in the evening. The guy who runs it is a bit of a psychic, in fact he's the one who thought up the 'spiritual kick up the arse-part', and I'm thinking that perhaps he might give us some answers to what has been going on here." He paused for a moment and then added, "It might be a good thing, also, to invite Beth over. She's sure to have some good insights. What do you say?"

Anna smiled and nodded, "Okay," she said, "but give me an hour or two to smarten myself up, will you?"

"That will suit me. I've got to feed Charlie, get out of these gardening togs, have a bath, shave, iron a shirt, ring Beth. All in all that should take me about ten minutes?" She hesitated, so he laughed and said, "Alright, give me a call when you're ready, but not too posh, mind, remember this is Cornwall. When I first came down here I was told you're dressed up if you're wearing a tie when you've got your wellies on."

"That's good, 'cos I've not brought much with me, and I'm afraid I've not got any wellies at all."

"I think we can make an exception in this case." He smiled as he walked her to the door.

Chapter Ten

ANTHONY WAS SO BUSY fussing and tutting and clucking as
he moved from table to table that at first he didn't notice their
arrival, but when David discreetly coughed he turned gracefully
towards them, one eyebrow theatrically raised, his left hand
delicately resting on his waist. "Hello, darlings! David, dear boy,
do come in. Such a pleasure to see you. And you're not alone!
Congratulations!" He walked forward, took Anna's hand and
delicately kissed it. "Of course you know she's much too good for
you, dear boy." He winked at Anna and led them to a table in the
corner of the room, where Beth was already seated, waiting for
them. "Here make yourselves comfortable whilst I go and see if
the chef has got out of bed yet."

Anna stood and watched, fascinated, as the little man she took
to be the waiter winked at her again, turned and with hand on hip,
scurried into the kitchen. Laughing she looked at David. "Who
was that?" she asked.

"Sorry, I should have warned you. That was Anthony. He runs
this place with his partner, Ben, the chef. They're a couple of
sweeties. They used to have a comedy act on the holiday camp
circuit, and gave it up to run this place. They've been very good
to me since my wife died."

Beth had already stood and was waiting patiently with a
welcoming smile on her face.

David was surprised by his feeling of relief when there was no
awkwardness in the introductions. Both the women looked directly
at each other and there appeared to be an instantaneous bonding,
a recognition of something that neither would have been able to
put into words, but which left both feeling totally at ease.

They immediately began such an animated conversation it
seemed to David that they looked as if they had perhaps, at some
time in the past, been close friends whose conversation had been
interrupted and which they were now continuing as if they had
never been apart.

He smiled as he looked at them, for they were so different.
Beth, in her bright floral gown with beads and bangles quietly
tinkling as she moved, her long hair a mass of curls and her

complete lack of any make-up, contrasted sharply with Anna's understated elegance, her single row of pearls emphasising the smooth perfection of her neck.

Fortunately for him, just as he was starting to feel a little excluded, Anthony made his reappearance and handed to each a huge, heavy menu.

"Take your time, my darlings. The chef is still rubbing his twigs together, or whatever he does to get the fire going. So there's absolutely no rush." Smiling sweetly he pirouetted and disappeared into the kitchen.

*   *   *

The evening was one they would remember for a long time to come. The food was delicious, perfectly cooked and served with taste, discretion and not a little humour. There was just one small incident, which at the time seemed of little consequence, but which was later to give David and Beth cause for concern.

They had been discussing Anna's 'visions' and Anthony was just about to pour the coffee. Beth and David were arranging the cups and saucers and Anna was happily watching the world go by out of the window, which looked out onto the main street, when David heard her quickly suck in her breath. He looked up to see her staring at him, her eyes wide open in what looked like terror. He quickly looked at the window and, seeing nothing untoward, just a few holidaymakers walking by and the rear end of a Rolls Royce slowly disappearing, looked back at her and asked, "What's the matter? Are you having another vision?" Anthony scurried away to the bar calling out as he went, "What you need, my dear, is a lovely double brandy. Be nice to her, David."

Beth reached across the table and took her hand. Gazing directly into her eyes she said very quietly, "It's okay, Anna. You're safe."

Anna looked back at her wide-eyed and surprised. Then a moment later she said, "It's nothing, really it isn't. I'm perfectly alright."

And then suddenly Anthony was back tutting and fussing as if she were the most important person in the world.

"Here, drink some of this. It's the very best and it's going to make you feel better, and it's going to make David feel even better to know that it's on the house." Anna smiled her thanks and sipped her brandy. As colour gradually returned to her face Anthony went on, "And you must tell me about your visions. I'm sorry, darling, I

couldn't help but overhear a lot of what you've been talking about."
David looked at him in mock surprise and as he defended himself
with, "After all, you've not exactly been whispering, you know."
David laughed and put him at his ease with, "It's alright, Anthony. It
really is. We were hoping you could give us some idea of what the
hell's been going on. I know you're a psychic and you've studied
these things. That's one of the reasons we came here this evening.
That, and of course the wonderful food."

"Flattery will get you practically anything you want, dear boy.
Now tell me all about it." He quickly took a chair from a nearby
table and sat with his legs crossed and hands clasped together over
one knee.

Fortunately for them business was slow at that time of the
evening, so for the next ten minutes Anna was able to give him a
complete, uninterrupted description of the visions she had had.

"Fascinating," said Anthony when she had finished. "Tell me,
when did these visions start to become a nuisance?"

"I suppose, since I got married. I'd had them off and on for a
long time, but they only became serious for me after that."

Anthony pursed his lips as he thought and then staring intently at
a spot on the tablecloth, said, "This is interesting, because there's
always a reason for spontaneous recall of this nature. It very often
happens at a time of great stress, a time when one is undergoing a
period of great mental pressure, when there is a resonance between
what is happening now and what happened in the past." They were
all surprised by a change in their host. Gone was the flippant,
superficial, theatrical restaurateur. In his place they were looking at
a very serious, profound and concerned man who seemed to have a
great understanding of all that Anna was experiencing.

"Now I'm not going to press you about your problems, my
dear," he continued. "I can see they are serious. I can also see that
they are bound up to some extent with problems you have
undergone in the past with this one here." And he waived his hand
at David. "It would seem you have unfinished business together.
Let us hope that this time round you'll get it right."

"Are you saying that the visions Anna had were memories of a
time she and I spent together?" David asked. For, although Anna
had already explained as much, he was still finding it difficult to
take in. He was also looking for some kind of confirmation of what
she had said to him.

"And made quite a mess of it from what she says," added
Anthony. "Also, I have a feeling that there will be more you will

uncover. I can sense at least one more very painful series of events nestling deep down in your memory, Anna."

"But what about my memory?" asked David. "If I was there how is it I can't remember any of it?"

Anthony thought for a moment and then said, "That's a complicated one, but I think I can, for the moment, say simply, that it is because for you, at this time, there's no need to remember. 'At this time', I say, for there will be times to come when you will wish that you had never wanted to see in that way."

David stared hard at him as he felt ripples of discomfort in his stomach.

Anthony continued, "For you, for the moment, the attraction is quite enough, and there's no need to look like that. It's quite obvious there is something between you, and if what Anna says is correct it's not surprising that there's an enormous bond between you. It's almost as strong as the bond between you and Beth. I could see it as soon as you walked in. Now, for the moment, Anna is the one who needs to remember, for as I said, her other problem is connected with all this."

"This ties in wonderfully with what we were talking about on the beach in Perranporth, David," said Beth as she smiled at him. "Anyhow, it's already started, hasn't it?"

Anthony frowned and was about to say something to David when Beth continued, "And, Anna, I should think that from now on you won't be troubled very often with this dream. What do you think, Anthony?"

"I think you're right. Now that the connection has been made with this one," he said waving an arm at David, "I should be very surprised if you were to have many more problems with that episode."

"Thank God for that," Anna said smiling. "It was becoming a bit of a nuisance."

They were quiet for a few moments and then David said, "I wonder." He paused and looked at Anthony, "I've just remembered. Twice since Anna's arrival I've experienced a level of guilt, and I don't know what it's all about. Have you any ideas?"

Anthony licked his lips and his intelligent, soft features creased into a smile. "Again," he said, "it's a question of resonance. There appears to be something coming up for you to do with the way you behaved with her, either in that life or one of the many you've had together."

Beth gave David a 'told-you-so' look, arching her eyebrows and smiling.

Anna frowned and pressed her lips together giving an impression of great sadness. "Yes," she exclaimed, "There was another one. You remember, David. I told you about it this afternoon. After I'd had my bath, when I came over. It was in Naples. I killed myself because my family wouldn't let me marry you."

David nodded and looked across at Anthony.

"I think you must be prepared for a few of these," he said, and then, seeing the look of horror on Anna's face, hastily went on, "Oh, they won't all be so gruesome, my dear. There's bound to be one or two good ones in between." He giggled in such a delightful way that they all couldn't help but join him.

"You must be exceptionally psychic, my dear. Have you had any other weird and wonderful things happen to you?" Anthony was sitting back in his chair with a slight smile on his lips and one eyebrow lifted.

Anna looked at David and Beth with her mouth open. "Well," she whispered. "Well." She licked her lips and swallowed. "I really don't know what to say. I mean, I hadn't really thought about it like that. I mean, that I'm exceptionally psychic, as you say."

She looked away and stared out onto the street.

"Do you know, this is amazing. I'd not thought about it in those terms. Not ever having met anybody like all of you, I suppose." She turned to them and smiled.

"None taken," said Anthony.

"What?"

"Offence." Said Beth.

"Oh!" Anna covered her mouth with her hand. "I'm so sorry. I didn't mean . . ."

"It's okay," said David. "You may not have noticed it, but you're sitting with a load of pachyderms here."

They all laughed, totally at ease with each other.

"I'm just a bit surprised that I didn't pick up on it," said David, frowning.

"Don't worry, David," said Anthony. "There were a lot of conflicting emotions and messages jamming up your senses."

"I've always been able to sense people," Anna said very slowly. "When I meet someone I always know whether they're genuine. And I usually pick up on their main characteristics." She hesitated. "It's only failed me once," she said, and immediately her face changed, the fear again showing in her face.

Anthony's voice was sharp. "He's not here, Anna. You are safe."

"But he is here, I know it. He's close, very close." She shivered and folded her arms protectively across her chest.

David stared out of the window, but all he could see were ordinary people enjoying the evening, laughing, talking together, walking the dog.

Beth reached across the table and took Anna's hand.

Suddenly, to the surprise of all, Anna stood up abruptly.

"I'm sorry. I'm afraid I've got to leave." She was trembling and, without looking at Beth directly, she said, "We came in my car this evening, so would you please give David a lift home, Beth. I don't want to break up the party completely, but I really must go."

Turning to Anthony she said, "Thanks for a wonderful evening, Anthony. Please tell Ben he's the most wonderful chef."

"Alright, my dear. I'm sorry you have to rush off like this, but I do understand."

David started to get up, but Anthony surreptitiously waved him down. "I'll show Anna to the door," he announced.

Taking her arm he led her to the door. Whilst she was putting her coat on David was surprised to see their heads close together. Anthony was very serious and appeared to be explaining something to Anna extremely energetically.

As she left, Anna turned to Anthony and kissed him lightly on the cheek. She spoke quietly, but David just managed to hear, "Thank you, Anthony. I'll remember that, I promise."

"You do." He said as he closed the door.

"We have to be very careful with that one," Anthony said softly as he returned to the table. "She's on the edge."

"History could repeat itself," Beth whispered.

"Exactly," said Anthony.

David looked at Beth and was surprised to see tears in her eyes.

"What's the matter, Beth?"

"The feelings that come with her are terrible. I can sense all sorts of nasties."

"All I have is a wonderful feeling of a marvellous person," said David defensively.

"I don't mean that she's nasty, you idiot. She's surrounded by feelings of evil, of awful things about to happen." She paused. "All around her is a terrible feeling of terror, of a really determined hatred."

"Then why can't I feel these things?"

"Because all you are sensing are the good feelings she evokes for you," said Anthony. "In the past you've been very close many times, good and bad times, and on one level you sense something is not right, but that just increases the desire to nurture and protect. Thus it increases the attraction."

David looked at Beth, smiled apologetically and shrugged his shoulders.

"It's okay, David, it really is." She smiled and took his hand.

"What were you saying about Perranporth beach?" Anthony asked with a slight frown.

"David and I were there the other day. Whilst we were talking it came out that he has been having some experiences of his own."

Anthony smiled and raised his eyebrows. "Like?" he said softly.

David took a deep breath and stared out of the window.

"There's nothing definite yet," he said. "There's been something awful coming up in my sleep that I've not yet been able to remember."

He was surprised to find himself becoming slightly irritated as he spoke.

"What's the feeling you get when you wake up?" Anthony asked, frowning.

"I feel terrible for a while, as if someone's been doing something really bad to me." He felt the irritation increasing.

"Is there any actual pain?"

"In my chest, groin, hands and feet. But it only lasts for a few moments." He had started to breathe a little quicker and could feel his armpits becoming moist.

"And when you . . ."

Both Anthony and Beth were taken aback as David suddenly stood, pushing back his chair, his knuckles tight and white as he pushed his fists against the table top.

"Oh, for goodness sake don't go on about it," he cried. "Let me sort it out."

"I'm sorry, my love. No-one's wanting to push you." Beth reached across the table to hold his hand, but he walked rapidly over to the till on the bar.

"Come on, Anthony, I'll pay the bill," he called over his shoulder.

Anthony pushed back his chair. "He's fighting it," he whispered to Beth as he followed him to the little bar where David paid the bill in silence.

"I'll give you a lift home," Beth said as he opened the door.

David turned to her and said, "No thanks, Beth. I think I'd like to walk home. I'll give you a ring very soon." With that he disappeared into the street leaving Beth staring, perplexed, at Anthony.

"He's getting into a bit of a state," she said. "Should I go after him?"

"No, my dear, let him be. As you said, he's got some stuff of his own coming out, and as you know it can result in some pretty wild mood swings."

He pushed the till drawer shut and stared up at the ceiling. "It won't be long now. He'll soon find out what it's all about." He smiled ruefully.

"It's a big one, isn't it?" she asked quietly.

Anthony turned to look at her. "Terrible," he whispered. "Just terrible."

* * *

David left the restaurant feeling his anger tight across his forehead, dampness on the palms of his hands making it difficult to pull on his gloves. Forty-five minutes later when he reached the cottage he realised with some surprise that he remembered hardly anything of the walk home, however the irritation he had felt had subsided and he felt quite tired as he climbed the steps that led up to his garden. He did notice that the Audi was not parked outside the holiday cottage, but, knowing how concerned Anna was about the possibility of it being stolen, he assumed that she had put it in the garage. It was when he was standing in the garden, whilst Charlie was relieving herself, that the thought came to him that perhaps Anna was more concerned about it being seen than about it being stolen. But seen by whom? By her husband? At that moment, as if in answer to his question a large black Rolls Royce very slowly and very smoothly drove by, and as it disappeared up the hill in the direction of the pub David remembered Anna's face in the restaurant. She had been looking out of the window just before she had gone white and the look of terror had come onto her face. He remembered seeing the boot of a Rolls as it disappeared past the window. He hadn't associated her fear with the Rolls at that time but now the thought came to him that very possibly the two were connected. He shivered, suddenly cold in the late evening air and realised he was feeling very nervous and that, again, the palms of his hands were sweating. Calling Charlie he hurried indoors and prepared for bed.

Chapter Eleven

THAT NIGHT HE DIDN'T sleep well at all. Tossing and turning from side to side he sweated profusely. Once, at about two o'clock, he woke himself up shouting, "No!" in a loud, terrified voice. Switching on the light he sat on the edge of the bed and tried to make some sense of the dreams he had been having. For him this was strange and unusual, for all his life, even when his wife died, he had been blessed with deep, refreshing sleep. Normally he didn't remember dreaming at all, so the experience of having what amounted to a nightmare was a new and very unwelcome experience for him. In the dream there was a beautiful girl he was trying to reach. Each time he drew near to her she retreated, calling out to him. Faces leered at him, laughing and jeering at his fright and frustration, and then he realised he was tied down, helpless. Struggling, in a panic, he awoke just as one of his tormentors was about to thrust a sword into his chest.

The dream had been real to him, too real. He could still feel the bite of the ropes tying him down, and the smell of the man bending over him about to thrust the sword into him seemed to still linger in his nostrils.

Slowly David forced himself down the stairs into the kitchen and made himself a hot, sweet cup of tea. As he made his way back into the living room he glanced out of the window and was surprised to see lights on in the cottage opposite.

"I hope Anna's having a better time than I am," he thought. On the spur of the moment he quickly dialled her number. After waiting for what seemed a long time he was about to ring off when the phone at the other end was picked up and a man's voice said very softly, "Pronto." A cold, tingling feeling shot up David's back and he quickly replaced the receiver. Switching off the light he looked out of the window and saw a large black Rolls Royce parked in the road outside the gate of the cottage.

"Why am I sweating?" he thought. "So her husband's turned up. So what?" He sat down in the darkened room and tried hard to calm his thoughts, but, however hard he tried, the picture of Anna's terrified face as she sat in the restaurant kept coming back to him. What he couldn't understand was his own feeling when he thought of this man.

"My God," he thought, "I haven't even seen him, never mind met him and the thought of him makes me shake."

For a long time David sat in his armchair stroking Charlie's head, trying to make sense of the situation, until his eyes grew heavier and heavier and he finally climbed the stairs and fell on his bed into a deep, dreamless sleep.

*　*　*

The following morning he awoke feeling surprisingly bright and alert and after a quick breakfast took Charlie out for her morning walk. As he walked down his path onto the road he noticed that the Rolls was no longer parked outside the cottage opposite. Quickly scanning the windows and seeing no sign of life, he called the dog and walked energetically up the hill and onto the heath.

He didn't often dwell on the past, but sometimes on a perfect spring morning like this memories of his former wife, Tina, would come flooding back. It was here, walking in a soft sea breeze on the path down to the beach where they used to lie for hours on the cool sand, that he would experience his fondest memories of her. Today, however, he realised that the memory of her had faded and in his mind's eye all he could see was a picture of Anna, but not as he would have liked to have seen her - laughing and seemingly full of fun and joy, but sitting in the restaurant, staring at him with her eyes wide with terror. Sweating he ran as fast as he could down to the beach where he threw stone after stone into the waves until both he and Charlie, who had chased every one of them, were quite exhausted. Then, sitting on a large rock just above the line of sea-weed that marked the extent of the last high tide, he gently stroked Charlie's ears and thought about this woman who had suddenly arrived to change his life irrevocably. For he had the feeling that from now on his life would never ever be the same again. Not only had she affected him profoundly as a woman, she had caused him to rethink the very basis of his philosophy of life.

His father had been an engineer, a 'respectable' job at a time when 'respectability' was still the commodity demanded for anyone hoping for middle class status. And this is what he strove for more than anything, to escape from the shame he felt at his working class background. Outside of his job his only passion was the local church, the Church of England, where he would spend all his free time, to the despair and bewilderment of his wife, who, although proud of his abilities and his work as a church warden, could not accept that the post should take up as much of his free time as he insisted that it demanded. She herself, the daughter of a coal miner, was also desperate for social recognition. She played the cello adequately enough to be accepted into the ranks of the local symphony orchestra and supplemented her husband's wage by giving lessons to a few local children. Unfortunately, neither of these activities filled her time enough, and she ever increasingly sought solace in the 'Good Book'. Both she and her husband tried their utmost to instil Christian principles in their son. However, when it looked as though they were not succeeding they would resort to beating into him the love of God.

When he looked back David was amazed sometimes at how he was able to resist their attempts to brain-wash him. Even the beatings he received for his 'wickedness' never changed his innate opinion that what they were telling him was wrong. It wasn't so much that he didn't believe in God, he just didn't believe what they were saying about God. So he retreated into music, and to a great extent this was his salvation, for, although his parents despaired of ever saving his soul, they could not help but be in awe of the beauty of his playing.

This morning, as he sat on his rock, David found himself wondering what his parents would think of him now as they struggled with their frustrations and bitterness in their retirement. They may have been 'Godly', but it had certainly brought them no peace or contentment in their old age. A part of him, a tiny part of him, perhaps that part that was still affected by his parents' orthodoxy, was just a little surprised by Anna's story, but mainly his reaction was one of calm unquestioning acceptance that what she had said was perfectly reasonable. The only part of her story that gave him a real surprise was his part in it, as a soldier, for he couldn't think of any time in his life when he had experienced enough anger to cause him to want to fight anyone. Suddenly he felt himself grow cold as a memory of an incident in his youth flashed before his eyes.

He had been eleven, self conscious in his brand new shiny uniform, on his way to his first meeting at his new scouts' group. As he walked across the large park that separated his parents' house from the scout hall he had met another boy in scout uniform who belonged to a different troop. He had been astonished when the boy, who was smaller than he, had started, without any provocation, to insult him.

David was surprised that he could picture in such bright detail the other boy's spiteful little face twisted in contempt as he poured scorn on his uniform. He also experienced the shame he felt on that day when the boy offered to fight him, 'to prove which group was the best.' He also felt his legs and arms go suddenly weak as they had then when he had stammered out an incoherent, pitiful refusal. The boy's jeers of derision as he shamefacedly walked away rang in his ears for many years after. It was an incident he never really understood, for he had never, before or since, experienced circumstances when his courage had been called into question. He also knew that at that time he had been, for his age, very athletic and strong, a 'natural' at many sports, including judo and wrestling. He knew that, had he wanted, he could have fought the other boy and, being so much stronger and more experienced than he, would most likely have won easily.

He was brought out of his reverie by Charlie, impatient to be on the move again. She nudged his knee, barked and ran towards the path that led up onto the heath.

"Okay, girl. Let's be off," he said and slowly followed her as she ran ahead, perhaps encouraged by thoughts of tit-bits to come when they got to the pub.

At the top of the climb up from the beach he stopped for a rest, and, temporarily blinded by the sweat running into his eyes, he was only made aware of the presence of the two men by Charlie's low growl. They were tall and even the expensively tailored suits they wore could not hide the fact that they were very heavily muscled. Holding Charlie, who continued to growl, David stepped to one side to allow them to pass but was surprised when neither of them moved. Thinking they were perhaps a little nervous of the dog he smiled reassuringly and said, "Don't worry about the dog. Her bite may be worse than her bark, but she's had a good breakfast, so she's not at all hungry."

His attempt at humour brought no reaction at all from the men, so David slowly edged his way past them keeping himself between Charlie and them and only let her loose when he was a good fifty yards further on. Only then did he turn to look at them, but they had by now disappeared. Shaking off a feeling of disquiet caused by their unexpected appearance he hurried across the road to the Green Man.

Inside the pub he felt his spirits lift as he saw all the familiar faces turn to look at him.

"Morning David," shouted out Norman, "how're you managing with the princess, then?

"Not much going on there, I'm afraid, Norman," David said, and, hoping to change the drift of the conversation, walked to the bar and ordered a pint of bitter.

"You lyin' bugger." Called out Norman, "You've taken her out to dinner you have. You're going to have to take care now her husband's shown up." He took a long swallow from his pint glass. "Right oily sod, he is, too!"

Tom handed David his beer and, leaning over the counter, quietly said, "I'm afraid I may have made a mistake, David. I don't know. You see, yesterday evening these two gentlemen came in. Real smart, city suits, one of 'em foreign. Bought drinks for everybody. Said they were on holiday, looking for a friend. Showed a picture of Anna. Well, I directed them to the cottage opposite you. I hope I did right."

David sighed and said, "I suppose so. He had to turn up one day. Anyhow there was no future in it for me. She went off in a bit of a huff, last night. Don't know why."

"You got no idea," called out Norman who had been straining to hear the conversation at the bar. "If I'd had a chance at her it would've been a different story, I can tell you. I wouldn't be sitting wasting my time here. We'd have been in Monte Carlo by now."

"Don't you be taking any notice of him, my 'ansome," called out George, his face round and ruddy and smiling. "Silly bugger's no idea of where 'tis."

"I do, too," Norman yelled. "'Tis foreign somewhere."

The roars of laughter were brought to a sudden halt and an abrupt silence fell on the bar as the two men that David had met on the path walked in. Immediately Charlie stood, softly growled and moved away, her tail tucked between her back legs.

"Good day, gentlemen, what'll you be having?" asked Tom, pleasant even though he instinctively disliked the men.

They ordered gin and tonic, and as Tom served them he asked, "Have any success last night, then?"

Neither of them said anything in reply, but turned to look directly at David.

"You are David Henderson?" The smaller of the two had spoken, confident of his power, his face arrogant. It was more a statement than a question.

David found himself irritated by them, and then realised he was sweating a little under the armpits, so he replied, "Why do you ask? What do you want?"

The taller of the two smiled and moved a little closer. "I am Antonio Taverna and I've come down to join my wife for a few days holiday." His English was almost perfect, just the way he pronounced his name and a slightly rolled 'r' giving away his nationality. "Unfortunately, she doesn't appear to be at the cottage. You live opposite. I wonder if you have seen her?" On the surface he appeared calm, pleasant, a man concerned about his wife.

David felt his hands start to sweat and the blood rush to his face as he felt the two men staring at him. His mouth was suddenly very dry. He turned to the bar and took a quick mouthful of his beer.

Turning back to them he tried his utmost to appear natural.

"Well, I saw her when she arrived, and the following day I lit a fire for her." He saw the man's eyes narrow and as David thought he was going to ask a question he went on lamely, "I look after the cottage whilst the owner is away. Your wife wanted a fire." He smiled and then, seeing no change of expression in their faces, stammered, "She didn't know how to make a fire so invited me in to light it for her." The Italian still didn't say anything. David, his mind in a whirl, felt himself falling into a panic, so it was with a great sense of relief that he heard Tom ask in his deep Cornish baritone, "Isn't your wife there at the cottage then, sir?"

Antonio ignored him completely and continued staring at David for a few moments. Then without another word both the men swiftly turned and walked out of the pub leaving their drinks untouched on the bar.

The door of the pub closed noisily behind them. David turned, leaned heavily on the bar. "My God," he thought, "I'm shaking like a leaf," and, realising his throat was parched dry he took a long drink from his glass. Suddenly, everyone started talking.

"Bugger me," shouted out Norman.

"Don't think I fancy that, Norm," called out George.

Tom leaned on the bar, his face as close as possible to David's. "What's going on here, David?" he asked.

"I don't know, Tom, but I think I'm beginning to get an idea about what was worrying Anna."

"You be careful, my 'andsome. That one's dangerous and he didn't believe you."

David could still feel his legs shaking as he said, "I'm afraid you're right, my friend. I'm very much afraid you're right."

"If no-one's 'aving they gins, I'll 'ave 'em," shouted Norman. He hurried over to the bar and carried them triumphantly to his friends by the fire.

"You're not as stupid as you look, Norman," muttered Alfred, a bit vexed that he had been outdone by his normally slow friend.

David quickly finished his drink and, to Tom's surprise, ordered another.

Tom had just started to pull the drink when the phone rang. He let it ring until he had finished then picked up the receiver.

"It's for you, David." He silently mouthed, "Beth."

"You can take it in the back if you want."

As he hurried into the back room Norm shouted to him, "That's right. You keep your other one sweet. Don't know how you do it, boy. Ugly bugger like you, and two on the go."

"You're just jealous," cried out George, "just 'cos you've had nothing since that 'ippy in 1965."

Shutting out the roars of laughter, David closed the door to the 'snug', as it was called, and picked up the receiver.

"David," Beth's voice was low and sweet. "Tried your place without success, so I thought I might catch you there in the pub. How are you?"

"Hi Beth, thanks for the call. I'm feeling a little better, thank you."

There was an awkward moment of silence before he continued with, "Sorry about last night. I was surprised by what happened. I treated you very badly, and I really feel bad about it."

"Don't worry about that. The important thing is, has any more come out?"

David jumped slightly as a picture of the man in his dream, ugly and foul smelling flashed into his mind. "As a matter of fact, yes, things have started to happen."

Quickly he told her of the events of the night and his meeting with Anna's husband.

"I can see what is causing her to feel as she does," he said. "He's a real evil sod. Made me sweat just talking to him."

"We're going to have to be very careful from now on," she said slowly. "I can't see this ending happily at all."

"No." He paused for a moment. "Have you any idea where she is? I mean, she can't have been in the cottage last night, so where is she?"

"Perhaps she booked into a hotel for the night."

"Perhaps. And then, maybe she's gone home."

"I think not. Not without saying goodbye to her soldier."

"Oh dear. I suppose I'm never going to hear the last of that."

"I like the picture in my mind of you dressed up in centurion's gear. Dead sexy." She chuckled and David felt his face go red. Closing his eyes he let the sound of her gentle laughter wash over him. Then, suddenly, all the tension that had tightened the muscles of his body since his encounter with the gangster drained away, and he smiled.

"Do you know of any fancy-dress shops in the area?" he asked.

"I'll ask around."

They both laughed.

"And what about the dream?" Beth's voice was quiet and solicitous.

"As I said, the details are a bit vague. I'm just left with a horrific feeling of something really terrible about to happen."

"You said something about a girl. Any ideas about her?"

"No. Just that I was in a panic, trying to find her. She kept slipping away."

He stopped talking as he felt a hard burning feeling in his abdomen. Then a moment later he gasped as a picture flashed into his mind of a beautiful girl with her flaxen hair in tight ringlets. She was staring at him with a tiny frown on her forehead.

"What is it, David?"

He took a deep breath.

"I think I've just seen her, pretty, hair fair, in curls."

"Well, my dear, you really are coming on. Oh, it's getting quite exciting, isn't it?"

"Do you think so? I'm not so sure. In fact I think it's going to give me a good dose of diarrhoea before it's all over."

"Remember what I've said before, 'You're never alone. Don't be afraid or feel awkward about asking for help'. It will come, believe me."

David sighed. "Yeah, I remember. Okay, I'll try not to forget that."

"You see that you do. Oh, and when you go back into the bar, see if any of the guys there have any idea of where Anna could be."

"Good idea, if anyone knows they will." He laughed as he suddenly started to feel lighter. "Yes, they knew already that we'd had dinner with her last night at Anthony's."

Beth laughed. "Well, this is Cornwall."

"So it is. See you soon, my dear."

"Yes, bye."

David walked into the bar and saw Norman, Alfred and George standing facing the fire. As he reached out to claim the beer that Tom had poured for him in his absence, they turned towards him and in near perfect three-part harmony, for they were all members of one of the many local choirs, they started to sing a version of 'Tea for two.'

"Tea for three and three for tea,
Me for both and both for me, but
What the hell you're gonna do with he?"

They all broke into uncontrollable fits of laughter, staggered to their seats and lifted their glasses to each other in self congratulation.

"Thank you very much, fellers," David called to them wryly. "Just don't give up your day jobs."

"You're just jealous, 'cos you can't sing. All you can do is plonk away on that piano and let the gorgeous Beth do all the hard work," shouted George. They all bent over the table loud and raucous in their laughter.

"I may not be able to sing, but I know bum chords when I hear them," David said, laughing.

"Bum chords, Bum chords!" Alfred appeared outraged. "That was bloody perfect, that was."

"No it wasn't, and you know it. One of you, and I think it was you, Norman, cocked up the second line."

Alfred and George lent across the table and pretended to hit Norman with their caps. "Bloody cloth ears," howled George. "You want to get that ear wax scraped out," yelled Alfred. "The conductor's been telling you for weeks now."

"T'was not my fault," cried Norman. "My false teeth fell down with that high note."

By now everybody in the bar was laughing and cheering them. David turned to Tom.

"Give them a pint each," he said. "It's the only thing that'll shut them up."

Chapter Twelve

A LITTLE WHILE LATER David slowly walked down the hill towards his cottage and was not a little relieved to see the Rolls Royce was no longer in the lane. He was, however, very surprised to see the battered old Ford Fiesta tucked up against his hedge.

"Hello, Denzil," he called out. "To what do I owe this pleasure?"

Detective Sergeant Denzil Stevens slowly eased his massive frame out of the car. "I really must change this old banger. You know, I dream of a car that will take someone like me. Something I can sit in without feeling like a sardine in a tin. Something like that Roller that's just moved off." He smiled wryly and then quietly, "Mind if I come in for a minute or two?"

"Official, or social," David asked as they walked up the path and into the cottage.

"Bit of both I'm afraid," said Denzil. "As a friend I came to tell you to be careful. As your local bobby I came to tell you to be bloody careful." He paused for a moment and then said quietly, "Are you going to stand there for ever with your mouth open, or are you going to put the kettle on?" Denzil turned a chair round, sat on it with his arms resting on its back and gave Charlie a rough, friendly welcome.

"Have you met the slime-ball from across the road, yet?" he called out. David walked through to the kitchen. His knees started to shake again as he filled the kettle.

"I've just spoken to him in the pub. I'm afraid he put the fear of God into me."

"He didn't threaten you, did he? If he did I'll bang him up quicker than you can say Jack Robinson."

"No, he didn't say anything really. He didn't need to. He just looked, and the way he looked was so evil, he made my skin creep."

Denzil glanced out of the window. "I can't say much, David, and I suppose I really shouldn't be here talking about him, but we've been mates for a while now and I wouldn't want anything to happen to you, you know. Just be bloody careful how you deal with this fellow. If you knew just how dangerous a bastard he is you'd not sleep for a week, believe me."

"Thanks a lot, Denzil, it really feels good to hear that," David said wryly as he carried two steaming mugs of tea into the living room. "It is four sugars, isn't it?" he added with a smile.

"Now don't you start on at me, David. I have enough problems with the missus about that."

They sat for a few moments in silence drinking the tea before David's curiosity got the better of him. "So who the hell is he? He must be a mighty big fish for you to come down here to warn me off. It's the first time you've been here for ages. And I know my tea making isn't that good."

"As I said, I was just concerned about you, and don't knock yourself, the tea's really good. Hearing what I heard, and knowing what I know, I thought it'd be a good thing to come for a bit of a chat."

"So what did you hear and what do you know, for Christ sake?" David stood up and was just about to sit down again when the phone started ringing.

Later, when he had had time to think, he wondered why he reacted to the ringing in the way that he did. His normal reaction, knowing how his agent hated to be kept waiting on the phone, was to rush to pick up the receiver as quickly as possible. That morning, however, he froze and stared at the phone, for some inexplicable reason unable to move.

"Do you want me to answer it?" asked Denzil quietly.

"Christ, what's the matter with me?" David muttered under his breath, picked up the receiver and abruptly said, "Hello."

Even before she spoke he knew who it was.

"David?"

The intensity of the joy and relief he felt took him completely by surprise, so a few moments passed before he was able to blurt out awkwardly, "Anna? Anna, where are you? What are you doing? What's going on?"

"I'm sorry, David. I really am, but last night I had to go. I suddenly realised the danger I was putting you in."

"That doesn't matter. How are you? Where are you?" David heard a groan behind him and turned to see Denzil staring at him in disbelief. "What the hell are you doing, David?" he whispered. "Are you crazy?"

"Have you someone with you? Is it alright to talk?" She was speaking very softly as if she didn't want to be overheard.

"It's okay, it's just my friend Denzil. Where are you? What the hell is going on?" He felt his face suddenly become hot. He knew he was blushing and hoped that it wasn't too obvious to Denzil how awkward and guilty he felt.

"I'm sorry, David, I really am, but now I've had time to think I've realised I do owe you an explanation. Could we meet? Perhaps at the restaurant in St. Agnes?"

"Okay, when? In an hour?"

He hung up the receiver and wiped his sweaty palms on the sides of his trousers. Turning, he was surprised to see Denzil looking at him in horror.

"David, have you really been messing about with his wife? Do you know what you're playing about with? If you want to commit suicide just take a gun and blow your brains out. It'll be a damned sight quicker and a lot less painful, believe me."

"I'm not 'messing about', as you call it, Denzil. We just met, had a talk, a bite to eat, and that was it."

Denzil slowly lifted his massive frame from the chair and looked hard at David. "I'm not stupid, my 'andsome," he said very quietly. "I just saw the effect she had on you on the phone, and I really don't know how to impress on you what you're messing with here."

He slowly walked to the door and then turned and said, "There was one bloke, a couple of years ago, who expressed interest in her. Didn't meet her, didn't talk to her, didn't have a bite to eat with her. Just expressed interest. Disappeared for a few days. Then he turned up, in a yard, behind a restaurant, in some bin-liners." He waited for a moment, perhaps wondering whether to add any more details, or perhaps just for dramatic effect, and then, staring directly into David's eyes, added, "Cubed." He opened the door and again looked hard at David. "Leave it alone, boy," he said as he let himself out.

Chapter Thirteen

SHE WAS SITTING IN a corner of the restaurant hidden so well in the gloom that David had difficulty in recognising her immediately when he walked in. As he approached her he could see that she was showing signs of considerable strain. It was almost as if she had shrunk slightly. Certainly her face was thinner and her fingers were nervously playing with the silver salt pot. She was so withdrawn and totally engrossed in apparently studying the bubbles floating on the surface of her cup of coffee that she hadn't noticed his arrival and jumped when he quietly said, "Hello Anna. It's good to see you again. Where've you been hiding?"

"David! I'm sorry. I didn't see you come in. Please, sit down. Have some coffee. I took the liberty of ordering some for you. Would you like something to eat?" As she spoke, her face became brighter, and as he looked into her eyes it was obvious to him how happy she was to see him.

"Thanks," he said as he sat facing her, "but I had something to eat before I came out. What about you?"

She smiled and said, "I'm not hungry at the moment."

There was an awkward moment, so David said, "I left Charlie at home gnawing a bone."

He couldn't help but notice the slight tremor in her hand as she poured him a cup of coffee and added a dash of cream with two spoons of sugar. "You see, I remember how you like it." She smiled nervously as she passed him the cup.

"Thanks." He slowly stirred the coffee, "Well, how've you been? Where are you staying? I notice you've not been at the cottage."

"No, you're right. I'm not at the cottage, but I don't think it would be a good idea for you to know where I've been staying." She looked down, embarrassed, and David noticed her fingers nervously pulling at the tablecloth.

"Why not? I promise I won't breathe a word to anyone, and I'm very resistant to pain, so I'm very good under torture."

Quickly she looked up at him, her eyes wide. "For God's sake don't ever joke about things like that." She was suddenly sharp and brittle. "You don't know what you're dealing with."

David felt his body press back into the chair, responding to the force of her attack. "That's the second time I've heard that today," he said. "So what am I dealing with? Or rather, what are you dealing with? Come to think of it, what are you really doing down here?" David felt himself getting slightly irritated. "Why are you running away from him? Why has he got you so almighty scared? Have you nicked his gold cards or something?"

Anna sighed and smiled. Reaching across the table she lightly touched his left hand. "If only it were that simple, David." She stared at a spot on the wall directly behind David's head, for a moment lost in thought, and then nodded and looked at him. "Yes, you could say I've taken something away from him. Something he will move heaven and earth to get back, even torture, maim and kill to get back. Something he considers his prize possession." She paused and looked nervously out of the window. Then, turning to David, quietly she said, "Me. I've taken away me. And he wants me back, and I don't want to go." She looked down as tears welled from her eyes.

"Can't you get a divorce?" he asked, frowning.

Anna shook her head. "No," she said emphatically, "No one gets divorced from that family." She reached down, picked up her handbag and pulled out a tissue. "The only way out I'm afraid is in a very ornate wooden box." She sighed and delicately wiped away her tears. "God, what the hell am I going to do?"

"Well, the first thing is, you don't panic. We'll think of something." He tried to sound confident, but the truth was that, contrary to what she thought, he knew exactly what it was he was dealing with. Just thinking of his disastrous meeting with her husband in the pub made him break out in a cold sweat. Memories of his stay in Italy rubbing shoulders with, and working for, men who had been just like Antonio Taverna came flooding into this mind. He knew just what kind of animal they were dealing with, what these men were capable of. On the surface they were smart, urbane and sociable, some of them even very likeable. However, underneath the facade they were totally self-seeking, greedy and ruthless, prepared, without a second thought to do absolutely anything to preserve their power and wealth.

Anna looked at him, smiled and lightly touched his hand. "Thank you, David. I know you're trying to make me feel better, but I'm afraid there's nothing you or anyone else can do to help. I'm going to have to work this out myself."

They sat quietly for a few moments and then Anna looked at him and went on, "You asked me what I was really doing down here. Well, you know, when I came down here, I had absolutely no idea at all what I was doing. I acted in total panic. I thought it was in some way an escape, that I'd find an answer to it all." She paused and looked out of the window. Then, leaning back in her chair, her eyes dancing with amusement she said, "Well, at least I found out who my Roman soldier is. That problem is apparently solved." A moment later her face grew serious and very quietly she murmured, "But he's not going to get you this time round."

David shook his head, perplexed. "I'm sorry, I've got absolutely no idea what you're talking about," he said. "I may have given you the impression that I did, but if I'm really honest I've got to admit there's a host of things I don't really understand." He hesitated and then continued, "For instance, how on earth, if this bloke is such a bastard, did you get hooked up with him in the first place? And what is all this stuff about a Roman? What's it got to do with you in the here and now?"

"Okay," she said taking a long deep breath, "let's take Antonio for a start. First of all, from a woman's point of view this guy had everything, looks, charm, wealth, social standing and even on occasions a great sense of humour. When I first met him I was completely bowled over, head over heels, totally smitten by his . . ."

"Okay, you've made your point," David interrupted dryly. "I take it you liked him."

Anna laughed. "Sorry if I laboured it a little, but you must realise I had never met anyone like this before."

"So what ruined it for you?"

She sat apparently deep in thought for a while and then slowly went on, "At first everything was wonderful, like in a fairy-tale, until, one day I had a call from a dear friend, an agent, asking me to do a show. It seemed they had been let down by a model and were in a bit of a panic. Of course I said I would be delighted to help them out, but when I told Antonio what I had promised he went mad, crazy. I've never seen anyone lose it quite so completely. I thought he was going to attack me. Of course I had to then ring my friend, go back on my word and cancel the booking."

"Ouch, agents don't like that sort of thing."

"No, but I'm very lucky. He understands."

"You're extremely lucky. There aren't many people in my business who would be so understanding."

"We've been colleagues and friends for a long time now, and I've helped them out quite a bit in the past."

"And since your old man lost his rag, what?"

"Since then, I learned pretty fast not to question him at all about his work, or anything, for that matter. I don't know whether it's that he's changed, or I've just found out a bit more about him, but over the last couple of years I've been seeing him in a totally different light. Oh, he's just as charming as he was, but," she hesitated as if not knowing how to express what she wanted to say. After a few moments with the fingers of her left hand gently twisting her lower lip in her concentration, she slowly continued, "I started to sense something different about him. It's difficult to explain, but it was a general air of menace. Particularly when I saw him dealing with business associates. I started to feel that, even when he wasn't saying anything he was exuding a threat of violence. It was the things he didn't say when he was on the phone. The threat always seemed to be implied."

She paused as if there were something she wanted to say but didn't know whether to or not. Then, with a sigh she whispered, "And then he started to beat me."

David stared at her, horrified, not knowing what to say.

"He was very careful never to leave marks where they could be seen," she continued, "and it was only now and then, but, God, it hurt."

"Is there nowhere you can go, nobody you could see to get help? The police, social services . . ." He stopped in frustration as he looked into her eyes and saw her utter helplessness, her understanding that there was nobody to help her, nowhere to go for shelter.

"God, he's even more of an evil bastard than I thought when I met him."

Anna's mouth sagged open and her eyes opened wide in horror and fear. "He's spoken to you? When? How?"

"He and another goon followed me into the pub. Apparently he went there yesterday asking after you. Showed them your picture and asked if anyone had seen you. Of course they weren't to know what was going on, so the bar man told him about you and the fact that I had spoken to you. I must say, I've mixed with gangsters and even mafiosi in Italy, but your husband managed to put the fear of God into me with just one look."

"Oh, my God! David I'm so sorry. What can I do?" Suddenly she was sobbing and shaking uncontrollably, holding her hands to her face. "Oh, I'm so sorry!"

David was taken completely by surprise by the swiftness of the change in her and for a few seconds was unable to respond. However he then stood up, and moved to her side. Putting his left arm on her shoulder he softly said, "It's alright. There's no harm done. He asked me the questions and when he realised I didn't know where you were he went away."

"Don't you realise, he doesn't give up! He'll be back!" As her fear increased so did the level of her voice. Then she swiftly got to her feet and put her arms around his neck. "I'm so sorry my dear. I can see there's only one thing I can do." Desperately she clung to him and kissed him hard on the lips. "Please don't think bad of me. I'll never forget you." With that she put her hands on both his cheeks and lightly kissed him again. Then, suddenly she was gone, leaving him again bewildered, staring at the wall, not able to react at all to the sudden turn of events. He turned just as Anthony emerged from the kitchen.

"Dear boy, what's going on? I heard raised voices. Where is she? Where's Anna?"

David looked at him in astonishment. "She's done it again!" he cried out. "She's bloody well done it again!" With that he started to run to the door just as Anthony himself started to walk there. They collided, but by the time they had recovered enough from the collision, opened the door and stumbled out into the street there was no sign of her.

Chapter Fourteen

DAVID HAD NO IDEA how much time had passed, nor did he remember how he got there, but, as if he were waking from a dream, he suddenly became aware of himself sitting near the cliff edge high above St. Agnes village. Perhaps it was the rain that brought him to his senses, for his neck had become uncomfortable as the water dripped on to the collar of his shirt, and his hands were so cold they were beginning to become painful. The rain must have only just started to fall, for his clothes were only lightly dusted with tiny droplets of water. Below him the Towanroath engine house marked the site of the shaft down which, according to ancient legend, the fearsome monster, Bolster, tricked by the cunning of St. Agnes, allowed his blood to flow, not knowing that the shaft had no bottom and emptied out into the sea. Out to sea a huge, dark cloud hung over the water, with rain cascading from it diagonally onto the waves which were beginning to be whipped into a froth by the savage gusts of wind sweeping around Godrevy Island. Normally David would go to any lengths to avoid getting cold and wet, but today he slowly stood, walked, uncaring, back over into the lee of the ruins of the old Wheal Coates engine house and sat on the ground. Not thinking about anything at all, he just watched the rivulets of water trickle down the side of the hill, cross the path and disappear into the dark depths of the prickly gorse.

After a while pictures started to form in his mind and without any conscious effort David found himself immersed in a pool of memories. Suddenly he was back to his first meeting with Tina. He had been playing the piano for a cocktail party on board the P&O ship Canberra. Almost in a dream state he had allowed his fingers to go their own way, just a small part of his mind dictating the broad sweep of harmonies and melodies, so that the result, the outcome of years of tight discipline and practice, sounded light, melodious, and unobtrusive, a gentle flowing stream of sound below the dissonant chatter of about six hundred voices fighting for attention and supremacy.

Lifting his head he glanced around the crowded room. Everything appeared to him to be boringly normal. People in clothes they were, for the most part, wearing for the first time, trying to make conversation with total strangers, some of them striving to create a favourable impression, above all, most of them, trying their best to come to terms with the totally foreign environment in which they would have to exist for the following two weeks. For, the first captain's cocktail party can be a frightening affair for the socially conscious. There is an instantaneous comparison of dress and accent, a sizing up, an organizing of the relative positions in the new social context.

David had been studying the crowd for some time when he realised that someone was standing silently behind his left shoulder. Turning his head he looked up and found himself staring into the most strikingly beautiful eyes he had ever seen, dark brown, almond shaped and laughing in a kindly, I'd-like-to-be-friends way. Her face was pale with very little make-up, soft, round cheeks and shoulder length blond hair. Her eyelids widened in surprise as David stopped playing and held out his right hand across his body.

"Hi," he said, holding her gaze, "I'm David."

She awkwardly reached out and held his hand and, embarrassed, spluttered, "Oh, please, don't stop for me. Won't you get into trouble?"

"Not at all. Look around. There are only two people who've noticed, that woman in the ghastly pink over there by the bar. And, of course, the captain."

"Won't he mind, then?" she asked, astonished.

He laughed. "No. Part of my job is to keep the customers happy. So, as long as I don't make a habit of it or stop for too long he won't care." David waved at the captain who nodded and delivered a lascivious wink before turning to deal with a pretty, pearl-laden middle-aged, social climber, who was directing her large chest up at him as if for appraisal.

"Is this your first cruise, then?" David asked. And then quickly, before she could reply, "I'm sorry, I didn't get your name."

"Tina. My name's Tina, and no, it isn't my first cruise. We come on every year."

"We?"

"My parents. They're the short, bald man over there." She quickly pointed to a group standing near to the captain. "Mum's opposite him in the sparkly green."

David looked across the room at them and noted the stern disapproving looks on both their faces as they looked across at him. He smiled, waved and started to play 'Isn't she lovely?' Neither of the parents seemed to understand and continued to glower at him. Tina lightly punched him in the back in an attempt to cover her embarrassment.

* * *

As he sat beneath the towering walls of Wheal Coates' engine house David remembered how they had never approved of him, even after the wedding, even after seeing how happy their daughter was, even after the months and months of love and care he had devoted to Tina before she had died.

He had been there for about an hour when Anthony found him staring out to sea, apparently totally oblivious to the cold and wet.

"Dear boy, what on earth do you think you are doing? Come on then, come with me. I've got the car down in the car park in Chapel Porth. I'll take you home and run you a nice hot bath. You can pick up your car in St. Agnes car park another day. What a good job you didn't bring Charlie with you. Poor thing would have died her death of cold." Chattering in this fashion he helped David stand up, and, supporting him, they both stumbled and staggered down the steep path, past the Killas, the quarry which had produced the stones to build the buildings in Wheal Coates, past the White Rocks and down onto the beach.

* * *

Later, as David lay in his bed, warm and dry, he realised he had very little memory of what had happened to him between the time of Anna's sudden departure and his feeling the shock and pain of the change from peeling off his wet, cold clothes and getting into a very hot bath. Then he remembered he had been thinking of Tina and how they had met. Smiling he wondered whether the captain had ever managed to get rid of the woman at the cocktail party. Relaxing with that thought he realised he owed a debt of gratitude to his friend Anthony and as he wondered how he would ever repay him he fell into a deep, dreamless sleep.

* * *

Later, much later, he felt as if he were being dragged up out of a bottomless pit. Something was pressing against his throat making it difficult to breathe and as he struggled he realised he was completely helpless. He tried to open his eyes but found himself blinded by the light of a very strong torch. Someone was very firmly slapping his face.

"Wake up, wake up! Porca madonna, but you sleep the sleep of the dead. Which you may soon be if you do not tell me what it is I want to know."

David was seized by a terrible fear, a fear which sucked all the strength out of his body, to such an extent that, even if the person who was holding his throat had loosened his grip, he would have been unable to retaliate in any way at all. He tried to say something but could only produce a gargling sound.

The silky voice was calm, yet terrifying. "Do not try to talk. I shall ask you a question and when I want you to answer I shall loosen my grip on your throat."

David again tried to speak, again only managed a gurgle and a moment later winced as his face was sharply slapped.

"Perhaps you are deaf as well as stupid. Listen!" and the voice grew just a little louder. "I shall say this just once more. Do not speak. I shall ask you a question. You will answer it, and you will tell me the truth, or my friend here will kill your dog. That would be a pity, because I am a great lover of animals. I love them, baked, boiled or fried." He laughed, the short disdainful laugh of the bully in command.

As he spoke the beam of the torch flashed away to illuminate Charlie held very tightly by another man. His right arm was wrapped around her body and his left hand held her jaws tightly closed so that the only sound she could make was a pathetic whimper in the back of her throat.

"Now, do you understand me? If you do, blink twice."

David blinked twice.

"Good. I see you are not deaf. Let us see if you are stupid. Now, you will tell me what it is I want to know. Where is my wife? Where is Anna Taverna?"

Slowly he moved his hand just far enough away from David's throat so that he could, with an effort, answer.

Again, just as he had in the pub when he first met Antonio Taverna, David felt the cold grip of fear in his stomach. His throat dried out completely and again he found he could not speak.

"What is the matter with you? Have you lost your tongue? If you do not find it again very quickly I shall go looking for it, and when I find it I shall rip it out and feed it to your dog. That is, if she is still alive."

It was as if all the strength was oozing out of his body. Never before had David felt so totally powerless. He was afraid that if he told the truth he would end up 'cubed', as his friend Denzil had so graphically described. He also knew that he was incapable of lying well enough to pull the wool over this gangster's eyes.

"I'm waiting."

Slowly and painfully David swallowed and said, "I honestly don't know where she is."

He gasped as his head as jolted back onto the pillow by the force of the slap he received.

"How the hell am I supposed to know?" he cried out. "If she isn't in the cottage I have no idea where she is. How could I know?"

"She might have told you when you saw her. You have seen her, I know you have, so there is no use you denying it. This is Cornwall, remember. You do something and everyone knows." He waited a moment and then quietly said, "Kill the dog."

"No, wait!" David shouted. "Okay. I've seen her." He was now bordering on hysteria. "She called me and said she had to talk to somebody. She sounded upset, very upset."

"Where did she call you from? She was not in the cottage."

"A cafe, in St. Agnes."

"Why would she call you. You are an insignificant nobody."

"I don't know. Perhaps it's because I'm the only person she's met here. I have some of the keys to the cottage. I look after it."

"Why was she upset?"

David hesitated knowing that if he told Antonio the truth there was the likelihood that both he and Charlie would have their throats cut immediately.

"Well?"

"She has been having a dream."

"What? Do not play games with me. I do not like games."

"It's true. She's been having a dream for a long time now, a terrible frightening dream."

There was a long pause during which Antonio stared at David as if trying to penetrate his skull and discover if he were telling the truth.

"Tell me about this dream." His voice was now very quiet, but also the level of menace appeared to get stronger.

David knew that if he told the truth exactly that it would sound ridiculous and he would never be believed.

"She's afraid," he managed to croak and coughed again as if it were difficult to speak. "No, not just afraid, she's been terrified for some time now by a dream in which she gets killed."

"Killed? How? Who kills her?"

"I don't know what it's all about." At least that part was true. "I just know she gets killed, stabbed to death. She can see it all, feel it." David suddenly realised that what he was saying had had an effect on Antonio, for the gangster released his hold on David's neck and stood away from the bed so that he couldn't be seen in the dark.

"It's been getting worse and worse recently . . ." David had started to get a little more confident and there was a danger of his spoiling everything, but he was abruptly cut short by Antonio's violent command, "Silenzio! Zitto!" Lying in the bed David felt himself start to shiver as if with cold. He was surprised because a part of him was aware of being quite warm in the bed. He strained, trying to make out the shape of Charlie, but the light in his eyes was too strong. His blood pounded loudly in his ears and his throat felt dry and painful from the punishment it had suffered from the hands of the Italian. Suddenly he gasped, then immediately gagged as the hand again whipped out of the darkness and gripped his throat.

"You will say nothing of this to anybody." The voice was silky smooth and petrifying in its implied menace.

And then, suddenly, they were gone. The light was extinguished and swiftly, smoothly, silently they had moved to the already open bedroom door, casually tossing Charlie onto the bed before closing it.

David lay for a long time in the dark, unable to control the shaking of his body. Then slowly, painfully he sat up and reached out for his dog. Surprised to find that she too was shivering he held her close and both of them lay down together till their fear subsided, their bodies warmed each other and they fell into a deep, dark sleep.

* * *

It must have been quite early in the morning, for it was still pitch black outside, when David struggled to wake up out of another horror. Slowly he sat up and reached for the comfort of Charlie's warmth. In his dream he had been lying on a cold rough table in a frightful room of dark grey stone, the walls of which glistened with tiny rivulets of water. The picture in his mind was still vividly clear, the evil leering of a black-haired, pock-marked face, ugly beyond belief in the delight it was taking in inflicting pain. David could still feel the agony in his chest; a sharp, bright, deeply searing pain, which started in the sternum and swiftly, spread throughout his body. As he had woken, terrified by the horror of what he had experienced, the scene had imprinted itself on his memory. Now, detached from it, he could see himself spread-eagled on an old rough table, his arms and legs tightly tied to metal rings bolted down on the four corners. A large, grossly fat man was bending over the table with his left hand pressing down on the chest of his pathetic figure, presumably to stop him from arching in the agony of the torture. In the man's right hand was a sword, which he was very slowly pushing into the sternum horizontally, so that it was gradually being directed towards the throat of the poor wretch.

Very gradually David became detached from the scene, viewing it as he would one on the television, but, even though he ceased to be part of it emotionally, he could not help but gasp as, just as the picture in his mind started to fade, he caught sight of a sinister figure standing in the gloom by the doorway. The man was very well dressed in expensive, brightly coloured clothing of a period of history David remembered very well, about the time of Henry VIII, for he had only recently seen a re-run on television of the film *A Man for all Seasons*. His elegance stood out in sharp contrast to the dirty, dinginess of the rest of the room. However, although he was immobile, not taking part in the torture, there was an air of menace about him, the stillness of the predator waiting for the kill. David shuddered, gripped by fear, for, although he was unable to see his face in the gloom, he had a feeling that, somehow, he knew the man, had known him for a long, long time, and had suffered at his hands many, many times.

David was brought back to the reality and the warmth of his bed by Charlie gently licking the back of his hand as if she understood his need for comfort. He lay dozing for a couple of minutes, gently massaging her throat, before falling away into a deep, dreamless, healing sleep.

Chapter Fifteen

THE NEXT MORNING HE awoke very slowly, almost painfully, wanting to stay for a long time in the womb-like comfort of the bed, but as soon as he moved and gently grunted a hoarse greeting to Charlie, she leaped from the bed and, standing by the bedroom door, barked an insistent demand to be let out. Slowly he struggled down the stairs, opened the front door, stepped out into the garden and, with some difficulty, for his throat was painful from the punishment it had received during the night, breathed in the sweet smell of morning air. Charlie seemed not to have been affected by the events of the night, for she hurled herself into the hedge in a frenzy of barking, driving away a couple of heavy cows in the adjoining field. The cottage opposite looked forlorn and empty and David was tempted for a moment to go over to see if there were any signs of Anna. Then, feeling a little foolish at his adolescent yearnings, he turned and went back into the cottage for breakfast.

He had just finished the last mouthful of porridge when there was a loud knock at the door. David felt a sudden surge of fear in the solar plexus as the door was gently pushed open.

"Who's there?" he shouted, rising nervously from the table. Charlie rushed to the door barking her most vicious threat, and as it opened a little further backed away.

"Are you all right, David?" Denzil tentatively poked his head inside and Charlie immediately calmed and ran to greet him as he walked into the room. "I was in St. Agnes, saw your car parked there this morning early on, and as I was passing thought I'd just check to see if you were okay."

David stood nervously at the table and hesitantly mumbled, "Hi Denzil, good to see you. Yes, I'm okay."

"Are you sure, boy? You look bloody awful. What've you been up to?"

"I'm alright, I really am, just a little tired."

"Nonsense. If I looked as bad as you do I'd make a booking with the undertaker. Come on now. You pour me a cup of tea and tell me all about it." Denzil sank his huge frame into the armchair by the fireplace, and as it became immediately obvious to David that he was not going to be deterred he poured him a cup and joined him.

Slowly he described everything that had happened, except for the dream that had caused him such pain and terror. Denzil listened with keen attention, and when David started to describe the events of the early morning when he had been interrogated by Antonio, he leaned forward staring unwavering at David's face.

"Well," he said dryly, when David at last got to the end of his sad story, "at least I know why you look so bloody awful. And I'm not going to tell you 'I told you so', but at least perhaps now you understand fully what it is you're playing with." Denzil shook his head and took a gulp of his tea.

"You know I've been around more than most people," David said a little wearily. "Worked very happily with gangsters and mafiosi in Italy, but it's never really registered what kind of men they are. The evil they put out is beyond description."

Denzil stabbed the air with a forefinger. "This is obviously the first time you've crossed one of them."

"Obviously." David paused for a moment. "I remember once in a hotel south of Milan, we were on a long contract in the night club and living in the hotel. There was a group of 'business men' living there with whom we got very friendly. They were wonderful to us, sent us champagne every night, took us out to dinner in the town during the day. Wouldn't accept any payment from us."

"A real bunch of regular guys, eh?" Denzil laughed and rolled his eyes up.

"Yeah. Well, one night a girl arrived late during a thunderstorm and booked in. She was English so naturally I had the job of translating for her. It turned out that she had been living with an Italian boy in a flat in town." David stood, picked up Denzil's empty cup and walked over to the table. "One day she was taken ill and had to spend a couple of weeks in the hospital. When they let her out she returned home only to find her boy friend had moved someone else in in her place." He quickly refilled Denzil's cup with tea and heaped in four spoons of sugar.

"Don't tell me – she was broke."

"Spot on, not a lira to her name," David said as he walked over to Denzil and handed him his cup.

102

"So did they boot her out of the hotel?"

"No. By the time the owner found out, she was heart to heart with Mario, the chief 'business man'," he said sitting down and staring into the fireplace.

"Cosy," said Denzil, noisily sipping his hot tea.

"Yes, but you must realise this was the first time I'd come across people like this. So when she came to me one day and said Mario had agreed to pay her bill and give her a train ticket to England I believed her."

"God, but you were green." Again Denzil looked up at the ceiling in a gesture of disbelief.

"Yes, and didn't I look stupid," David said looking away, "when, after she'd gone, I was talking to the owner, and I mentioned in passing how great I thought Mario had been to pay her bill." He laughed and shook his head. "He quietly took me by the arm, led me into his office and showed me heaps and heaps of bills on hooks all around two walls." David stood and waved his arms around the room as if to show just how many shelves of receipts there had been. "'They have been here two years and not paid a single lira', the boss explained to me very patiently. 'Two years. Every night in the night club, champagne and girls. Food in the restaurant. Four double rooms they take up'."

"Can't you go to the police? I asked him. I can tell you, Denzil, I was absolutely outraged."

"And rightly so, my friend." Denzil nodded.

"He'd laughed. 'Sure,' he said, 'but tomorrow they burn down my hotel'."

Denzil stood up having noisily finished his tea. "Nice people," he muttered. "I've met 'em."

"But that's it!" David exclaimed, also standing up. "To us they were marvellous, generous and kind. It was only after that, that I realised that whenever they took us to dinner in the town we had the best service, the waiters were obsequious, everything done at the double and no-one ever paid as we left."

"And they never asked anything of you?"

"No, never. I suppose it was because we were the entertainers. They always said it was enough for them to be seen with us."

"There's none so queer as folk." Said Denzil as he bent down to pat Charlie. "That's why I love your dog so much. She's so uncomplicated."

With that he walked ponderously over to the door, opened it and turned to David. "If I find this Italian I'll have words with him. I'll be wasting my time, I know 'cos he'll be well covered. I just hope you've learned something. See you." The door closed quietly behind him.

Chapter Sixteen

"DAVID, DEAR BOY! HOW are you? I can see you've not fully recovered yet." Anthony was being his usual diplomatic self.

It was now mid-morning. David had soaked for a long time in a hot bath in an attempt to repair some of the physical and psychological damage he had suffered during the night. Then after dressing in a leisurely fashion he had decided to walk with Charlie into St. Agnes to pick up his car.

"Thanks, Anthony, but Denzil has already made it very clear how awful I look this morning."

"He should keep his thoughts to himself. Such a gross man. Agh!" Anthony shuddered at some unspoken thought and waved David to a table. "Sit down. I've something to talk to you about." David slowly took off his coat and sat down as Anthony poured him a coffee.

"Here you are. A bit stronger than normal, cause I'm afraid I'm the bearer of bad news."

David groaned. "Oh, no, what now?"

"I'm sorry to have to tell you, dear boy," and he hesitated as if reluctant to continue, then he whispered, "she's gone."

"What do you mean, gone?"

"He came for her early this morning."

"Who came for her? What are you talking about?"

"The Neanderthal, her husband, of course."

"Here? He came here. But why? I don't understand!"

"Anna was staying here. Somehow he worked it out, or someone told him. You know how it is around here."

Suddenly it became so clear to David. "Of course," he whispered, "I remember now. The first time we were here, when she left, she held back talking to you. You fixed it up then."

"Yes. I'm sorry we had to keep it from you. Subterfuge always makes me feel awful. She thought everybody would be a lot safer if no one knew."

"How was it? I mean, was he violent? Did she resist? Couldn't you stop it?"

"Dear boy, there was no drama, no histrionics. As I opened up the front door to air the place, there he was. With his goon, of course. He just said, 'Tell her I'm here', came in and sat down, and what could I do? He just fixed me with a psychopathic stare and I'm afraid I just felt as if I was starting to melt."

"I'm sorry, Anthony, I know exactly how you felt. They came to see me in the middle of the night."

"Oh, God, he didn't hurt you, did he?"

"Not really, just scared the daylights out of me, even put the frighteners on the dog." David stopped and stared out of the window. "I hope I didn't give anything away."

"How could you have? You didn't know. That was the whole idea of not telling you."

"Yes, of course, that's right. So what did you do?"

"I didn't have to do anything. She just appeared, said something in Italian to him, I didn't understand, and then said to me, 'Thank you, Anthony, you've been most kind'. Very formal she was, very business-like. Then she gave me a huge wadge of money and said, 'This should cover everything', and before I could say anything she swept out of the door, and she was gone, and he with her." Anthony walked over to the till and took from behind it a sheet of paper.

"Hidden in the money was this note. It's for you, dear boy."

He handed the paper to David and walked away into the kitchen.

My dear David,

> *Well, I really made a mess of things this time, didn't I? Here you were gently living your country life, a little lonely perhaps, and I'm so sorry about that, but generally without a care in the world, writing your music and loving your dog. And then along I come and turn you upside down and inside out. Here's where I feel I should say I'm sorry, but instead I feel as if what has happened has had some purpose in it, that there's been a damned good reason for it. However, I feel so very sad at the moment that I can't for the life of me think about anything deep or meaningful.*

> *My dear, I'm afraid I can see only one way out of this. I'm going to have to go back with him when he comes for me, which I know he surely will. And I'm going to have to make the best of a very bad job. I just feel so very sad that I couldn't get to know my Roman soldier a bit better. I truly think we could have done some lovely things*

together. However, remember what I said to you shortly after we first met – that I believe there's a purpose for everything that happens to us. So, never give up hope. Do not think too badly of me. Give Charlie a lovely big hug from me and tell Anthony and Ben they will always have a place in my heart. Give Beth a huge kiss and tell her I hope you'll both be very happy.

Love, Anna

* * *

For what seemed a long time David sat at the table staring into an empty lonely void, not moving or caring about the tears streaming down his cheeks, and, at last, when Anthony came out and silently exchanged his cold cup of coffee for a fresh hot cup, he made no attempt to drink.

Anthony stood before him for a while and then very softly said, "Come on, dear boy. Take a sip or two. It'll do you good." So he absent-mindedly sipped the coffee for a while, and then quietly stood up, motioned to Charlie to follow him, put on his coat and walked out of the door into the gently falling rain without saying another word.

Anthony picked up his coffee cup and shook his head.

"It's not going to be easy, dear boy," he murmured.

Outside, on the wet pavement David put Charlie on a lead and they walked slowly through the village, which was surprisingly busy in spite of the rain. He had no clear idea of where he was going, but after he had walked down the steep incline alongside the picturesque Stippy Stappy cottages, and found himself staring, not seeing anything, into the window of a gift shop, he realised that unconsciously he was being drawn to Beth's cottage.

Swiftly, as if a decision had been made, he walked down the tree lined Quay Road leading to Trevaunance Cove, but before getting there he turned right onto a steep coastal path, and struggled up towards the old Wheal Kitty mine and Beth's cottage.

Chapter Seventeen

BETH HAD BEEN STANDING at the window looking out at the magnificence of the view when she had seen David struggling against the force of the wind, his face twisted as the rain lashed against his back. Immediately she saw him she sensed that something dreadful had happened, something that had affected him to the very depths of his being. Quickly she opened the door to him as he hurried down her path, her round face smiling a welcome, her long colourful gown, blown back by the keen sou'westerly and pressing against the curves of her statuesque body.

"Hi, David, you must have known. I've just put the kettle on." Tossing her ringlets back she turned and walked into the darkness of her cottage. "Don't hang about," she called. "That wind's driving the rain in."

David forced the door back closed, took off his coat and hung it up. There was a towel hanging behind the door for Charlie so he gave the dog a vigorous rub down. Nevertheless she still energetically shook herself, spraying what was left of the wet on her all around the tiny hall. David took off his wet, muddy shoes and followed Charlie into Beth's sitting room. He had been there many times, but never tired of the array of drapes and wall hangings, the multitude of hues of blues and greens, the soft cushions and bright carpets, glistening crystals and tinkling glass wind chimes. He sank into the softness of a welcoming settee, and, enveloped in the warmth of the spluttering log fire, surrendered to the peace. In the background he could hear Beth gently arranging mugs, opening and closing cupboard doors. He closed his eyes and tried to calm the chaos of his mind.

"So, what's happened?" Beth had come in and put the tray down on a small table so quietly that he hadn't heard her movement at all. She sat down on a cushion on the floor by his legs and with her left arm stretched across his knees, she turned towards him and took hold of his right hand with hers.

"If you don't mind my saying, you look bloody awful," she whispered.

David stared into the fire and without looking at Beth said, "She's gone."

"What do you mean?"

"Anna, I mean, Anna. The bastard's got her, and she's gone."

"Where to?"

"Back to wherever she came from, with him."

Beth squeezed his hand. "Oh, my God, the poor girl!"

He turned his head slightly to look at her, his face now wet with tears, "He took her back with him and I couldn't do a damned thing to help her!"

Beth stood up crossed the room and returned with a fist full of paper handkerchiefs. Sitting down beside him on the settee she very carefully wiped his face and then wrapped her arms around him holding him tightly for a long time as he wept out his sadness and frustration. Then, as she felt his body relax, his anger and sadness for the moment spent, she carefully stood up, stretched him out. Taking a soft throw from an armchair, she covered him as he sank into a deep restful sleep.

She woke him at lunchtime with a plate of ham and cheese and salad, which she insisted that he eat. For Charlie, who had spent the time sleeping in front of the fire, she opened a tin of tuna, which the dog wolfed down in a few seconds. Then, after the meal, contented, they sat in separate armchairs, cosy in front of the fire, sipping hot, sweet coffee and he told her all that had happened to him since their conversation on the phone in the pub: Denzil's visit, meeting Anna at the café, being rescued by Anthony on the cliff top, Antonio's night time visit, which made her gasp in horror, his dreams and visiting Anthony at the café. He ended by showing her the note that Anna had left him.

"My God. You poor thing. All that has happened since yesterday?"

"I'm afraid so."

"No wonder you're so shattered."

She quickly read the note, folded it and handed it back to him.

"What's going to happen to her, then?" she asked quietly.

"God only knows, I don't."

They sat staring into the flames in silence for a while.

David broke the silence with, "I remember that when I last saw her, she said that there was only one thing she could do. Now I know what she meant. She knew that she had to go back to him."

A thought came to him suddenly. "You know, I bet it was she who let him know where she was. She told me she couldn't divorce him. 'There's only one way out of that family – in a very ornate wooden box'. That's what she said."

"She's not going to top herself, is she?"

"I don't know," he said frowning, and then a moment later, "no, I don't think she would do that. She seemed too," he hesitated and thought about it for a moment, and then found the word he was looking for, 'resigned'."

Beth was quiet, staring into the fire. "She's waiting for something. Don't ask me what. I just have a feeling of her sitting back and waiting," she said.

Charlie stood up, stretched, turned around in a circle and flopped down again in front of the fire.

Beth poured them out another cup of coffee. "What about your dreams?" she said, "You seem to have something really frightening coming out there."

"Yes, and it looks as though it's something to do with a girl. I feel it's tied up with a dream I had a while back about a girl I was looking for. She was there for one moment, but it was too quick. However, even though it was only for an instant I did get a good look at her."

"Yes, I remember you said you had seen her when we were speaking on the phone. Well, come on, tell me again. What was she like."

David thought hard for a moment. "It's hard to describe. She was, I'd say, in her late teens. Pale faced, er . . . sandy coloured hair, in ringlets hanging down, like yours, but not as long. Shoulder length. The dress and the feeling all round is Tudor, I think."

"Make up?"

"None that I noticed."

"No, but you are a man."

"Thank you. And so therefore, I wouldn't notice things like that?"

"Exactly."

"Chauvinism works both ways, you know."

"Yes, I know, but, close your eyes for a moment."

David frowned but after a moment's hesitation closed his eyes.

"Okay," she said, "now what colour eye shadow do I have on now? And keep your eyes shut!"

"That's simple. You don't have any on. You never do."

"Now open them, and take a good look."

Slowly he opened his eyes to find her standing, bent over, leaning on the arms of his chair, her face just an inch or two away from his.

"Now tell me," she whispered in a smooth breathy voice.

111

He could now see clearly how delicately she had applied her eye shadow.

"Okay, you win, howev . . ." he was stopped from saying anything further by her lips, soft and warm pressing gently on his mouth.

They stayed like this for what seemed a very long time, but was in fact only a few seconds, before he felt her mouth leave his. He opened his eyes to see her standing in front of him, her hands on her hips, her eyes laughing.

"No further today," she said. "You're in no fit state to defend yourself."

She laughed, and both of them had the same thought, *but it won't be long now.*

For the first time David found himself actually looking forward to making love to her without any feeling of guilt.

"Time to go, my dear," she said.

Reluctantly he agreed, "I suppose so," he said slowly tearing himself away from the comfortable embrace of the armchair. "Come on Charlie. Time to go home." Charlie looked up at him, wagged her tail, yawned, stretched and stood up.

It was as he was putting on his still-wet coat that a thought suddenly came to him, and he laughed.

Beth looked at him, her eyebrows raised. "What is it?" she said.

"I've just remembered," he murmured. "I came out to pick up my car from the car park in St. Agnes." He sighed and shook his head in disbelief.

"And you walked here in the pouring rain, got wet through and messed up my nice clean porch," Beth reached out to him and folded him into a tender embrace. "What a dodo," she whispered. They held each other close, relaxed and happy in their intimacy. "By the way, I'm not teasing," she whispered in his ear. "I just know, we have to wait a while."

He slowly broke away from her.

"So, how long?" he asked and smiled.

"I don't know. All they tell me is, 'Wait'."

"I wish they'd mind their own business."

"They are, my dear. They are."

*   *   *

Later, when she had returned from driving them to the car park, Beth sat in her favourite armchair and stared into the gently flickering flames of the fire, watching the pictures that flashed into her mind.

She was a natural psychic and medium. From her early childhood in Ongar, Essex, she had both seen and heard people and voices that she very quickly realised other people didn't see or hear. Fortunately her parents neither ridiculed nor chastised her when she behaved strangely. They were both very busy professionals, her father a doctor, her mother a head of department in a large college. Young Beth was left to the very tender mercies of a West Indian nanny, Claudette, who was large, jolly and comfortable, so Beth's young life was full of love and laughter. At first the nanny didn't pay much attention to Beth's imaginary playmates, but when, one day, she overheard her talking to someone in a very grown-up way whilst sitting alone, and she realised that Beth was talking to Claudette's mother, who had died a year ago, it dawned on her that she was dealing with a very extraordinary little girl. Claudette herself had a highly developed sixth sense, and had previously considered herself to be 'psychic', but found herself in awe of Beth's wonderful powers.

Beth smiled as she pictured Claudette standing before her, her arms folded against her generous bosom, "Until you're a big girl," she said, "don't you go telling nobody about what you see and hear. This is going to be our secret. Do you understand me?" Beth remembered how she had nodded, not understanding, but so adoring her huge nanny that she told nobody of the strange, invisible people who formed a large part of her childhood world. She kept it hidden even from her parents who had no idea they had such a gifted child. Even when she, eventually, gave them some inkling of her abilities, they, like so many, refused to accept the possibility that their daughter was any different from all the other children in their world.

As she sat by the fire, half aware of the howl of the wind as it beat against the walls of her cottage, Beth almost laughed out loud as she remembered her mother's face when, at a family dinner party celebrating Beth's fourteenth birthday, someone had mentioned that they had not heard from her favourite uncle Tom. He was a research biologist working somewhere in West Africa, nobody knew exactly where. Information about him was received only rarely, but he always managed to send something for Beth on her birthday, no matter where he was in the world.

"Perhaps he's lost in the jungle," said her father.

Someone else chipped in with, "Most likely run out of stamps."

"Or can't find a post box!" The laughter was so loud that they almost missed Beth's contribution.

"He died last week," she said very quietly.

The laughter stopped immediately.

To Beth at the time it seemed that time had stopped for a moment. Her mother's eyes were wide with astonishment, her mouth hanging open. After what seemed an age her mother stood up and looked imperiously down at Beth. "That is the most tasteless, thoughtless remark I have ever heard you make, and you've made some beauties in your time, my girl," she said, at last.

Beth was looking down but very aware in her peripheral vision of her father trying not to look at anything in particular, and Claudette, staring at her hard, shaking her head just once. All the other guests were intently and silently studying their laps.

"You dropped a really good one there," Claudette said later, her mighty chest bobbing up and down as she laughed in her good-natured happy way. "Did you see your mother's face, girl? Good job there were no mirrors near. They would have cracked into pieces."

"But, didn't you see him?" Beth had asked.

Claudette stopped laughing and slowly shook her head. "Who?" she asked.

"Uncle Tom. He was standing behind dad, laughing fit to burst. Didn't you see?"

It was only then that the aloneness of her path finally sunk into her. She was fourteen and she was the only one in a world of blind people, the only one with sight. Of course later she found out that this wasn't true. There were many like her. It was just that most of them kept very quiet about it.

It was shortly after this that she found she could sing. She had been fooling about in a classroom with a friend, pretending to sing through an imaginary microphone, when a teacher had walked in. She had stopped singing, embarrassed and expecting to be told off, but was astonished when the teacher had said to her, "Don't stop. That was terrific. You're a natural."

She laughed, now embarrassed even more, so much so that no amount of persuasion would get her to continue singing.

"Okay," he said at last, "but if you want to sing through a proper mike, come and see me and I'll fix it."

She and her friend had gone away giggling and she hadn't thought about it at all for a couple of weeks. Then, one day, as she was preparing to go home, the same teacher stopped her in the corridor. "I've been looking for you," he said. "At the end of the summer term we'll be putting on a show and I want you to sing in it. I'm not going to take no for an answer."

What he didn't tell her was that he had her earmarked for the lead. That came later when he had shown her how to use a mike and she had become aware of the fact that when she sang people stopped to listen. And applauded.

Her parents were delighted when she came home and told them that she was to be the star of the school show. What she did not tell them was that she already knew that she was going to be a singer for the rest of her life.

She stayed at school until her A levels at eighteen. Her results were poor, which didn't surprise her at all. Too much time had been spent gigging and building a formidable reputation throughout Essex.

She hadn't expected a positive reaction when, finally, she told her parents of her choice of vocation, but nothing had prepared her for the torrent of abuse thrown at her by her enraged mother, when she realised that her daughter wasn't going to follow her footsteps into university. Phrases like, 'spitting our sacrifices back in our faces', 'throwing your life away', and, 'ungrateful little cow', rang in her head for many weeks afterwards. However her mother's attempt at control through guilt failed and shortly afterwards Beth moved out of her spacious family home into a small, but comfortable, flat in Harlow, from where she soon earned herself a very comfortable living singing in clubs in and around the area and, later, in London.

A harsh, violent gust of wind smashing the rain into the glass of the kitchen window brought Beth out of her deep reverie with a start. Yawning she slowly lifted herself out of her armchair and padded into the small entrance hall, where she bolted the front door. The door catch was in the habit of slipping and she didn't want the now gale force wind blowing it open and filling the hallway with water. She smiled. Even on days like this she never regretted the move to Cornwall. The winters may be wet and sometimes violent, but she found more than enough compensation in the multitude of kindred spirits, the peace and the beauty of the cliffs, beaches and countryside of the county.

Chapter Eighteen

DAVID SPENT THE REST of the spring and the summer in a form of trance, going through a routine of work in the evening and walks to the beach during the day. The loss of Anna affected him more than he would have liked to admit. From time to time he would think of the Roman soldier, but no matter how hard he tried he failed to recall any details of that experience for himself. Constantly, in spite of his growing feelings for Beth, he found himself wondering how Anna was coping with the atmosphere of anger and hatred in which she was having to live, and, perhaps as a result of this, the magic moment he had enjoyed with Beth in her cottage that stormy day didn't repeat itself.

The games with Charlie on the beach helped him expend the energy generated by his own anger and frustration. Sometimes he played for so long and so strongly that even Charlie would have to stop and, finding a delicious pool of sea water, lie panting, her legs stretched out in front of her, her tongue lolling from the side of her mouth. When that happened David would trot round and round the small beach until, exhausted, he would fling himself down onto the wet sand where, oblivious to discomfort, he would lie with his face to one side staring, unthinking, at the pebbles and the grains of sand and the slow trickles of water draining away to the ocean.

*　*　*

And then the autumn came bringing with it a sudden change from warm, lazy, people-filled beaches to rainy, gale-filled walks on paths poached heavy by horses' hooves.

One day, towards the end of September, as the summer season was drawing to its close, David awoke early in the morning, his head throbbing and his body drenched in sweat. The dream during the night was still bright and clear in his head. The fear that it had caused him still lay heavy, like a rock, in his stomach. He reached out in the dark and gently rubbed Charlie's ears.

"What the hell was that?" He spoke aloud but Charlie just groaned and rolled over in her sleep.

In the dream he had found himself strolling easily in a meadow full of wild flowers, lush green grass, plump broad leaf trees. It sloped down before him towards a wide, lazily swirling river. In his hands he carried a lute, his prize possession, in fact his only possession. But for all that, he was quite well dressed, filled with the satisfaction of the knowledge that he was young, fair of face and figure, talented and well known as a lutenist, singer and composer and part of the household of the very rich and powerful Powell family of Windsor.

Suddenly the mood of the dream changed, for he was on his way to an assignation, one that he knew, without knowing exactly why, was full of danger, both for himself and another. He struggled for a while to remember who it was he was hoping to meet. Then, as the recollection came to him – Francesca, the daughter of Lord Powell – the scene changed. Powerful, coarse hands roughly seized him from behind and he felt a sickening blow in his back just below the kidneys. He caught a glimpse of Francesca's beautiful, frightened face frozen in terror before he awoke with a cry, immediately conscious of his body soaked in sweat, his throat rough and dry. The pain from the blow remained with him for several seconds before thankfully dying away.

During the summer he had from time to time had frightening, disturbed nights when he had woken with most of the bedclothes on the floor, but with no understanding of what had happened to him during the night. Sometimes on these occasions he would stumble downstairs, breathing deeply, his tongue heavy in his dry mouth, and out into the soft darkness of the garden, where he would stand staring into the night soaking in the calm peace. Usually he would quickly regain equilibrium. These nights came and went and in general didn't affect him during the day at all. Each time, after he had wandered about the garden or made himself a cup of tea he had been able to go back to bed and continue the night's sleep without further problems. But this was different. This had a reality that disturbed him profoundly. For the first time he could understand completely how Anna had been so deeply affected by her experiences with her Roman soldier.

A second dream, when it came a week later, was even more real and horrific than the first. It was as if he had woken up in his sleep, both a viewer and a participant in the events.

He found himself in a small, cold, draughty room without any furniture or decoration. To his left there was a palette of straw, which he knew was the only bedding he was allowed. The only other item in the room was his lute, propped up in the corner. *Well, at least they allowed me that*, was the thought that came to him. He knew that he was in Scotland, but where exactly he wasn't sure. He wondered what had happened to Francesca. Surely they hadn't beaten her as they had him? His body ached as the memories returned, of being seized, savagely punched and kicked about the body and especially in the face, and when they considered they had done enough damage, of being dragged before the master and humiliated. Francesca had been there too. He could still see the look of horror as she saw what they had done to him and especially to his beautiful face. But what had surprised and bewildered him the most, to the point of almost total disbelief, was just the fact that it had happened to him! To him! The most talented lutenist in all England! He knew that the lords, especially, and some of the ladies too, considered him so far below themselves on the social scale that he was hardly worth consideration, but he, on the other hand, had always felt himself to be their equal, in fact superior to some of them. He would never bow down to them and they hated him for it. They hated him too for his popularity, especially with many of the ladies, so he knew the delight they had felt at making his face unsightly. And all he had done was to make an assignation with Francesca! Francesca Powell! The fact that she was the lord's daughter was neither here nor there to him. They had fallen in love at first sight, and as far as he was concerned, that was that. They should be together, for as long as they lived.

His thoughts were abruptly interrupted by a door behind him being thrown open. Three soldiers with knives drawn, kilts swirling over heavy knees, marched in and pushed him roughly against the hard, granite wall. They were followed by a small, but well built elderly man, a man of authority, used to command and obedience. He walked over to a small opening in the wall, the only source of light for the room, and stood for what seemed a long time, his mouth twisted in what looked like contempt and distaste. When, at last, he spoke, his voice was quiet, but so thick was his accent he was difficult to understand.

"My cousin has sent you here, firstly because he is not a violent man and saw killing you as a waste. He thought your punishment would be much greater and his knowledge of it more pleasurable to him, if you spent the rest of your days here in Scotland and learned from me from time to time how you were bearing up under the strain, so to speak."

"But . . ."

"Do not dare to speak to me." He whispered contemptuously, still staring out of the window. He then continued to speak, quietly at first, but then becoming gradually louder and more forceful, his voice rising as his anger became very visible. "In Windsor you may have been valued highly for your voice and talent on this instrument, but I wish to impress upon you that here you are nothing, less than nothing. Do you understand me? Nothing!" His voice had risen to a scream. He strode over to his men-at-arms, as if for support. His eyes bulged and spittle shot out from his ugly twisted mouth. He turned away and, clenching his fists, took deep breaths for what seemed a long time. The soldiers smiled at each other and then leered with cruel satisfaction at the helpless prisoner. Composure regained, the man walked to the window again and, as if he were talking to no-one in particular, continued talking in a chilling, matter of fact way, "You will remain alive only for as long as you are useful to me. They say in the south of England that you are talented and have a fine voice, but I'll wager you have nothing to sing which we in Scotland will find acceptable." He walked away from the window and still continued speaking as if to no-one in particular. "You will come to us this evening, and sing and play. If you do not please us," he hesitated for just an instant, "well, in that case, we will make other arrangements for you." Without another word he turned and quickly left the room. His men at arms swiftly followed him, smiling in a chillingly lecherous fashion.

In the dream David had felt himself engulfed with wave after wave of fear that stayed with him and continued to pulse through him as he awoke with a start. His head was a ball of throbbing pain and his body was again, as after the first dream, bathed in sweat. Groaning he hurriedly went downstairs to the bathroom, started to run himself a deep hot bath and sank down onto the cold toilet seat to wait. Normally when coming out of a dream the events begin to fade as soon as wakefulness returns but after both these dreams the memory of what had taken place remained with him with crystal clarity. Again he was shocked at the reality of what he had experienced. He could still feel the pain of the beatings for Christ's sake! And the fear instilled by the Scottish Laird and those evil men-at-arms! Fortunately, the physical hurt only lasted a few moments. However, what he felt most strongly was the deep, bitter resentment he had experienced in his 'dream' at the contempt with which he had been treated by his Scottish hosts. It was obvious to him that to them his life had no value; his body merely an object to be dealt with like any other commodity, to be used as they desired, and, when it no longer held any prospect of further enjoyment or profit, to be immediately got rid of, without any hint of compassion or pity. For the first time in his life David really understood what it was to be valued as nothing. Never before had he felt so lost, so completely worthless.

This was his lowest point, the nadir of his experience. For months, since Anna's disappearance, he had felt as if he had been slowly disintegrating, as if he had been breaking into thousands of pieces, scattered far and wide into the universe. But as he climbed into his bath, and began luxuriating in the warmth of the water, with his eyes closed, staring into the universe of his mind, he realised that what he had experienced had been the source of something that had been for him a problem for most of his life, a problem that had lain, deep in his subconscious, hidden from him, yet driving him like the wind drives the yachts down the Carrick Roads to Falmouth, unseen, yet forceful and relentless. He recognised the deep feelings of dislike and antagonism he had always had for people in authority and particularly for those who used their power to crush others. God, how he hated bullies! Immediately a strong wave of relief surged through him so powerfully that it brought tears to his eyes. Lying in the scalding hot waters of the bath he let the natural healing properties of the waters gently lapping against his shoulders relax the tension from his body and calm the anger and frustration of his mind. Then, as he let his mind drift and settle into a state of calm and peace he found himself astonished at how much lighter he became, how much more tight and together, as if all the pieces of himself that had been scattered far and wide had been drawn together into him again. Quietly he lay and breathed deeply, marvelling at the way the dream-which-was-more-than-a-dream had finally made him understand, not only how deeply he had allowed himself to sink into the pit of self-pity, but also how low his sense of self worth had been for most of his life.

Chapter Nineteen

LATER HE SAT IN the café in the village with Anthony and Beth discussing the events of the past few months and the experiences of the two dreams. He had begun immediately on his arrival by apologising for his behaviour over the summer, only to have it swiftly brushed aside as of no consequence whatsoever.

"My dear friend, it is not even worth a mention. You did what you had to do at the time and that is all, so let us not speak of it again." Anthony smiled and absent-mindedly carried on wiping a glass till it shone.

Beth smiled and reached across the table to take his hand in hers.

However, when David described his dreams and how they had affected him they became intensely interested and animated.

"Dear boy, it's wonderful how it works, isn't it?" Anthony was sitting with his back perfectly straight, his eyes shining brightly.

"What do you mean, it's wonderful?"

"Synchronicity, dear boy. The way that people's lives intertwine with one another. Anna experiences terror with her husband, which resonates with the terror she experienced in that former existence, bringing up the memory of that terrifying death. This fear eventually drives her down here where she meets you, the other part of that life, or should I say, that death. This helps her to remember even more and come to terms with what happened to her so long ago." Anthony was now in full flow and there was no stopping him, even if David had wanted to. "But with her she brings the source of her terror in this life, her husband, and this horror now spreads over to you. That causes you to resonate with a terror that you experienced once before. So you, in your turn, drag up a memory of experiences that are still causing you problems, or rather, they have been causing you problems for most of your life, until now. For, having experienced those events and the terrible emotions, having brought them up and faced them, and having come to terms with them, they are no longer a problem to you, are they?" He sat back in his chair with a triumphant expression on his face, his arms held out to an imagined audience, waiting as if for a round of applause.

It came, but unexpectedly from the doorway to the kitchen. Ben, his partner stood there, his head to one side a sardonic smile on his lips. Twice he clapped his hands together in mock applause.

"My dear, you really should stand for parliament. Honestly, if votes were given according to the amount of bullshit that is produced, you would be our next Prime Minister."

Anthony looked in mock despair at David. "Do you see what I have to put up with in this place?" The back of his right hand flew up to his forehead. "What is the matter, Ben? Why are you not slaving over your hot stove?"

"I'm so sorry. I just decided to drag myself away from the heat, give myself a breather and cool down a bit, and here I am met by enough hot air to send a balloon into orbit." He carefully put a hand over his eyes as if shading them from the sun and peered at David. "Oh, it's you. My God, you look awful. What have you been doing? You really should spend less time in that pub and more in here. And I see you've brought that dreadful hound of yours in." He sighed a theatrical sigh. "I suppose it wants something to eat whilst it's here." Crouching down he slowly showed Charlie a delicious bone he had been hiding behind his back. "Here, doggie, get your chops around that." As Charlie, carefully, as if afraid of breaking it, took it from him, Ben stood up, turned and walked into the kitchen. "No mess, mind," he called over his shoulder, but Charlie, already in bone gnawing mode, paid no attention.

Anthony looked at David and smiled. "We were a good act together at one time, you know."

"You still are, my friend. You still are."

Beth squeezed David's hand. "David, I'm so glad you've finally managed to bring something out," she said her eyes shining. "Now, perhaps we can get back to being normal."

"Not much hope of that, I'm afraid, my dear," said Anthony. "There's a lot more of where that came from."

"And here I was hoping I'd dealt with the worst of it," David sighed.

"I'm afraid it doesn't quite work like that," said Anthony. "Life and, what is more to the point, spiritual development, don't run in a straight line, dear boy. You have to think more in terms of a spiral. You keep on coming back to the same problem, almost to the same point, but of course, on a higher level," and his hand described one sweep of a spiral, "but with the benefit of the experience gained on the way round you look at it in a different way each time. Already you've seen this particular problem from different viewpoints and already you're looking at it in a different way from the way you did when it first appeared to you. Am I not right?"

David nodded.

"So, I'm afraid, there will be more."

They were silent for a few moments and then Anthony stood up and quietly said, "I'll be right back. Don't go away. There's something I have to show you." He swiftly strode into the kitchen area, and a couple of minutes later reappeared with a very expensive-looking suitcase.

"Not having any forwarding address I have no idea what to do with this lot." Seeing by the questioning look on David's face that he had not understood, he added, "It's Anna's. She left in such a hurry she must have forgotten it."

"Oh, God." David felt his stomach start to churn as he looked at the case. "What the hell are we going to do about this?" He moved as if to touch it, but then his hand hesitantly withdrew.

"What's in it?" he lamely asked. "Have you had a look?"

"Good lord, no." Anthony was horrified at the suggestion that he would have intruded into somebody else's property without permission.

"I'm sorry. I shouldn't have asked that. It was just such a shock, seeing it."

Anthony shrugged. "There can't be anything of value, or anything she's missing badly or we would have heard from her."

"Or the Neanderthal."

"Yes, there's always the Neanderthal. May a nest of hornets attack his scrotum!" Anthony smiled as his imagination ran riot.

"She obviously just wanted to get out of here as fast as possible," and seeing the quizzical look on Anthony's face, David hastily continued, "and to save you any trouble or embarrassment, of course."

"Yes, but she still could have sent for it."

All three of them stood and looked at the case whilst Charlie, her back to them, carried on her relentless attack on the unfortunate knuckle joint.

"I think it would be a good idea, dear boy, if you were to take it home and get in touch with her friend. Oh dear, I've forgotten her name. What is it? The one who owns that cottage opposite yours."

"Sylvia"

"Yes, Sylvia, her. Anna's bound to have got in touch with her, isn't she? Whilst she was here she told me all about this friend she'd had from school." He stopped for a moment and then hurriedly continued, "But of course she's been here a few times, hasn't she? Small, attractive, very bubbly, journalist. Yes, now I remember. Apparently they used to talk for hours on the phone. Drove the Neanderthal wild, she said. Perhaps she could get in touch with Anna and find out what she wants done with it."

"Yes, I think you're right. She's bound to know something. I'll give her a call when I get back."

Chapter Twenty

HOWEVER, WHEN DAVID DID manage to ring Sylvia the next day he was shocked to be told that she hadn't heard from Anna at all.

"I'd heard she was back, but I haven't had a word from her since she left to go down to Cornwall. Frankly I'm worried. She always gets in touch when she gets back home, and she must have been back for about three or four months at least."

"Have you tried ringing her?"

"Of course! I got fed up with waiting and tried ringing her. All I got was some idiot saying she wasn't available. Wasn't available! What the hell does that mean? I've no idea what's going on."

"Have you thought of going over to see her?"

"Well, yes I have but I'm afraid Antonio doesn't like visitors just bowling along and showing up. Strictly appointments only, I'm afraid."

"God, what a miserable sod. How do you normally get to see her, then?"

"Usually we talk on the phone a lot, and then when she's coming up to town we usually arrange to meet for a bite to eat."

"So you've no idea what happened down here, then?"

"No, not a sausage. What did go on? You've got me worried now. Was she alright?"

David hesitated for a moment. "She arrived in a bit of a state, as you know," he said.

"Well, no, not really. She just rang me and said she needed to get away for a bit to think things out. She didn't give any details, so of course I offered her the cottage. She did ask me not to tell anyone of her whereabouts, so I thought she was just trying to get away from her old man for a bit." There was a moment's silence and David realised from the sound of her swallowing that Sylvia was having a cup of something.

"Is the coffee good, then?" he asked with a grin.

Sylvia guffawed and spluttered, "No, it's rubbish." She laughed loudly once more. "God, is it that obvious?" she cried. "As a matter of fact, you just caught me as I was having a quick break. It's been bedlam here all morning."

"I'm sorry if I interrupted anything," David said hastily, "but a few of us were in the café yesterday, talking about Anna and I wondered if you'd heard anything. That's all."

"Oh, dear, I'm afraid I'm absolutely no help to you at all, and here I am a bloody journalist and supposed to know everything there is to know about everybody." David heard her swallow some more coffee before she continued dryly with, "Or so my editor seems to think."

She sniffed loudly and took a deep breath.

"So," she said, "when Anna arrived, did you manage to find out what the matter was? Was it to do with Antonio?"

"Mostly, it was Antonio, but there was also the dream."

"Ah yes, the dream. She told me about that. Did she get any more?"

"Well, yes she did. It seems she worked out I was the Roman soldier."

"My God, you're kidding! How extraordinary!"

"You're right, especially as I hadn't a clue what she was talking about at first."

"Oh, you poor thing. I expect you thought you were dealing with a bit of a lunatic, didn't you?"

"No-one who's met Anna could think that for one moment, but . . ." he paused, wondering whether to explain further, and then continued hesitantly, "the big problem was that, although she was only here a few days, we got kind of close."

Sylvia gasped, so David hurried on with, "Nothing went on. That's to say we didn't . . . do anything. There was just something between us, that's all, a feeling."

"Oh, God! What happened when Antonio turned up? I take it he did turn up?"

"Oh yes, he turned up, alright. In my room in the middle of the night. Scared me half to death, Charlie as well."

"He didn't hurt Charlie did he? She's alright, isn't she?"

"She's fine, thank you. She just had her ego dented for a while, that's all, but she's got a good memory." David smiled, "She'll know that bastard when she sees him again."

"Well let's hope that she doesn't have to see him again. He's bad news at the best of times. But what about you? What did he do to you? Did he hurt you?"

David hesitated for a moment wondering what to say, for, although

128

Antonio's visit had been a painful episode, he had been affected more by the dream that followed it. He could still sometimes feel the ropes that tied him down and see the awful pock-marked face of his tormentor leering over him in the satisfaction of his power.

He decided not to say anything about his own problem and turned the conversation back to Anna.

"Not much," he answered, "just enough to know a little of what Anna is going through."

"God, you poor thing. You must be feeling wretched. What are you going to do?"

"At the moment there's precious little I can do. I suppose I'm just going to have to wait and see what happens. There is one thing, though, I need your advice on. She was in such a hurry to get away when Antonio came for her, she left a suitcase here full of her gear. I've no idea what to do with it."

Sylvia thought for a moment. "If I were you I'd sit on it for a while. If she's not been in touch about it there can't be anything she needs in it. No, you just keep it and if I manage to get in touch with her I'll find out what she wants done. There's one thing I'm sure of, though. She knows it's there with you and she's left it there on purpose."

"Do you think so?"

"Sure. She knows exactly what she's doing. It's there for a reason."

"Now you intrigue me. I'm going to have sleepless nights wondering what her reasons are." David thought for a moment and then said, "Okay, I'll hang on to it. It's no bother, or as they say down here, 'Don't eat no meat'."

"Charming. I can see you're totally immersed in the local culture." She laughed a rich throaty laugh. "Now, I'll tell you what I'm going to do. I'm going to do some research on Mr. Antonio. I've got contacts everywhere. One of the perks of the job. I'll let you know what I come up with."

"Please do, and if you hear from Anna, let me know what's happening to her. Oh, and give her my love."

Sylvia chuckled. "I'll do that," she said.

Chapter Twenty-One

DAVID HAD EXPECTED TO have to wait quite some time before hearing news of Anna so was surprised when it arrived a week later, and from an unexpected source. He had just fed Charlie her evening meal and was settling down to an evening in front of the television when the phone rang.

"David, Denzil here. You going down to the pub tonight?"

"Well I was just getting ready for an evening's oggle at the telly, actually. What have you in mind?"

"Never mind the telly, my boy. You just get your fat ass up to the Green Man and have a pint of best bitter waiting for me when I arrive in ten minutes time, and I'll have a bit of news of extreme interest to you."

"What's this then? A nice bit of bribery and corruption?"

"You bet. See you in ten."

Reluctantly, but also with a certain amount of excitement brought on by the feeling of intrigue that Denzil's message had generated, David quickly put on his overcoat, persuaded Charlie that going out tonight would be an unpleasant affair, and, leaving her curled up in front of a roaring fire, hurried out into the night. Fortunately there was no rain and the wind that had been blowing for a few days had lessened, so that the walk up to the pub was pleasant.

The bar was fairly quiet, with just a few of the regular soaks and refugees from dysfunctional families huddled round the bright warmth of the fireplace.

"Evening, stranger. Not seen you for a while. Half of the usual?"

"Thanks, Tom, and in a minute or two pull a pint for Denzil, will you? He'll be along directly."

"You heard from the princess, then, recently?" It was Norman wearing a supercilious smile on his thin, cracked lips.

"No, Norman. No joy there I'm afraid." David tried hard to hide the irritation that rose up in him in response to Norman's attack.

Norman turned his infuriating smirk back to the fire, which, as if in response spat out a spark in his direction. Alfred, sitting next to him, turned to David, shrugged, smiled and lifted his watery blue eyes towards the smoke stained ceiling.

At that moment the bar fell silent, an instinctive response to the appearance of Denzil's enormous, official bulk.

"Ah, good, you made it!" He strode in at a speed surprising for his size and grasped the pint of bitter that Tom passed over to him. "Cheers," he whispered, lifting the pot up to his lips, "up your nose!" He was slightly gasping for breath but still managed to empty half the glass in one swift gulp. Grasping David by the elbow he steered him purposefully to a table in a corner, as far away from the others in the bar as he could, where, in his usual fashion, he turned a chair around and sat with his arms resting on its back.

"I can't stay long, my 'andsome, but I've heard a bit of news I think might be of interest to you, and, I should imagine, be a bit of a relief for you, too."

David found he had to lean forward to hear what Denzil had to say as he had, out of habit, slipped into conspiratorial mode and was speaking at a volume only just a little louder than a whisper.

"I've been keeping my ears wide open for information concerning the activities of that Italian gangster who came down here chasing his wife."

David was surprised at how immediate his response was to the mention of Antonio as he felt the palms of his hand break out in sweat. A knot started to form in his stomach, hot and hard.

"I've got contacts in the Met. That's how I knew of him in the first place. Apparently he came over here a few years ago as a result of some trouble he was having with some other gangs first over in Milan and then Australia. Really heavy stuff, and if he hadn't got out when he did he would have been topped for sure. It seems, in Italy, some Mafiosi moved up from the south and there was a lot of mayhem went on, murders and kidnapping, the usual Mafia stuff, you know."

"So it would have been just after he got here that he met Anna, then."

"I suppose so. She wouldn't have had any idea of the kind of psychopath he really was."

"So what news have you? What's the 'scumbag' been up to then?"

"First of all let's get our priorities right, shall we?" Denzil lifted his now empty pint pot.

Groaning, David hurried to the bar, ignoring the speculative looks from the group around the fire, and waited impatiently, drumming his fingers on the bar as if playing an imaginary keyboard as Tom slowly and carefully refilled their glasses.

Back at the table, he then had to wait again in an agony of nervous anticipation as Denzil poured half his glass of beer down his throat with, amazingly, just the tiniest twitch of his Adam's apple.

Denzil sighed as he carefully placed his half-empty glass on the table. "Better than sex, that." He smiled resignedly. "Got to say that. In my state there's no chance of even the quickest, tiniest, most inactive bunk-up imaginable. One of the joys of having a delicate frame like mine."

"Denzil! For Christ's sake! The scumbag! What's happened to the scumbag?" David had finally exploded.

"He's gone, my friend."

"What do you mean, gone?"

"He's upped and left. Gone back to Italy."

"Permanently?"

Denzil nodded. "Could be. Looks like it."

David stared at him, frowning, his mouth open. "Anna, what's happened to Anna?"

"Gone with him."

David tried hard not to show the devastating effect the news was having on him as he felt the familiar sickening knot form in his stomach.

"Do you happen to know where exactly in Italy he's gone to?" David asked. He felt the muscles at the back of his neck tighten and the start of a sharp pain above his right eye.

Denzil moved his head forward and lifted his hands. "Milan, I think," he said.

David stared at him. "Does this mean he is no longer in any danger of being topped, as you put it?"

"It certainly looks that way. What has happened is anybody's guess. There's always a lot of shuffling about with these people, power moving from one faction to another and then back again, but you can be sure of this, that there's a tidy profit in it for him somewhere, and he must know that things have swung his way again." He picked up his pint and the rest of his beer disappeared in an instant. Standing up he turned the chair round to its normal position. "Anyhow, you can now rest easy knowing he's festering in some hell hole in Milan and not here wondering how he can cause you enormous amounts of grief." He turned and walked to

133

the door. "He would have, you know. Sometime, somehow, somewhere. He'd have had you." With that he eased his bulk out of the door calling out, "Cheers!"

"Sure, thanks Denzil. That's really good to know," David murmured, but his mind was already far away drifting through the square in front of the imposing facade of the Milan cathedral, listening to the superb music of the tiny orchestras that play for the patrons of the cafés, pushing through the throngs of people idly window shopping and then standing on the marbled floor of the Galleria Vittorio Emmanuele.

A loud burst of laughter from the fireplace brought him back to the reality of the pub and so, draining the last of his beer he quietly got up, said good night to Tom at the bar and to the regulars, and walked slowly down the hill to the cottage. Charlie, as usual, greeted him enthusiastically when he opened the front door and hurled herself into the cold night air barking furiously at nothing at all. David followed her up the garden path and sat silent for a long while on an old wooden seat, gazing up at the breathtaking splendour of the crystal-clear heavens, trying to imagine Anna, confident and elegant, walking through the covered walkways surrounding the piazza in front of the elaborate cathedral of Milan. He wondered whether she would be free to do this, or would her gangster husband maintain his grip on his prize possession. Certainly if he did allow her out there would be a minder assigned to her. "Even if I could get near her I wouldn't be able to speak," he found himself musing and sat up straight with a start. "Don't be stupid. That's over with. There's no future there," he muttered.

Standing up abruptly he called Charlie away from the hedge and they both hurried indoors out of the crisp night air.

Chapter Twenty-Two

HOWEVER, DAVID'S ATTEMPT TO put Anna out of his mind came to nothing, for a week later as he got back from his usual evening walk across the heath there was a call waiting for him on his answer-machine. It was Sylvia. "Hi there David. Sylvia here. I'm coming down for a couple of days. Just a quick visit. Should get there tomorrow at about four in the afternoon. Will you turn on the water and switch on the water heater, please? I've got lots of really good stuff to give you about you-know-who. And I've heard from Anna. At last. Thanks a million. See you soon."

It took him several hours of tossing and turning in bed that night before sleep finally came, but the following day he awoke, nevertheless, with his head crystal clear and full of energy and optimism. However, in spite of feeling so energised, he found it impossible to concentrate on the work he knew he should be doing, such was his excitement at the thoughts of Sylvia's impending arrival. So, when he had switched on the water, turned on the heater, lit a fire, and opened the windows to air her cottage, he decided to take a long walk along the side of the stream, further down the lane that leads down to the sea and Chapel Porth beach. There, he spent the day idly watching the powerful breakers dashing against the rocks and helping Charlie in her search for the ultimate smell. He was surprised, once during the morning, to find himself wondering whether Anna had now stopped having her dreams about her tragic Roman soldier, and whether he would ever be able to tell her of his 'visions' of a lutenist, pining for the love of a beautiful, young medieval maiden and banished away to a grim castle in a hostile, wet, cold Scotland. He realised that he hadn't thought about that 'dream' for what seemed a long time and wondered how that little episode had ended. "Had they finally got together and lived happily ever after?" he mused. There would come a time when he would remember thinking these thoughts and wishing he had never found the answer, but for the moment he just allowed himself to sink back for a short while into the mood of that episode. He realised with some astonishment how easily he was able to immerse himself again into the feelings he felt as the unfortunate lutenist. "What the hell is going on?" he thought standing up, embarrassed by the tears that flowed down his cheeks and shocked by the intensity of the emotion he felt, the sense of loss and despair made stronger by the hint of a feeling of guilt, that somehow what had happened had been his responsibility. Luckily the beach was not crowded and the few people that were there were wrapped up in their own enjoyment of the sea and did not appear to notice his discomfort. Calling Charlie he hurried back along the track, wiping his face dry with the flap of his shirt. Luckily the path was deserted, for, as he hurried back towards the road he found himself uncontrollably sobbing. The ground was stony and uneven and as he stumbled his way up the hill his foot caught a rock and he fell heavily on his left side, twisting his arm beneath his chest. As he lay in the dust, shocked by the fall, his mouth thick with the taste of the dirt, he was surprised by an unexpected feeling, a thought, which was almost a memory, of lying, at some other time, in just this way. Unsuccessfully he tried to remember when it had been. The memory only lasted a moment for the pain in his arm very rapidly focused his mind into the present. However it had lasted long enough for him to be aware of it and the disturbed emotions it brought. Quickly he stood up and looked around him. There had been nobody to witness his indignity, except, of course, Charlie, who stood before him, uncertain, with tail wagging and front legs splayed out before her, as they usually were when she sensed some form of game. Seeing the look of carefree optimism on Charlie's face David forgot his pain and his memories and, after dusting himself down, he slowly and carefully made his way back to the cottage.

Sylvia arrived at 6 o'clock, a couple of hours after he had got back home. He had, by then, been able to wash and change out of the dusty clothes he had worn at the beach. He was in the process of mixing up Charlie's dinner when she knocked at the front door.

"Hello gorgeous, sorry I'm a bit late," she called out as she strode in, gave him a quick hug and continued into the kitchen. "Hello my darling, Charlie! It's me. Your auntie Sylvia!" Charlie acknowledged her existence with a quick look and a wag of her tail and immediately continued staring up at her dish on the drainer where David had left it to answer the door.

"You really should feed this animal more often, David," she said as she watched the dog, admiring its single-minded focus. "Starvation is making her very anti-social."

"Now you know it's nothing at all to do with starvation. She's always been anti-social. It's one of her most endearing qualities." David followed her into the kitchen and quickly finished mixing Charlie's food.

"There you are girl," he said as he transferred the bowl from the drainer to the floor.

He smiled at Sylvia. "You're looking great," he said. "Would you care for a drink of something? Tea or coffee?" He started to fill the kettle in anticipation, but stopped when she surprised him by saying, "If you don't mind, I'll skip this one and get back over the road. The journey down was a bit horrendous and my poor body's screaming out for a luscious long soak in the bath." She bent down, patted Charlie and walked through into the living room. "Later on we'll go out for a bite to eat. On me. I insist. And I'll fill you in on all the sordid details I've scraped up about dear Antonio." She walked over to the door, where she turned to him and said, "It's good to see you again, David, even though you do look a bit rough. You should get out a bit more. Find yourself some totty."

"Thank you for the advice, but as a matter of fact I have got myself some 'totty' as you put it."

"Then what's she been doing to you, for God's sake?" She glanced into the mirror hanging on the wall by the door. "God, I need a serious make-over." She opened the door. "It's going to take me at least two hours to get myself into some sort of acceptable state so, would you be a darling and make reservations for 8 o'clock? You can pick the place. I don't care where it is so long as it's Anthony's. By the time we get there I'll be so hungry I'll most likely eat the napkins for starters. Just make sure they've got some really good Bolly ready for me." She stood on the doorstep, took a deep breath and, gazing out across the fields towards the sea, she sighed and cried out, "God, but I love this place. Heaven!" And as she crossed the road towards her cottage David heard her repeat, "Heaven!" several times before he closed his door and sank into the welcoming arms of his favourite chair. He had forgotten just how powerful a personality Sylvia was, and although he liked her directness and admired her strength he almost always found himself quite drained of energy by the time she left after her hectic stays at the cottage.

Chapter Twenty-Three

BY THE TIME THEY got to the restaurant it was quite late and most of the clientele were on their final course, however Anthony was just as welcoming as if they had been the first customers of the evening.

"Dear boy, so good to see you again. You always manage to turn up with some lovely glam on your arm. Good to see you again Sylvia. Do come this way." David experienced a peculiar sinking feeling in his stomach as Anthony directed them to the same table he had occupied with Anna when they had come for their first meal together.

"Sorry we're a bit late, Anthony. I'm afraid I was unavoidably detained."

"Not at all, dear boy, you know you are welcome at any time."

"I'm afraid it was my fault entirely," Sylvia said with her most dazzling smile as she sat at the table. "The older I get the more time it takes me to repair the damage I do to myself."

"You do yourself a grave injustice. You look so much younger than the last time you were here." Anthony said as he smoothed an imaginary wrinkle away from the perfect surface of the tablecloth, handed them the menus and left them to make their choices.

"Thanks for bringing me here." She reached across the table and squeezed David's hand. "He always does wonders for my poor downtrodden ego."

"Now that I find almost impossible to believe. Of all the people I know you are the least downtrodden I've ever met. I'm sure, anyone trying to tread you down would end up with a broken leg at least."

She smiled and slowly nodded. "That's true, but it doesn't mean I don't appreciate a little pampering now and then, especially coming from a master in the art like Anthony. So, believe it."

"Okay, I believe," David said, "but let's order. I'm starving and, besides, I don't want to upset Ben. I can see he's already had a hard time of it this evening."

They quickly chose and then kept conversation to the minimum whilst they ate in order to fully enjoy their food and the bottle of champagne that Sylvia had demanded that David order, so it was towards the end of the meal that she said, "I've got a very special Italian friend, works for the Corriera Della Sera. He's a lovely, gorgeous hunk of Italian manhood. Unfortunately I don't turn him on but he'd drive Anthony wild with desire, if you know what I mean, Ben or no Ben." She carefully wiped the corner of her mouth with her serviette. "He's been finding out things for me, at no small risk to himself, I might add, about our friend Antonio, who, it seems, turned up a few years ago and began operating out of a small night-club on the outskirts of Como."

"Como! I thought Como was a boring little holiday resort for genteel retired school mistresses."

"Just what I thought, but, do you remember at the end of the sixties there was an earthquake in the south of Italy? No? Well, there was and Como was one of the places that, out of the goodness of their hearts, agreed to accept a large number of refugees. In amongst them were a few undesirables, about whom the good people of Como discovered too late, and because of whom, have been suffering ever since. Antonio was one of them."

She took a sip of her champagne and closed her eyes in appreciation, before continuing. "The main business at first was smuggling cigarettes from Switzerland. He was quite small and posed no threat to anyone at first. However in a very short time he managed to expand very rapidly and got a foothold in Milan. By that time the cigarettes business had become small-time and Antonio appears to have become involved in drugs, protection, extortion and at the same time building up a reputation for a ruthlessness that made the SS look like a bunch of school girls." At that moment Anthony arrived with their coffee and hearing Sylvia mention the name Antonio, looked at David and said, "I'm dreadfully sorry my dears, but I couldn't help but overhear you mention that thug Antonio. May I listen in here? I know it's not the done thing, but . . ."

Quickly looking round the restaurant, David saw that nobody else remained in the place, so he stood and drew up a chair for him. "Of course, Anthony. Sit down. The place is just about closed now, anyhow, isn't it?"

Anthony quickly strode over to the door, locked it and drew down the blind. "It is now," he said with a satisfied grin.

As Anthony poured their coffee Sylvia continued, "Very soon he became extremely strong, so strong, in fact that he became a threat to several of the old guard, who put out, first a warning, and then, when he ignored it, a contract. Antonio soon found that a lot of the support he thought he had suddenly evaporated and he disappeared. They think he went to Aussie for a year, where he has relatives, but he managed to upset even them by trying on some of the tricks that had made him so unpopular in the old country. The next we hear of him is in London."

"And that's where Anna got caught by him," David whispered.

Sylvia smiled at him "That's right," she said. "And apparently in the end he'd started to become a threat to quite a lot of people there too."

"Seems it's hard being a successful crook these days," David said with a smile.

"The competition is fierce. Apparently there were a couple of attempts on his life just before he upped and left."

"What made him think he could make a go of it back home, then?"

"Two of the really old guard died and Antonio came to an arrangement with some of the up-and-coming youngsters in one of the factions. At the moment things are quite quiet but a lot of my friends there are on tenterhooks knowing an explosion is due and most likely imminent."

They sat for a while in silence and David was about to speak when he just caught the sound of Anthony's voice very softly say, "Anna is in great danger."

"What was that? What did you say?" Sylvia had also heard him.

Anthony looked away from them, his eyes quite blank, unfocused. "She is in great danger. They are watching her, waiting to pounce; like predators in the jungle. If they can they will take her and use her to get what they want."

"Who are they, Anthony? How can they get her? Doesn't he watch her like a hawk?" David cried out.

Anthony turned towards them his face now quite normal. "I'm sorry my dears, but that's all I could get this time. She's in danger, and there is a way they could get her. I'm sorry."

Sylvia picked up her handbag and pulled out a sheet of flimsy airmail writing paper.

"I think that maybe the answer's in this."

"What is it? Is it from Anna? Yes, I remember you said you'd heard from her." David realised his muscles had tensed and the palms of his hands were wet with the sweat of fear.

He stretched out his arm towards the letter.

"I'm afraid that even if you read it you wouldn't be able to understand it, David. You see, because Antonio is so jealous, we had to make an arrangement whereby we could communicate and even if he read it, which he most certainly did, he wouldn't be able to understand what it was she was really saying."

"You mean a kind of code?"

"Yes, but not anything that could be recognised as a code as such."

"So how do you do it?"

"You know we were at school together? Well, whilst we were there we devised this system of writing whereby whenever we wanted to disguise what it was we wanted to say, part way through a letter, we put in a mark. Everything in the sentence past that mark was to be the exact opposite of what we really wanted to say. And then when the mark appeared again everything after it would be taken at face value."

"Very clever. So even if you only wanted to hide one fact in a long letter it would be possible," said Anthony smiling.

"Exactly."

"But you had to arrange this sign in advance, surely?" said David frowning.

"Yes, that's so, but there was one way which was our favourite and I think, no, I'm sure, this is the way she has chosen in this letter. It's a peculiar way of dotting the letter 'i'. Instead of a dot she does a tiny little circle. She does it normally, it doesn't matter who she's writing to. It's only when she's writing to me that it has any significance. However, as far as Antonio is concerned it's just her normal way of writing, so for him, there's nothing strange in what she does."

"So, what does she say? How is she? What's she doing with herself?"

"Well, for a start she's bored out of her tiny mind. They have no friends, so she has no social life. When she goes out she's always accompanied by some heavy or other, so she never gets out on her own. She misses all her friends here, especially those in Cornwall. You get a special mention, David. She wrote, 'Thank God I'll never have to endure another night in that ghastly cottage and spend my time trying to avoid that boring, ugly bloke you had looking after it'."

David stared at her, his mouth sagging open in disbelief and horror.

"Sorry, David, couldn't resist that. She wrote that after the peculiar dotted 'i'. So what she's really saying is that she wants to spend a long, long time in the cottage, preferably with that lovely, interesting bloke who lives opposite."

"Christ!" exclaimed David. "It's at a moment like this that I really wish I still smoked." He picked up his cup and took a long drink of coffee.

Anthony looked at him in disbelief. "I didn't know you ever smoked."

"Many years ago, I did, but I gave it up one time when I was seriously short of cash. But," and then he looked from Sylvia to Anthony, not knowing how to continue. "What the hell am I going to do?"

"I can't see that there's very much you can do," Sylvia said as she frowned. "You're here, and she's there. There's no way you're going to be able to swoop in there and scoop her up."

"And even if you did, where could you go to. There would be no place to hide. Not from him with his connections." Anthony, usually bright and optimistic, sounded more gloomy and pessimistic than David had ever known him to be.

"I don't know, my friends, I don't know, but I do know this is not the end. Somehow I'm going to find a way."

Chapter Twenty-Four

LATER THAT NIGHT AS he got ready for bed relaxed and happy, the result of the excellent food, wine and good company, David looked out of the window just as a large, deep brown dog fox trotted across the garden. As it got to the hedge it paused and turned its head to look up at his window, almost as if it knew that he was there. David didn't know if it could actually see him, but they seemed to stare at each other for what seemed to him a long time, before it slowly turned away and in an instant had disappeared from view. However, as he had watched it he had become aware of an idea that seemed to come from nowhere and instantly grow into an awareness, a realisation that he was going to have to do something that would change his life forever. Exactly what it was he couldn't quite grasp, but the thought made him suddenly lose all the strength in his legs. In the pit of his stomach he could feel a strong band of fear start to grip him. Clutching his stomach he fell on the bed and moaned, "Oh no! For Christ sake no, not again." He lay there for a while until the pain subsided to just a dull ache, then slowly he sank into a deep sleep.

Three hours later he awoke into a dream whose clarity astonished him. For, again he was both participant and spectator. He was lying on the bank of a swiftly moving river, wet and cold, with the pain of hunger in his stomach. He raised his head and saw his lute a few yards away. He had a memory of a hall full of men and women, richly dressed, but without the quality he had become accustomed to in Windsor. They were screaming at him as he tried to sing and play for them, hurling abuse and food at him, until he fled from them, their jeers and taunts and scathing laughter ringing in his ears. The next day they had thrown him out, penniless, hungry and sore from the many kicks and punches he had received from the soldiers as they had woken him. He had wandered in what he thought was a general southerly direction for two or perhaps three days before collapsing on the bank of this river, too weak to move any further. His left arm was twisted painfully underneath his body, so he very carefully and slowly turned over onto his back, releasing the arm and sighing with relief as the pain subsided.

The transition, when it came was surprising. One moment he was lying on the ground staring into the sky, the next, he found himself lying in his bed, in the dark, in his cottage in Cornwall. It took him several moments to realise what had happened, where he was, and then a series of emotions swept through him bringing tears to his eyes. The feeling of relief was overwhelming, but at the same time he experienced the humiliation he had felt lying, defeated, on the bank of the river. "They had laughed at him! Ridiculed him!" David sat up in bed, put his hands over his eyes and took a deep breath. "Come on, now," he said aloud. "Pull yourself together, for God's sake!" Charlie turned her head towards him and softly growled in her throat. "It's OK Charlie, I'm just having a problem with a guy who doesn't understand his limitations." He swung his legs out of the bed and stood up. "Or his public," he added. "It's only three o'clock. How can I possibly feel so damned hungry?" Yawning, he carefully made his way down to the kitchen, leaving Charlie lying on the warmth he had left, and made himself a couple of pieces of toast.

Taking a chair he sat by the window looking out at the garden. A soft rain was falling and the hedgerows were gently swaying in the breeze blowing from the south west. He slowly ate the toast, savouring the sweetness of the jam he had liberally spread on it, and thought about the character he had been 'dreaming' about. He realised that he knew this guy very well indeed, so well, that he found himself, very reluctantly, accepting the fact that he could have been experiencing episodes from a life he had lived before. He also realised that there were many things he didn't want to accept about the guy, and about the situation the guy in the 'dream', found himself in.

David realised he had finished his toast, but, as he was still hungry, he walked back into the kitchen and popped another two slices of bread into the toaster. "Boy, wouldn't 'he' be surprised to see one of these," he said to no-one in particular. Whilst waiting for the bread to brown, he started to review in his mind what had happened to the boy so far. It was then that he realised that he had no idea what his name had been. He knew the name of the girl – Francesca, and the name of the family – Powell, so why couldn't he remember the boy's name? He tried hard to concentrate on the memory of the dream, but after a minute or so gave up.

The sound of the toast popping up brought him immediately to the present, but as he reached out to pick up the hot toast a name suddenly flashed into this mind.

"Peter Cavanagh!"

"He was called Peter Cavanagh, Charlie," he announced but Charlie, who had quietly sneaked down stairs having been awakened by the smell of the toast, just looked up at him imploringly.

"So you approve do you, do you, Charlie?"

Charlie wagged her tail and licked her lips enthusiastically.

"I think I'm going to have to have a session with Anthony," he said to Charlie, who apparently approved with another quick wag of her tail, and gratefully accepted half a slice of toast.

Chapter Twenty-Five

LATER THAT MORNING THE three of them, David, Sylvia and Anthony sat in the cafe drinking coffee and discussing his experiences of the previous night.

"I seem to be getting, bit by bit, an episode in a life I had in the Tudor period," David said. "It seems that this guy was a musician in the employ of a large, rich household in, I think, the district of Windsor. He played the lute and sang, pretty well, as far as I can remember."

"Well you lost that ability somewhere along the way," muttered Anthony with a smile.

"Forgive my abysmal ignorance, my darlings, but what's a lute?" Sylvia asked apologetically.

"It's a string instrument, bit like a guitar, very ancient," Anthony turned to David, smiling. "Am I right, dear boy?"

"Yes, Anthony, you certainly are. It's a very old instrument. There are pictures of lutes on the walls of Egyptian tombs. It was the favourite instrument of the troubadours in Medieval times."

"So, let me get this straight," Sylvia said, staring into her coffee cup. "This guy, did you get his name?"

"As a matter of fact I did, just this morning."

"Good for you!" cried Anthony. "What was his name?"

"Peter Cavanagh! And he wasn't a troubadour, although I have a suspicion that he was at one time. He was employed by a family. Had a proper job. Didn't spend his time walking all over the place annoying the local populace."

"And they treated him like shit," muttered Sylvia.

David nodded. "You could put it that way, I suppose," He said smiling. "Musicians have rarely been very high on the social scale."

Without waiting to be asked, Anthony refilled their coffee cups.

"The thing that amazes me more than anything else," David said, "is how incredibly real it all is."

"And it's made so real mainly because of the levels and the intensity of the emotional involvement." Anthony had sat down and was staring intently into his coffee cup as he spoke, using it as a focus for his concentration.

"But it's somehow even more real than the life I'm living now!" David cried.

"Of course it is, because you are experiencing it on more levels of yourself, consciously, than you do your normal life. You are experiencing it as it was, but with a much keener focus than you experienced when you actually lived it for the first time."

"How can that be?" Sylvia laughed a little nervously.

"Because he's viewing it as it happened, and also from the view point of today. He's had four hundred years or so of experience and development since."

"But when I'm in the 'dream' I'm not aware of today, so how can my today-state affect the way I'm seeing it all?"

"Because of what you yourself said. That you are both in it and viewing it at the same time."

"So the part of me that is viewing it is affecting it in some way."

"That's right."

"But doesn't that mean I'm not seeing it as it really happened. If my today-awareness is changing it."

"I don't think it's necessarily changing it, as much as altering the way you see it and react to it." Anthony stared again into his cup. "Take, for instance, the point you've just got to, by the side of the stream. You are lying there and feeling very nervous, am I right?"

"Right, but considering I'd just got away from a potentially life threatening situation, and was back to the state I was in before I got the Powell gig, i.e. young, foot-loose and free, I was feeling a lot more fearful than I should have been."

"That's so. And that's because. . . ?

There was silence as David sat deep in thought. Then, as understanding came to him he looked up at them, his eyes wide open. "Part of me knows what's to come," he said in a subdued voice, feeling again the tentacles of fear gripping his stomach.

He and Anthony looked at each other.

"I'm afraid most of this is beyond me," sighed Sylvia. "But what I'd like to know is, who's the girl?"

"What do you mean, 'who's the girl?'" David frowned.

"When Anna had her experience it turned out that you were the Roman. So?" The question hung in the air as she turned her face from David to Anthony, her shoulders and her hands lifting.

The two men looked at each other for a few seconds and then David's eyes widened once more and his mouth gaped open as Anthony nodded and smiling said, "It seems you and Anna have had more connections than you at first thought, dear boy. I did say when you first brought her here that you had had many lifetimes together. I think that in a lot of them you took part in situations in which you had very great problems. Problems that caused you both a lot of grief." He paused, and then, "And I remember also saying something to the effect that I hoped that you were going to make a better job of it this time."

"It hasn't started as well as I would have hoped," David said gloomily.

"Oh, I wouldn't go as far as to say that." Anthony was smiling. "Don't forget I'm the medium, and as far as I can see, things are going exactly as they should be."

"Oh, great!" David felt himself becoming irritated by what he saw as Anthony's smugness. "I'm here, she's over there in Italy, married, and not only married, she's surrounded by psychopaths, and you say everything is going as it should! Do me a favour!"

"I'm not saying that everything is going to be easy, or even pleasant, or even that it will all pan out as you think you want it to, but you will be successful in what you have come here to do. Believe me!"

"And what's that, then? What have I 'come here to do'?" David found his exasperation growing rapidly.

Anthony looked at him and slowly shook his head. "I can't tell you that, David."

"No, of course not!" David snorted. "That's the trouble with you people. You're always full of advice and knowledge, but when it comes down to the nitty gritty you don't really know anything at all."

"Hey! Come on David! Cool it." Sylvia reached across the table and tried to touch his hand, but David shrugged her off, stood up and strode out of the door.

"What the hell's got into him?" she cried out. "I've never seen him like that!"

Anthony shrugged his shoulders, stood up and closed the door that David had left swinging open. "He's had a rough time," he said with a sigh, sitting down again at the table. "He lost his wife and then Anna, and of course there's Beth. He's having a bit of a struggle there as well. On top of all that, the kind of experience he's been having at night reliving some pretty nasty events doesn't help at all."

He sighed and topped up his coffee cup. Sylvia was surprised to see his normally jovial face clouded with concern.

"He also knows deep down what he's got to do. He knows it's going to be very demanding in every way, and he's kicking against it."

"But he's usually such a nice guy!" Sylvia exclaimed.

"So he is, but he's come to a major turning point in his life, one which will not only change the way he views himself and the rest of creation, but will alter his very existence. Life has given him a mighty kick up the arse-part. It seems that that is the only way sometimes to get people to go in the direction that's best for them. It can appear to be cruel, but it's not. It's just necessary, for him." Anthony stood up and collected the coffee cups.

"Don't worry. He'll be back." He said as he walked over to the bar.

"So, how do you know?"

Anthony pointed under the table, where Charlie smiled and wagged her tail.

*   *   *

And come back, he did, full of apologies. "I'm so sorry, Anthony. I just don't know what the hell's going on. I don't know what to do, what I should be doing, where I'm going or . . . I'm just so confused."

"First of all, there's no need to apologise. Second, sit down and take a deep breath. Here's a coffee, hot and sweet as you like it."

David sat down beside Sylvia and sighed heavily as she laid a hand on his arm. Anthony handed him a coffee and sat facing him.

"Now, listen carefully, because the sooner you admit that what I'm going to say is true, the sooner you'll start to feel a lot better. Okay?" Anthony was speaking forcefully and staring directly into David's eyes.

David sighed deeply, "Okay."

"Your problem is not that you don't know what to do. It's not that you don't know where you're going. Your problem is that, on one level at least, you know precisely where you are going to and what it is you have to do. You are just not prepared to acknowledge it, to accept the inevitable. For you see, on one level you know that things are going to be somewhat difficult." He watched David as he slowly stirred his coffee. Then more softly, "Am I not right, dear boy?"

"Oh, bloody hell," was all that David could manage.

They sat in silence for a long while and then David sighed again and looked up at Anthony. "Will you look after Charlie for me?"

"I was hoping you would ask me that," said Anthony with a slight smile at the corner of his mouth.

Chapter Twenty-Six
Milan

ANNA SWIFTLY GOT OUT of the Fiat limousine and hurried into the Galleria Vittorio Emmanuele, not waiting for her chaperon, whose huge bulk often hindered him from keeping close to his charge. For her it was a game – to make it as difficult as possible for him to do his job properly. Of course it wasn't his fault, but, every week when she got to the centre of Milan she was still shaking with anger at the humiliation she felt at being escorted everywhere by what she thought of as some ignorant, mindless ape. Every Friday, she came to Milan, not because she particularly wanted to wander about the streets without purpose, but because she felt she had to break free of the constraints of living in the huge house outside of the city, always under guard, never seeing another woman, not being allowed any friends and surrounded always by ignorant goons, whose only interest was the comparative size and power of their weapons. Every week she insisted on one trip to town. Every week Antonio tried to forbid her. The battle that ensued left her shaking with fury and shame, so that by the time she arrived in front of the magnificent cathedral she was so drained of energy that it took at least an hour before she began to feel the benefits of having escaped her 'prison' once more. Sometimes she found relief by going into the cathedral and sitting in meditation, much to the discomfort of her 'escort'. However, that was a luxury often refused her because of her liking for short sleeves. She had been denied entry for her 'immodest' dress many times, and, in fact, this was a source of such amusement, albeit mixed with a touch of feminine resentment, that she would deliberately arrive at the entrance showing her bare arms knowing that a priest would very swiftly appear denying her entry because of her nakedness. On these occasions the hapless cleric would often receive the full force of the anger she had brought with her from her battle with Antonio.

However, this Friday she had decided to work off her anger with a brisk walk around the Galleria Vittorio Emanuele and then on to do some shopping. Sometimes this formed part of the game she played, particularly when she was accompanied by someone like Bruno, her escort for today, for he seemed to her to be fat and

153

very unfit, and appeared to find great difficulty in keeping up with her. It afforded her a measure of satisfaction that, even though she was, in a way, his prisoner, she felt she could still cause him some discomfort. Today, however, she found out exactly why she had been entrusted to the care of what she considered a true slob.

She had almost arrived at the centre of the cross that forms the Galleria and had just turned to see if Bruno was anywhere near when a strikingly handsome man accidentally bumped into her. He turned to speak, perhaps to apologise, but before he was able to utter a word he was roughly thrown to the ground. The speed with which Bruno reacted was as shocking to Anna as the violence with which he treated the poor man. She wanted to apologise to him, but before she could say anything her arm was gripped tightly by Bruno's calloused hands and she felt herself roughly pushed away to the other side of the Galleria.

"What are you doing?" she gasped struggling as fiercely as she could. "How dare you!" The palm of her free hand flashed up towards his face, but he easily checked her blow and smiled almost indulgently as he said, "I am sorry, but I have to defend you as best I can."

"Defend me, defend me?" she cried, loudly enough to attract attention from passers by. "Defend me? From what? Anyone could see he had bumped into me purely by accident. What's the matter with you!" A reaction from what had happened was now beginning to kick in and she realised that not only was she shouting but she was shaking uncontrollably.

"Maybe," Bruno's face remained completely impassive. "But I cannot afford to take the chance. If anything should happen to you, I'm afraid I would have to emigrate, very quickly indeed," he smiled, "and I still have family here. I wouldn't want anything to happen to them."

Anna realised that he was still holding her arm and so she pointedly looked down at his hand.

"I'm sorry if I was a bit rough, but I had to move you on fast. Just in case, you understand." His hand dropped down by his side. "Also it might be a wise thing not to say anything about this when we get back to the villa. I wouldn't want anything to get in the way of these trips into the city. It doesn't happen often for me to come with you, but when it does, I quite enjoy the break. Understand?"

She understood perfectly knowing the paranoia that sometimes gripped her husband, but at the same time wondered just what was the danger that Bruno seemed to think they faced in coming into town. Also the thought came to her that in spite of her former opinion of her minder there was perhaps more to him than she had thought.

"Okay," she said, "I'll keep quiet about this, but only if you'll tell me what it is you're afraid of." Her smile was a little coy and her raised left eyebrow held a hint of a challenge.

"I shall only say this – your husband has many enemies."

"But I thought matters had been resolved. He told me before we left England that all the old problems had been smoothed over."

"No situations are ever completely static. Oil can be poured on troubled waters, but eventually it sinks to the bottom, and the waters can then become troubled again."

"So what stage are we at now? Where is the oil, on top of the water, or has it started to sink?"

Bruno stared at her for a while and then turned away without saying anything.

Frustrated and feeling somehow more vulnerable she stared at his massive back for a moment.

"Come on," she sighed, "let's do the Via Montenapoleone. We'll both feel better."

Striding ahead she smiled to herself, hearing him call out, as he realised she had left him behind. Her smile broadened when she heard him quietly cursing under his breathing in the unique, imaginative way of the Italians.

Chapter Twenty-Seven

THE CLUB WAS DARK but suffused with a rosy hue from the discreet wall lighting. It made the 'consummation' girls' faces glow, hiding their natural pasty complexions, making them look younger, much more attractive than they really were. David sat in a corner waiting patiently for Ugo the club's owner to appear as he knew he would at ten to midnight, just before the start of the evening cabaret.

He had arrived in Milan the previous day early in the evening and had taken an apartment in an area he knew well from his previous time in the city. It was on the Viale Monza two metro stops away from the Piazza Loreto, where Mussolini's body had been displayed at the end of the second World War. It was cheap and warm, close to several shops and bars and within a short walk of the metro station.

It had been almost a week since the fateful meeting with Sylvia and Anthony at the café. He had realised then that he had to go to Italy, but without knowing precisely why. He had no idea of where Anna was, or what he could do should he be able to find her. He just knew that he had to go in spite of the doubt and fear that filled him when he thought of what he had to do.

For a moment he felt a touch of despair as he looked around the club and smelled the acrid cigarette smoke mixed with the staleness of the old champagne that had soaked into the carpets.

His mind drifted back to when he had visited Beth and told her of his intention. She had been strangely quiet for a long time. Sitting in her favourite chair in front of the fire, surrounded by her crystals and the fairy lights that burned all the year round, she had stared into the flames, appearing not to hear the gentle pulse of the music that seemed to swirl with the incense, soothing the atmosphere of the cottage. She closed her eyes and started to sink into a trance.

David, knowing her well, had sat and waited, allowing the sounds of the synthesizers, the tinkling bells and chimes to wash over him helping him to release the tensions that had gripped his body since making the decision to go.

As he relaxed he began to see again the infinite variety of breathtakingly brilliant colours and shapes that had long been a part of his inner world. Soon he felt as if he were sitting, supported by cushions in a very soft place, surrounded by light, whispery forms. Time stopped as he surrendered himself to the peace. Gone were his guilt, his fear, his loneliness. He felt himself filling with strength and power, and the knowledge that he was not alone. He was safe, secure. Then, out of the quiet came a sound, a single tone, monotonous, humming with a quiet urgency, and he found himself again experiencing the feel of the armchair, the smell of the incense, the warmth of the fire. Carefully he opened his eyes and saw Beth seated before him on a cushion gently rubbing a wooden rod around the edge of a Tibetan bowl.

"I thought it best to be gentle with you. You seemed to be in such a peaceful place," she whispered.

David waited a while to adjust himself and then said, smiling, "Thanks. You're right. It was very special."

"Feel better?"

"Thanks. A lot."

"Get anything?"

"No. It was just," he hesitated looking for the right word, "wonderfully soothing. And not only that, I felt so strong and supported." He shook his head unable to describe exactly how he felt. "It was a very special place I was in."

She nodded in understanding.

"Did you get anything?" he asked.

"No," she had said, getting up. She turned and walked quickly into the kitchen. "I'll put the kettle on," she called out over her shoulder and wiped away the tears that were flowing down her face.

* * *

As he sat in the gloomy Milanese night club waiting for Ugo, the boss, to appear, David remembered feeling the barrier between him and Beth, the awkwardness that was starting to separate them. His meditation had helped him, but nevertheless afterwards the guilt he had felt about what he had decided to do returned. What he didn't know was, that Beth had a sensing of some of the terrible events he was about to walk into. There had been times in her life when she had felt the heavy burden of her psychic abilities, but never had she felt such sorrow and so helpless as she had with David that day.

She had taken a cushion and sat facing him. Holding his hands she stared directly into his eyes.

He could still see clearly her eyes, full of concern and love, as they had looked at him.

"Listen," she had said quietly, but with great urgency. "I know that you have to go away. I know how torn you are about it, how afraid you are. No, don't say anything," she touched his lips as he was about to interrupt. "I just want you to understand that I will be with you, and so will a lot of others whilst you are away. So that no matter what happens, and I do mean that whatever," she gently squeezed his hands as she emphasised the word, "may happen, all you have to do is think of us and you'll find the answer, the strength to go on. And never forget, I'll be here when you get back, waiting for you. Do you understand?"

* * *

In the club David felt his eyes start to water and, even though he knew that none of the girls was the slightest bit interested in what he was doing or thinking, he ducked down below the edge of the table and quickly wiped his face on a handkerchief.

The club in the centre of Milan only had a tiny clientele, without exception male, all of whom were being attended to by a pair of girls. David had come in half an hour before and had been relieved to find that he knew a couple of the girls. He had been not a little surprised that one of them still recognised him even after an absence of several years. A couple of girls he didn't know, for they were very young, approached him and offered themselves to him 'for a bit of fun', but soon lost interest when he told them he was there 'on business' for they knew they would find no profit in him. He knew that most of them were bitter with what they saw that life, and men, had offered them. They had developed, for their work, a veneer of vivacious eroticism worthy of the most consummate actress, so that the men they 'serviced' gladly paid the extortionate prices asked for the 'champagne' they bought, little realising how much the girls despised them.

David watched the pair nearest him as they smoothly worked as a team. Sitting on either side of the grossly fat man it was easy for one of them to divert his attention from the other whilst she poured her glass of champagne on the floor. Then that girl would attract his attention with a kiss or demand for more drink whilst the first in her turn poured the contents of her glass on the floor. The aim was to drink as little as possible, but at the same time consume as much as possible, for what they were drinking was not champagne, but the cheapest fizzy plonk available, put into Moet and Chandon bottles in the club's kitchens. Drinking too much of it could result in internal bleeding, expensive visits to hospital and lost time off work, so with just a little trickery most of it ended up on the floor without the customer being any the wiser.

"Ciao, maestro, come sta? Bene?" David had been so engrossed in watching the interplay between the fat man and the girls that he hadn't noticed the arrival of the tall, slim, heavily muscled owner of the club. Startled, he rose to his feet and winced as he felt his hand crushed as Ugo greeted him.

"Benissimo, Ugo. Grazie." He had been pleased during the day he had already spent in Milan to find how easily he had slipped back into the racy conversational Italian he had accumulated during the four years he had worked with the Italians.

"I see business is just the same as ever for you."

Ugo laughed as he waved an arm and as if by a miracle a bottle of Barbera wine appeared on the table with two glasses. "Okay, so it's plonk," he said as he noticed David's wry look, "but it's honest plonk. Not like that muck." His head nodded in the direction of the fat man. Again he roared with laughter. "I wouldn't even try to clean the loos with that stuff."

He picked up the bottle and filled the glasses. "So what brings you to Milan? Hope you're not looking for work. Business is dead at the moment. I've had to cut down to just a duo."

He turned and waved toward the bandstand. "But they're good, these two. They may be Polish, but they know all the old songs." He took his glass and downed the contents in one. "And they're cheap," he added emphatically banging his glass on the table.

"Don't worry, I'm not after work," David said, trying his best to appear nonchalant. "I'm here on a little holiday. Hoping to see the guys I used to work with when I was here, and maybe meet up with a particular friend I've not seen for a while."

"A friend, you say. Someone I know?" Ugo asked, already aware that something was in the offing, knowing David wouldn't be in his club for the joy of it.

"I don't know. Maybe."

"What do you mean, maybe?"

"You may not know her, but perhaps you'll know her husband Antonio Taverna."

David felt a cold sweat break out on his forehead as he saw the expression on Ugo's face change from apparent bonhomie to a cold mask of suspicion.

"How do you know him?" His voice was carefully controlled and his eyes locked with David's so forcibly that it was impossible for him to look away.

David returned his gaze, but kept his hands beneath the table, afraid lest Ugo noticed the sweat on his palms. "I don't know him. It's his wife I'm interested in."

Ugo's look became more and more intense for what seemed to David an age, and then suddenly a smile appeared at the corner of his mouth and he smacked the table so hard that his minders, sitting at the next table, jumped to their feet, not knowing what was going on, but hoping to be ready for whatever might happen.

"Porca Madonna!" he swore and smacked the table again. "It's the woman." He reached across the table and pinched David's cheek, painfully. "It's the woman!" he shouted again and laughed so loudly the fat man turned to look at him, saw who was making the disturbance, grinned an apology and turned his attention back to the girls. The minders, slightly embarrassed sat down again and straightened the lapels of their jackets.

David had been wondering on the way to the club how to broach the reason for his visit and had been expecting some strong reaction, suspicion, perhaps some anger. However nothing had prepared him for Ugo's present behaviour. There was of course the normal Italian male reaction to the news of someone chasing another man's wife, but David suspected that there was more, much more, involved here. The Italian gangster's stare when he had first heard the name of Antonio Taverna, had managed to transmit a threat of danger, of unspoken threats of awful physical pain. The change to Ugo's present state of apparent delight had been so sudden, so surprising that David felt himself almost as concerned as he had been by the fear of the swift punishment that had seemed at first to be coming his way.

"You had me worried for a while there, my friend." Ugo sat back in his chair, his head on one side and grinned at David. "For a moment I thought you had been keeping the wrong sort of company."

"What do you mean the 'wrong' sort? In what way wrong?" David was genuinely interested in finding out what Ugo's interest in Antonio was. He obviously knew him and by the look he had given him David suspected that they were not in any way friends.

"It's the sort of company that could get your face altered." He smiled a humourless smile. "Very permanently, you understand?"

"I think so," David said.

"Good." He turned to the man on his right. "Bring us some beer," and then turning swiftly to David, "unless you'd prefer some of our excellent champagne?" he roared with a huge laugh. "No, I thought you wouldn't," he said seeing David's head shake slightly. "Wise man," he said still smiling, but the look on his face showed he was very rapidly weighing up several factors, assessing the situation, looking for threats, for potential dangers.

Then, abruptly, he appeared to relax and inspected his perfectly groomed finger nails.

"What's your interest in his wife, then?" he asked quietly. "If you're hoping to give her one you've no chance, I'm afraid." Ugo smiled wryly. "No-one gets near her." He paused, "unless you are wanting to donate your body parts to the Italian lakes." Again he deafened the sound of the band with his roar of laughter and the slap of his hand hitting the damp surface of the table.

This time his minders merely turned, glanced nervously at their boss, looked at each other and shrugged.

Respectfully smiling, David waited for an appropriate few moments before carefully offering his explanation. "I met her in England and we became friends. I thought I might renew the acquaintance, that's all." David diffidently shrugged one shoulder slightly.

Ugo looked long and hard at David, who felt his hands grow moist as the gangster's eyes bore into his own. Finally David managed to look away at the girls across the room. One of them had her arm around the man's neck and was stroking his face as the other emptied her glass of champagne on the floor.

"There's something you're not telling me, my friend." Ugo's voice was quiet now, and he leaned back in his chair, his right hand tucking into his left armpit whilst he folded his lower lip with the smooth fingers of his beautifully manicured left hand. "No, there's more to it than that. If you're an 'acquaintance' you know already what happens to men who merely think they can get to be even a tiny bit more than an acquaintance."

David felt the now familiar sinking in his stomach.

"Well, you're right, I suppose, from what I hear of Taverna, but she and I did get to know each other and we did become friends." David looked into Ugo's eyes and saw the disbelief there. "We did. Honestly we did."

"But you are here. Your skin is not stretched over some lamp standard in his front room as a permanent warning to others."

"I was lucky. When he met me he didn't know, and by the time he had found out, he had to leave England in a hurry. I suppose that had he known, when we met, that I had already taken her out to dinner . . ."

"What? You took her out to dinner? And lived!" Ugo stared at David in genuine amazement and with a great deal of admiration. "You are an amazing man, my friend. There are hidden depths in there." He pointed to David's chest. "I am genuinely full of admiration." He smiled and lifted his glass as if in a toast.

"But before we go any further with this I really must get the show on the road. We will talk some more about this later."

Ugo turned towards the stage where a man had been standing for some time now waiting for the signal to start the show. The nod he gave was hardly noticeable, but almost immediately the curtains around the stage slowly rolled back to reveal a stout man in evening dress with sparse hair neatly smoothed back in the old manner. The pianist started an introduction that David recognised after only a few notes to be the start of *Indifferentamente*. He looked around the club and noted that a hush had descended and everyone, even the girls and their clients, was looking at the singer, who stared back at his audience with arrogance and even a tinge of contempt in his face during the long introduction. But as he started to sing in a clear pure tenor voice in the manner made famous by the singers of Naples, David noted how he appeared to lose all his haughtiness as he immersed himself in the song, which had been at one time, it was said, the favoured song of most of the mafiosi in Italy. In the audience nobody spoke and when he finished the song the reaction was rapturous. Six more songs followed, all of them Neapolitan, and all of them met with the same mixture of respect and delight.

When the show was over Ugo turned back towards David, who had been listening critically to the singer and particularly the accompaniment, which he had to admit had been flawless.

"They never go out of date. One never tires of them. Will you, in sixty years time, be able to say the same of any of today's songs?" Ugo asked with a satisfied smile on his face.

"I honestly don't think I'll be around in sixty years." David's wry comment resulted in a huge roar of laughter from Ugo and his henchmen.

"I love your sense of humour, Englishman. Very funny. But if you are not careful with this woman, you'll not be around in sixty hours."

He stared at David for some time, again twirling his lower lip as he drifted away in thought. Then suddenly he stood up and said, "Come back in two days and I may have something for you. I'm not promising anything." Then he laughed, again loudly. "But of course, I never promise anything anyhow, to anyone. You know that." Surrounded by his men he walked away still laughing at his own joke.

Chapter Twenty-Eight

THE NEXT TWO DAYS David spent visiting old haunts and trying, without success to find former friends. They were all, without exception, working abroad, driven there by the lack of work at home. However, David found great delight in wandering in the gardens of the Castello and drifting aimlessly in the streets of the artists' quarter. Time and time again he found himself drawn to the Duomo and the Galleria, knowing from the letters that Sylvia had received that this was an area favoured by Anna, but each time he went there he was disappointed. In the evening he spent the time writing long letters to Beth and Anthony detailing his experiences.

Two days later he went again to the club in the city centre where Ugo managed his little empire. The same girls were sitting gossiping or filing their nails, their faces made lifeless by the emptiness and boredom of their lives. David wondered what rackets Ugo was specialising in these days, for it was obvious that the club on its own brought in next to nothing. Tonight there was only one customer, a round-faced, fat, sad little man squashed between two of the most predatory of the hostesses, who had already persuaded him to buy them two bottles of 'champagne'. David watched as a waiter offered a fresh bottle to the man who looked at the label as if to show that he understood the finer points of vintage. He nodded his assent and the waiter swiftly removed the metallic wrapping, the wire surrounding the top of the neck and finally the cork. He then poured a more than generous amount of champagne into the ice bucket, which was standing just outside of the customer's line of vision. David couldn't help but feel sorry for the poor wretch even though he could see the man's ego was working overtime to persuade him that he was smart enough, and handsome enough, and witty enough, and masculine enough to impress these girls that they really should end the evening between the sheets in a sagging, squeaky bed in a nearby hotel.

"He's got absolutely no hope at all," muttered Ugo as he smoothly slid into a chair opposite David. "And he won't leave here with a single lira in his pocket, either." He smiled. "But he'll leave here thinking he's the smartest, handsomest, funniest guy on this planet. That's what this business is all about, eh, David? Making people feel good?"

"Don't tell me you're doing this for altruistic reasons, Ugo."

"God, no. It's the money and that's all I'm interested in. The girls know how to work the customers even though most of them hate men. You see those two." He waved in the direction of the two girls, one of whom was gently stroking the man's neck and gazing into his eyes, whilst the other slowly poured her champagne on the floor. "They're both lesbian. Live together. They hate it when a man even touches them, but they're professionals. They know just how to part a man from his cash. Flattery works wonders." He looked back at David and raised his eyebrows. "Just look at Rosa there. You'd never think she hates his guts would you?"

He turned and made a sign to a waiter who immediately hurried over carrying a tray with a wine bottle and two glasses. Smoothly, expertly the man opened the bottle and poured about a centimetre of wine into one of the glasses. Ugo sniffed at the wine, took a sip, rolled the liquid around his mouth and after a moment or two, swallowed with a self-satisfied smile on his face.

"Excellent," he muttered and as the waiter poured out two generous glasses he said, "I think you will enjoy this. It's from my own vineyard."

"Have you gone legitimate, then?" David asked, smiling.

Ugo said nothing, but stared at David as if trying to make up his mind about something. Then after a moment or two he straightened up as if he had made a decision.

"Listen, I think we may be able to help you in the question of your problem with this *stronzo* Taverna. I must be honest with you, I'm not promising anything, but I could see that should we be able to remove the woman and thereby exert a little pressure on her husband a situation could arise which would be in our best interests, you understand."

David felt the blood rush to his head and for a moment he found himself unable to speak. Then he slowly stammered, "What do you mean exactly, 'remove the woman'? You don't mean..."

Ugo leaned forward and stared intently and very seriously at David and then burst out laughing so loudly that the little greasy man across the room stopped trying to kiss one of the girls and stared guiltily at them.

"I had you worried then, eh?" Ugo continued laughing, took the paper serviette from under one of the glasses on the tray, wiped his eyes and then noisily blew his nose.

"Excuse me," he said, "but I can't resist the temptation to have a little fun at the expense of the English. You take life too seriously, my friend."

"I'm sorry but you said . . ."

"I know what I said. I said 'remove the woman', but I didn't mean permanently." He laughed again as he slowly drew the fingers of his right hand across his throat. "I meant to snatch her for a while. Keep her in a pad somewhere, safe and secure, whilst we have a little talk with signor Taverna. You see it is almost impossible to get near him these days. Even getting a simple message to him is out of the question. Of course should we manage to take her she would need careful, considerate treatment, you understand. Do you know of anyone who could undertake such a delicate task? It would certainly be difficult, specialised work."

David smiled. "I think I know just the person who could do it." He laughed and went on, "And I think I know just the place where we could keep her out of harm's way."

They both laughed and shook hands, but David could not help but feel that he wasn't being told even half of the story. He stood up to leave but Ugo frowned and the two henchmen stood up and looked threatening.

David again felt the palms of his hands moisten. In his chest he could feel his heart pounding.

"You are not leaving?" The question was really a statement of fact. "We have not finished the bottle." Ugo was amused, "And the show is about to begin," he said nodding his head. He roared with laughter and turned towards the man on the stage who had been waiting patiently to start the show. David slowly sat down as the curtains opened to reveal the same singer, who sang the same songs in the same way, to the same rapturous applause.

*　*　*

And later, as he lay in his bed in the apartment he had taken in the Viale Monza, David felt himself starting to sweat, even though the bed was still cold. He had been experiencing a vast range of emotions since leaving the club. The thought of seeing Anna again filled him with a delightful joy and a keen excitement, but having no control over the means of bringing about their reunion filled him with a profound apprehension. He had tried to find out from Ugo what he was going to do and how he was going to take Anna in the middle of the city, but the gangster had just smiled and patted him on the back.

"Don't worry," he said. "I'll take care of it. All you have to do is sit back and wait. I'll let you know when to expect her."

And so David lay on his bed, unable to sleep, fighting the fear that ravaged his whole body and seemed to grow stronger and more uncontrollable as the time passed. Had he been at home he could have gone downstairs and made himself a couple of slices of toast and perhaps calmed himself in the company of his dog, but here he was alone with nobody to turn to. However the thought of his dog helped somewhat and after what seemed an age of staring into the blackness he felt at last his eyelids becoming heavy. Slowly he drifted off into a troubled sleep.

Two hours later he woke with a start, horrified by the scene he had just left. It was a repeat of one he had visited once before, but this time everything was more real.

He had found himself lying on a cold table. His arms and legs had been securely tied so that movement had been restricted and painful. His immediate concern on wakening was the state of the bed for in the dream he had, in his pain and the helpless horror, emptied his bowels. He breathed a sigh of relief when he found the bed dry and sat up to try to recover from his experience. He could still see very clearly the details of the scene. There had been two men who had been inflicting on him as much pain and degradation as they were able. Their foul imaginations and long experience had provided them with a huge variety of torture and David knew that in the dream he had been on the point of death. He realised that they had just arrived at the same point that had been reached in a previous dream he had had. They had just succeeded in pushing a sword underneath the sternum up to the Adam's apple without killing him and had been congratulating each other on their professionalism. David could still feel the pain in his chest and throat. Thankfully, as he took a deep breath, his discomfort eased and he was left shivering with the horror and revulsion he felt at what he had experienced. The room was cold so he slowly got back into bed, curled into a ball under the blankets and soon fell into a deep dreamless sleep.

Next day he awoke and was immediately amazed at how relieved he felt. It was as if a huge load had been removed from his shoulders and he luxuriated in the warmth of his bed, perfectly relaxed and at ease with the world. He lay for a while and listened to the sounds of the world coming from the street. The realisation came to him that what he was feeling was something that had been missing from his life for quite some time-he felt just how good it was to be alive. He suddenly realised how hungry he felt and how delightful was his hunger. So he quickly washed, shaved and dressed and hurriedly ran down the stairs out on to the street to buy fresh bread, cheese and ham from the corner shop.

Chapter Twenty-Nine

THE WEDNESDAY FOLLOWING DAVID'S meeting with Ugo, on the other side of Milan, Anna sat by her bedroom window and stared out onto the garden, just as she had for several days. The garden was beautiful, as carefully manicured as her nails used to be when she worked the catwalks of the major cities of the world, but its magic was totally obscured by the clouds of depression surrounding her. Her face had the same kind of emptiness that David had seen in the expressions on the faces of the girls in the night club. Her eyes, unfocused, staring out into the distance, saw nothing. Then, as she slowly became aware of the warmth of the tears trickling down her cheeks, she closed her eyes and gave herself up to the grief that had threatened to engulf her for so long now. For what seemed a long time she sat at the window, her head bowed and her hands clasped tightly together whilst great, gasping sobs racked her body. Then, slowly, she felt herself start to relax and, sitting up straight, she began to take in deep breaths of the sweet smelling garden air. With the scents of the garden came memories of the time she had spent in Cornwall and, with a clarity that astonished her she heard the voice of Anthony firmly insisting, just as he had when she had stayed with him and Ben above the restaurant, "Don't be a victim, my dear," he had said to her many times. "What you are experiencing is coming to you for a purpose. It is to help you to remember something. It's not an accident."

With that memory came strength and she found herself sitting straighter, stronger, more together. She started to see again the beauty of the garden, the bright colours of the flowers, the myriad shapes of the bushes and trees as they gently moved in the breeze.

"Thanks, Anthony," she whispered. "I had begun to forget."

"What was that you said?" Her husband had moved in his usual manner, silently like an animal stalking its prey.

Startled, she turned to face him and held his superior, almost contemptuous gaze without her usual apology.

"Nothing," she said quietly. "It was nothing." She stood up, moved past him and said confidently, "I shall be going into Milan tomorrow. I haven't been for a while and there are a few things I have to get."

"You know that if there's anything you want you only have to say and I'll send someone to get it for you. You don't have to go."

She turned and faced him. "I said, I shall be going into Milan." Her voice was strong and confident. She stared hard at him for a moment before turning away and sweeping out of the room.

"And when you return I shall have to teach you who is master here," he muttered at her retreating figure and viciously punched his left hand with his right fist. "Yes, you will have to learn a few painful lessons." He smiled, sure of his power and superior strength and thought of the stallion he had been 'breaking in'. "All she needs is the same kind of treatment, and she will come cringing to me like the horse does." His smile broadened as he thought of the pain he was to inflict on her beautiful body. "Yes, I'm going to enjoy myself very much."

Anna walked out into the garden, crossed the broad sweep of the lawn and sat down on a bench overlooking the magnificent lake. With the wonderful feeling of strength that had come to her in her bedroom had come the realisation that there was only one way for her to go. She knew that she couldn't go on in the same way as she had. He had been trying to break her using the same methods he used in the stables with his horses: the whip and what he liked to think of as his will power. But it was clear to her that his will power was only a single minded determination to get what he wanted regardless of how it was accomplished, and she knew that if she was to get what she wanted - her freedom - she would have to use some of those qualities herself. She felt growing in her a fierce determination to fight with all the strength she could muster, and she felt that strength increase as the understanding grew of how she been manipulated and bullied into following this man's lead.

Then, suddenly a thought flashed into her mind, a sickening realisation, that all that she had suffered at the hands of her husband, the beatings, the degradation, the pain, the humiliation, all had happened because she had allowed them to happen. In fact, on a very deep level, so deep that till now it had been hidden from her, was the awareness that she had wanted them to happen.

She gasped as she understood her complicity in the situation. And with this she realised that, as far as her part in the whole scenario was concerned, she herself had brought it on, indeed had welcomed it, because of her guilt, and through that, a desire for punishment.

Again Anthony's voice seemed to talk to her in her head. "Some day, my dear, when you've had enough, you will realise what it is that you have been doing and why it is that you have been doing it. When that happens you are going to have to stand up to him, you know. You will have to take control of the situation and escape from it, unless, of course, you wish to allow yourself to be destroyed. But I do not think you will want to do that."

"I wonder if he knows just how close I came to that," she said to herself. Then she stood up rapidly as if to banish the thought from her mind. "Enough of that. I've got to make a plan on how to get away and get help." She knew she would have to get a divorce and having got it, organise some form of defence for herself. For she knew that he wouldn't ever allow her to win at anything. It would be difficult, but there must be a way, somewhere, somehow.

*   *   *

The following day she found herself on the way to the Galleria as she had done many times before, but this time it was different. This time for the first time she had managed to leave the house without the usual histrionics from Antonio. There had been no shouting, no threats, no fists waving in the air, but on the other hand the way he had stood by as she got into the car and just smiled, unsettled her in a way she had not felt before. And even though her determination to get away was just as strong as the previous day she felt an enormous wave of relief sweep over her as the car drove out of the heavily guarded gates of the house. She had decided that, somehow, she would never return to that menacing but beautiful prison that had been her home for the last few months. Later she was to wonder whether that feeling she had had been just the result of a decision or more of a premonition.

Her escort this day was Franco, a bright friendly man from Rome who, every time they passed a pretty woman said in his quick, clipped Roman accent, "I'm going to get engaged, right now. No, not to her, to her." And then a few moments later, "No, to her." He was like a child in a toy shop and his enthusiasm infected her so much that when they arrived at the square before the cathedral her spirits had lifted and she had begun to feel light-hearted and free, as if she were going on holiday.

They came for her just as the car that had brought her had disappeared around a bend and she and Franco were standing on the pavement checking that they had taken what they needed from the car. It seemed for a moment that time had slowed down and she was seeing everything in slow motion. She heard a car screech to a halt behind her and as she and Franco turned round she was aware of several things simultaneously. She saw Franco reach inside his jacket in a futile attempt to get his gun out as he was felled by a savage blow from behind, and at the same time she felt strong hands seize her arms and thrust her into the dark interior of a Fiat limousine. She cried out, but someone, she didn't, in her confusion know who, said to her very firmly, "Don't do that. It's alright. No-one is going to harm you. You are safe now." Perhaps it was that last sentence that did it, but suddenly she felt calm and knew that they were not going to harm her. As the car accelerated away she had a fleeting glimpse of Franco lying on the ground with blood oozing from his head onto the pavement.

"Is he going to be alright?" she gasped out as she twisted to try to get a better look at her former escort.

"Don't worry about him. So long as he doesn't try to go back to the villa and explain to your husband what happened he'll be ok," said a strong confident voice. It came from the man sitting alongside her.

"He'll be off to the station to get himself a ticket to Rome in about five minutes, you'll see," the driver turned to her and grinned. "Are you ok? I hope we didn't hurt you, but there wasn't time to introduce ourselves. We had to do things in a bit of a hurry."

Anna looked around at the superb interior of the car, at the man beside her, now sitting back in the luxurious seat, relaxed, as if they were all going on a picnic, and then at the man next to the driver turning round to look at her and grinning like an excited schoolboy. The driver she saw glance nervously at her in the rear view mirror as he expertly wove graceful patterns with the car in the mid-morning traffic.

"Nothing behind, boss," he murmured.

"Good, I didn't think there would be, He's too sure of himself."

She realised that the 'boss' was the man beside her.

Anna now started to feel a reaction from the sudden, almost brutal way she had been snatched and bustled into the car.

"Who the hell are you?" she shouted. "What the hell do you want from me?" And then remembering that kidnapping was a way of life in certain parts of Italy she said, "You're not going to get any money for me from my husband. He'd rather hunt you down and kill you than pay you a single lira. Besides . . ."

"Besides what? He's so mean he'd rather see you chopped up into little pieces than put his hand in his pocket for anything other than a quick game of pocket billiards?"

All three roared with laughter. "Don't worry, we've not taken you for money as such, although I do believe that we will in the end find some profit in this." He smiled and looked out of the window. "There's someone who wants to meet you, an old friend of yours."

"Who? What's his name?"

"I'm sorry I'm not going to tell you that."

"You enjoy playing these silly games, don't you." Anna found herself irritated by the man's obvious enjoyment of the part he was playing, but now realised that these men didn't mean her any harm, so she started to relax and herself looked out of the window.

"I'm sorry, signora, but I'm afraid that just for the moment I'm going to have to put on this blindfold. It is just a matter of security, you understand, until we find out what the outcome of this is going to be."

He moved so swiftly that Anna had no chance to object in any way before she found herself looking out at complete blackness, her eyes being covered by a thick impenetrable piece of cloth.

Involuntarily she tried to tear the blindfold away from her eyes, but as her hands moved up to her face she felt them held very firmly.

"Do not do that, signora. If you promise not to take it away, there will be no need to tie your hands. You understand?"

As she nodded she felt him let go of her hands.

"That is good. Now, what do you want to talk about, art, music, literature?" Again he roared with laughter. "I am so funny. You will find I am so funny I even make myself laugh, and that, as my friends here will agree, is a very hard thing to do."

Anna, blinded as she was by the cloth, was unable to see the driver and his partner in the front solemnly nod.

"So sit back and relax. We will soon be where we want to go."

Chapter Thirty

THE SAME MORNING THAT Anna had left the villa for the last time, David had woken up feeling strangely buoyant and optimistic without having any idea why. The last few days he had felt aimless and some of the optimism of the last week after the meeting with Ugo had left him. The previous Monday he had received a strange message from the night club owner which had caused him to go to bed with his mood moving between acute anxiety and an optimistic curiosity. That evening, just after his evening meal, David had been surprised by a forceful knocking at the door. It turned out to be Roberto, one of Ugo's 'associates' with what was more of a directive than a message: "The boss says, 'Don't go out for the next few days'."

So for two days David had limited his excursions to the bread shop, knowing that nobody who wants to stay physically complete ignores a personally delivered command from such as Ugo. Roberto hadn't been threatening. On the contrary he had said what he had to say with a smile and then nodding in an absent minded way had left without any explanation. So that, although David had woken the following day intrigued, mystified and a little nervous, by the end of two days without any further contact or explanation from Ugo he had found himself becoming somewhat annoyed.

Thursday morning had come as a surprise to him, so relaxed and at ease with the world did he feel. He had woken quite late, enjoyed a leisurely breakfast and was just settling down for the morning with the papers when there was a gentle knock at the door. Not expecting anybody, but hoping very much for one of Ugo's men, the sight that greeted him left him unable for a moment to react in any way, except by standing motionless with his mouth and eyes wide open.

Anna, too, when she saw David had opened the door, reacted with shock and a little cry, and then stepped forward, wrapped her arms around him and buried her face in the side of his neck.

"Please, get inside and close the door both of you. If the old lady next door were to see you it could give her ideas she should have forgotten about years ago." Ugo gently but firmly pushed them both inside and closed the door.

Anna and David walked unsteadily into the room and sat down side by side, on the divan, silent in their shock. Tightly they clasped each other's hands as if afraid to let go.

"And they didn't even say 'Hello'." Ugo obviously had a theatrical bent and was clearly enjoying the effect he had created. "You English, you are so . . ." he walked about the room his head bent and hands clasped behind his back, searching for the right word. "I've got it," he cried, "so passionless. You have no passion for life. You are so immersed in being self righteous you miss all the fun."

"Now come on, Ugo. We did just have a bit of a shock."

"There you go, 'a bit of a shock'. It was earth shattering! Neither of you in your wildest imagination would have expected this." He laughed. "You must admit it was good, eh?"

David and Anna looked at each other and then at Ugo. "It was good, Ugo, very good," said Anna and then she bent forward and started to weep.

David stood up. "I'll get you some tissues," he said, but Ugo immediately pulled from his pocket a handkerchief.

"Tissues, tissues," he snorted. "A lady doesn't use tissues. My dear, use this. It is the finest Italian lace." Then he added as she took it, "Brand new and unused, of course."

He turned to David. "You will both stay here. I'm afraid it will be dangerous for her to go out for a while, you understand. So you will have to find things to do to amuse each other." He smiled. "Even for an Englishman that shouldn't be too difficult." His infectious laughter filled the room. "But if you have any difficulty, give me a ring and I'll send you some magazines."

He nodded to the other men and, grinning, they all silently and smoothly left the room.

* * *

For what seemed a long time David and Anna sat quite still on the divan not saying a word, not knowing what to say or what to do. Then David stood up and walked into the kitchen. "I'm putting the kettle on," he called out. Then as he reached for the kettle, he muttered, "God, how English can you get!"

"Would you like tea or coffee?" he shouted above the noise of the water pouring into the kettle.

"Tea will do fine, if you have any decent stuff, otherwise make it a black coffee."

He began to feel a little more at ease in the familiar surroundings. "I brought some tea with me when I came to Italy, so it's the good stuff."

For a while she remained quiet listening to the comforting sounds he made preparing the tea.

On leaving the house that morning she had had no definite plan, no idea of what she would do, where she would go. She only had a strong determination that she would never be returning to it, and now, even though she realised slowly that perhaps a solution to her predicament had been presented, she found herself beset with conflicting emotions. She felt outraged at the means by which she had been brought here, being still affected by the shock she had experienced at the violence of the snatch. But mixed with this was a certain relief on seeing once again her 'Roman soldier'.

Suddenly the questions burst out of her. "How long have you been here, David? Why did you come to Italy? Who were those men? Were they friends of yours?"

He walked out of the kitchen carrying a tray with two mugs of steaming tea and plates with two large portions of fruit flan.

"Here you are," he said, "get this down you. You'll feel better, and then I'll try to answer some of your questions, but I have to say that this has come as much of a surprise to me as it has to you."

As she took a plate and started to attack the flan with an energy that surprised him, David went into the bedroom and returned carrying the suitcase that Anna had left in Cornwall.

"I don't know why I did it, but I somehow knew that this would come in handy, so I brought it along," he said as he laid it down in front of her. "I think it will come in useful, don't you?"

She smiled even though tears had sprung to her eyes.

"Bless you, David." She quickly wiped her eyes and said, "You know, I don't really know why I left it there. I just knew that I had to."

"Well, I'm glad that you did. I don't know what's in it, but it'll more likely than not save me from having to go out and get embarrassed at having to buy all sorts of feminine gear."

He drew a chair up and sat facing her. "Now, in answer to your questions," he said with a smile, "it all began with the letter you sent to your friend Sylvia, telling her how much you hated the idea of coming back to Cornwall to that boring bloke in the cottage opposite."

Her eyes widened and hand flew up to her open mouth "But didn't she tell you about . . ."

"Yes, of course, I'm just pulling your leg." He smiled, "Eat your flan, you'll feel better. The shop downstairs specialises in it. It's the best in Milan."

She sat back in the chair and looked at him with one eyebrow lifted. "So?"

"So when Sylvia told us of the situation you were in I decided that I had to do something. What, I didn't know. I admit it was against my better judgement, but I felt as if I were being driven to come here. So I came to Milan with the hope of perhaps just seeing you, but even though I went to the Galleria quite regularly I'm afraid I had no luck. Then I went to a club where I used to work when I lived here several years ago, expecting to see some friends of mine who used to work there quite a lot, but they weren't there. They're working somewhere abroad." He took a sip of tea, stood up and walked to the window. "Whilst I was there the owner, Ugo, the one who brought you here, came and chatted to me."

Anna carefully brushed away some crumbs from the side of her mouth.

"You mean the dark, slinky one. Fancies himself as a comedian?"

"That's him. He got quite excited when I told him I had struck up a friendship with you and I wasn't at the bottom of Lake Como."

"I must admit I've had some bad nights wondering whether Antonio would try to get at you."

"Well, thank God he hasn't. But he certainly will if he finds out where you've been when you get back."

She put her mug down and looked up at him. "But I'm not going back."

David looked at her, astonished. "What do you mean, you're not going back?" and then swung round to the window again. "Of course, Ugo said we weren't to go out for a few days. It would be dangerous. Did you arrange something with him on the way here?"

"No, of course not. I'd already decided not to go back when I left the house this morning. I was on the point of running away when Ugo and his men took me outside the Galleria this morning. I certainly didn't say anything to him on the way here about my intentions."

"So he's brought you here, not knowing you were running away, but expecting you to stay here." David stared hard out at the courtyard below. In the shadows beside the main front door leading out to the street he caught sight of a movement and the glow of a cigarette.

"The sneaky bastard," he muttered. "He's got an agenda. But what on earth can it be? What can he possibly gain by having you here?"

He then remembered that the last time he had seen Ugo in the club the gangster had said that it would be a good thing to 'remove the woman and keep her in a safe place whilst they had a little talk with Antonio'. They had laughed about David's 'mis-understanding' of the word 'remove'.

At the time David hadn't paid much attention to what he had said, thinking that Ugo had been joking or playing the Italian macho game, but now he realised that the gangster had been serious and that both he and Anna were in the middle of what could be a very nasty situation.

"So, Ugo doesn't know that you were running away anyhow. That means he thinks he's kidnapped you."

"I should think so too. The way he got me was quite violent. He left my bodyguard unconscious and bleeding on the pavement."

"God, you must have been scared stiff."

"Yes, I was for a few moments, but they made me feel at home pretty quickly." She smiled. "He's certainly got the knack, you know. He may be a lousy comedian, but he knows how to lay on the charm."

"Yes, he does, but don't let that fool you. He's a killer, without any conscience whatsoever."

"So, what do you think he's up to? Why snatch me like this?" Then she remembered what Ugo had said in the car on the way. "Oh, yes I remember now. He said he hadn't taken me for money as such, but he thought there would be a tidy profit in it somewhere for him."

"I imagine that there will be, but I'm sorry I have no idea what he has in mind."

"Does it mean that I couldn't leave, even if I wanted to?"

"I'm afraid so. If you look out of the window you'll see he's left guards in the courtyard. Of course he'll say they are there to guard us from Antonio, but I'll bet we couldn't just walk out of here scot-free."

"So what do we do?"

They looked at each other and burst out laughing.

"I'd better put the kettle on again." David walked through to the kitchen.

"I see you've not been eating very well recently," he called out.

"What do you mean?"

"You've lost a lot of weight. Got quite thin, in fact. Are you alright?"

There was a moment or two's silence and then, very quietly, "I am, now."

"What was that?"

"I said, I'm fine. Just need some good home cooking. That's all."

"Right. I'll do you some pasta. How does Spaghetti Milanese suit you?"

"What's that?"

"The old girl who lives next door taught me how to make it. It's very light, just tomatoes, garlic and mushrooms with some herbs, done in olive oil."

"Sounds fine to me. Need any help?"

"No, you just sit back and relax. You've had a heavy morning."

David washed the cups, waited another minute or two until the kettle had boiled, then poured her another cup of tea and carried it through.

"I've just got to nip down to the shop and get some spaghetti," he said as he bent over the table, but her only response was a slight snore as she turned her face to the back of the divan and curled herself into a ball.

David fetched a blanket, spread it over her carefully and then silently let himself out of the apartment.

He crossed the courtyard and was about to open the large door, which led out onto the Viale Monza when two huge figures appeared and blocked his way.

"Where do you think you're going?"

"All I want to do is to go across the road to the shop over there and buy bread and spaghetti."

"The boss says you're not to leave."

"So what do we do? How do we eat?" David started to get angry.

The two of them turned away from him and talked quietly together for a minute.

"I tell you what we will do," said the bigger of the two. "Give me the money and tell me what you want. I'll go get it for you."

"Do you mean to say that we're prisoners here? You have no right to keep us locked up."

"No, you're not prisoners."

"Then I can go out to the shop." David started to pass them but they swiftly seized his arms very firmly and again blocked his path.

"I'm sorry," said the smaller of the two, "but we've been told that you mustn't leave. It could be dangerous for the signora."

David looked at them and seeing the potential power in their massive frames decided that perhaps it would be wise not to argue for the moment and gave in.

"Okay. For now, I'll agree. You go to the shop."

The men, obviously relieved that there had been no histrionics, relaxed their hold on David, smiled and the larger said, "Okay, I'll go. What do you want?"

"Spaghetti, four breads, onions, garlic, tomatoes, mushrooms, basil and fresh parmeggiano."

"Good." He turned, opened the huge door and was about to leave when he stepped back rapidly.

"What's the matter?" said the other quietly. "Is there someone there?"

"No, I forgot to ask. What size?"

"What size what?"

"What size spaghetti?"

"I don't know the exact number. Just make it medium."

"Okay," and he was gone.

David looked at the smaller man. He had a genial look about his face, black curly hair and bright, dark brown, intelligent eyes which returned his stare quite frankly. He was smiling, obviously trying to be friendly and relax the tension that David openly showed.

"I'm sorry it has to be like this," he said, "but we have our orders, you understand."

"Perfectly, but how can there be a danger to us here? Antonio has no idea that I'm in Milan, and he won't know where to begin looking for Anna."

The man smiled wryly and rubbed the first two fingers of his right hand against the thumb. "There are always people on the look-out for some way to make a little cash. Once he starts looking bits of information will come to him and very soon he'll know what you had for breakfast this morning." He took a quick look out of the doors. "I can see there's a lot of people in that shop, so Alfonso could be a while yet. Why don't you go back up and we'll bring you the goods up when they arrive."

David suddenly felt the sweat on his palms and realised that thinking about Antonio had had its usual effect. His stomach suddenly started to feel uncomfortable, as if the acid content had suddenly increased, and he could feel his armpits becoming moist.

"Okay, whatever you say, but don't be noisy. Anna's having a nap. She's had quite a stressful day already."

David slowly walked across the courtyard and then turned and asked, "Your friend is Alfonso, so what's your name?"

"I am, Pietro. I am from Napoli."

David nodded, "A great place," he said and turned and climbed the stairs to the apartment.

Chapter Thirty-One

ANTONIO SAT ALONE IN his study. All day he had had an unsettled feeling. Perhaps had he not had such a closed, set mind he would have been able to recognise his own psychic abilities, accept them and use them to his own advantage. He had always been able to know when things were not right, when danger threatened, when enemies plotted against him. Today he knew that something wasn't going as it should. The solution to the problem was elusive. Several times he thought he could be approaching the answer to what it was that was troubling him, but each time he thought he was about to understand he found himself staring into a black, empty space. And as the day wore on he found himself getting more and more frustrated and angry.

He got up and strode to the door. "Enzo!" he shouted. "Enzo! Come here, at once!"

Almost immediately he heard with satisfaction the hurried footsteps of his assistant.

Enzo hurried in, his face showing his apprehension.

"Enzo, as soon as my wife arrives home I wish to be told, immediately. Do you understand?"

"Yes, signore, as soon as she arrives."

"Who accompanied her today?"

"It was Franco."

He dismissed Enzo with a curt wave and sat down to wait, savouring the thoughts of what he would do to change his wife's attitude to him. He knew that she had reached a point in their relationship where she was close to breaking down. It would be just the time to exert a certain amount of pressure. If he played her correctly then she would be broken, just like that stallion. He smiled as he remembered his triumph as the horse, after a difficult, protracted battle, responded to his will, just as he knew it ultimately would. But it had certainly been difficult. The horse had been a real test for him, but it was on this type of challenge that he thrived: the type in which he pitted his will against that of another being. The battle to break his wife's will had been going on for a long time, but he was patient. He could afford to wait, and plan. In the end, he knew, he would triumph.

However, thinking of his wife brought back the unsettled feeling that had been upsetting the calm, methodical course of the day.

"She's normally back by now," he spoke the thought aloud.

"Enzo!" he shouted loudly, suddenly feeling very angry. without knowing exactly why.

Again the feet scurried down the corridor.

"Enzo, has the signora shown up yet?"

"No, signore, not yet."

"Porca madonna!" he swore. "Where has that bitch got to?"

He stared at Enzo as though it were his fault.

Enzo wilted under his boss's glare and stammered, "I'm sorry, signore, I don't know anything."

"Cretino! Deficiente!" Antonio screamed as he stormed past Enzo down the corridor to the large ornate dining room. Several of his men were standing in a group in the hallway cautiously watching their boss as, eyes bulging and fists clenched, he walked out of the dining room towards them.

He stopped abruptly in front of them and took a deep breath. He appeared to take a firmer control of himself and then in a quieter voice said, "If she is not home within a quarter of an hour, you will go out and find her and bring her to me. You may use any means you think fit. Any! Do you understand!"

They shuffled their feet and one or two muttered, "Sure boss, sure, any."

"And when you find her you will bring that bastard Franco to me to deal with personally. Do you understand?" he roared. And again, when no-one answered, "Do you understand?"

"Yes, boss," they answered, hesitantly for they knew that one of their number would be savagely punished, and Franco was popular among all the men for his humour and his ability to lighten the oppressive atmosphere of the house.

Antonio returned to his study and began to pace up and down in front of the window that looked out onto part of his beautiful garden. Again, however, he failed to see any of it so immersed was he in the anger and hatred that threatened to consume him entirely.

Occasionally, very occasionally, during his life, a thought would flit rapidly across his mind. It came and went so quickly that nearly always it failed to register in his awareness. It came with a question, together with an almost imperceptible desire to find the answer. It always asked, "Why? Why am I feeling this?" Always Antonio turned his attention away from it, for if he had stopped to think for even a split second the very basis of his life would have started to be destroyed, and on one level he was prepared to defend his choice of life, even though it could eventually lead to his destruction.

Today the thought came and went once more without him recognising it, and he turned even deeper into his hatred. For deep down he enjoyed it immensely. He revelled in the sense of power it gave him, the feeling of invincibility, the sure knowledge that he was right.

Into his mind came memories of all the women he had conquered. None had given him satisfaction of any kind. In fact, in using them he hadn't even been searching for satisfaction. He had merely used them to reinforce the concept he had tried all his life to build of himself as a man of power, a man who could stand alone and superior to all others, and in particular to women. For, as long as he could remember, he had hated them. They had always had the ability to make him feel weak and vulnerable. Perhaps the hatred stemmed from his childhood, perhaps it was an inborn characteristic, but certainly it began with his family and the women who surrounded him in the tiny, dirty cottage in Sicily. All his five sisters were older and stronger than he, and constantly punished him for his masculinity and his good looks. None of them was beautiful or even blessed with personalities that would over-ride their lack of good looks and make them attractive.

He remembered one event when he was just eleven, starting to feel his masculinity and recognise his own good looks. He had come home from school early, before his mother had returned from her work as a cleaner. The youngest of the sisters, Paula, had insisted on coming with him. It was not that he liked her more than the others. In fact, of all of them she was the one who made him the most uncomfortable. He didn't know why. Perhaps it was the way she looked at him when the others were preoccupied. Too many times he had caught her staring at him, her face expressionless, and when she realised that he had seen her she always looked away as if guilty about something.

That day she had heard a rumour which had infuriated her. It concerned a girl in her class and Antonio. The girl was pretty and overdeveloped for her age. In fact she had more on her chest at the age of twelve than Paula ever had in the whole of her life.

"I've been hearing things about you, Antonio," she cried out dancing around him in what she thought was a provocative way, but which Antonio only found silly and annoying.

"Don't be stupid," he sneered at her. "You don't know anything."

"Oh, but I do."

"No you don't."

"Yes I do."

He stopped in the hot, dusty street just outside the door to the house and stared at her.

"Well?"

She stopped dancing, unnerved by his look that seemed to penetrate into every part of her.

"Well, what?" she muttered as flutters of fear started to move in her stomach.

"What have you heard?"

She laughed nervously. "Just that you and Maria."

Later, as she told her sisters about what happened then, she realised that she had never seen anything move so fast as did his hand, not even when their cat, defending its prey, had lashed out at the neighbour's dog.

Antonio had caught her in a flash of movement by the throat, pulled her close to his face and very quietly, but with terrifying menace, had said, "If you say anything, anything at all about this to anybody – anybody, do you hear, you will wake up one day even uglier than you are now. And, believe me, that would a very difficult thing for you to do." With that he had scornfully pushed her aside and walked into the house.

Antonio, standing in his study, smiled as he remembered with satisfaction how she had howled with pain and shame as he had left her lying in the dust of the street. He could still see the side of her face streaked with dirt that turned dark as the tears dribbled down, her eyes screwed up, her mouth wide open showing her ugly teeth.

He walked over to the window and stared out, still not seeing anything there. His breathing slowed until it had almost stopped entirely as he remembered the day soon after when the sisters had taken their revenge.

He frowned, as he felt his heart start to beat fiercely and looked down as the memory of his shame returned. For she had blabbed. She had told her sisters of what he had said about her ugliness. They in their turn knew that, however ugly he may think Paula was, they were even uglier. So they had decided to 'pull him down a peg or two'.

They had cornered him one evening when their mother was out working. There were four of them, bigger then he and their combined strength was more than he could handle. They held him down and beat him as they screamed insults about him. Then they stripped him and pushed him naked out into the street, laughing and mocking his tiny manhood. The memory of the shame and helplessness he had experienced that day had stayed with him always, festering at the back of his mind, but rearing up whenever he felt that a woman was trying to better him. He had never had his revenge, a fact that made him even more ashamed, but he excused himself with the memory of his mother, who ruled the house with a cruel discipline.

She, made to look old before her time by the harshness of their existence in the poor South of Italy, was deeply embittered by the loss of her husband shortly after Antonio's birth. A deeply religious woman before his death, the tragic loss of the only man she had loved turned her away from the church and the God whom she blamed for her loss.

So Antonio grew up surrounded by hatred and spite in an atmosphere of harsh repression. Unable to defend himself from the torments he received from his sisters, for his mother always sided with them, he took satisfaction from the cruel treatment he was able to hand out to his peers. As a result he had no friends, but found that he really didn't need them, for he was stronger and more vicious than any of the boys in the neighbourhood, and though they didn't like him, they feared him and that fear gave Antonio more gratification than any friendship could give him.

He smiled as he thought of Anna and the satisfaction she gave him just by being there, where he could control her. In his arrogance he felt sure that she had no idea at all of his true feelings for her, how he despised her for her physical weakness and hated her for her femininity.

Now, he felt calm, at ease, in command of the situation, strong in the knowledge that, when she did return, he would be able to assert his power.

He sat in front of the window and looked out over his land, but still he didn't see what was really there.

Chapter Thirty-Two

DAVID AND ANNA SAT at the tiny table in the kitchen later that evening sipping wine and listening to quiet music on the radio. Alfonso and Pietro had brought them enough food and drink to last several days and David had cooked up a huge bowl of spaghetti. He had brought with him the case that Anna had left in Cornwall and she carefully emptied it, packing away her clothes as he cooked. They hadn't talked much as they ate, but now, feeling mellow, relaxed and happy, with a couple of glasses of wine taking their usual effect, they finally looked each other directly in the eyes.

"I don't know how or why this has been arranged, but, here's a huge thank you to the universe for it," said Anna.

"I'll second that," David said as he lifted his glass.

"It's amazing. There I was yesterday in the depths of despair, not knowing which way to turn, what I was going to do, where I was going to run to, and here I am now, safe and sound with my dear Roman soldier."

David, in spite of the niggling doubt at the back of his mind, smiled and said, "Yes, you never know what life is going to chuck at you, do you? By the way what happened to that Roman soldier? Did you get any more on that?"

"No, it seems that whatever the reason was for me having to re-experience that tragic event, there have been no further appearances of it." She smiled and looking directly at him she said, "However, many times, I did call on the soldier for help and strength when things got really tough."

"And did he come to your aid?"

"Every time."

They were now looking at each other and smiling, and gradually, as they looked, a feeling started to grow, a knowing, a deep recognition of the fact, already, before they had even touched each other, before they had even felt each other's lips, that they were lovers.

And, lovers they were, that evening, for the first time, after a wait of several centuries.

Later, much later, David stood up from the bed, in the darkness, and opened the curtains. At the front of the apartment there was light pollution caused by the street lights on the Viale Monza, and all that was visible there were the cars hurtling past and the glare of the shop windows. But here, at the back, all was darkness and they were able to see the stars in the sky shining brightly. After a few moments Anna joined him and together, in a tender embrace, they looked out and upwards into the heavens.

"We're lucky. It's not often that we can see the stars in the centre of Milan," David said quietly.

"Not like Cornwall though, is it?"

"Oh, no. There it's so clear I sometimes think I'll be able to see where we came from."

"What do you mean?"

"I was just thinking of a story Anthony told me."

David turned to her and gently kissed her cheek.

"Well, go on."

"Well, like all good fairy stories it starts with, 'Once upon a time'.

"So it's just a fairy story, is it?"

"Listen, and make your own mind up."

"Okay, go on then."

"Once upon a time there was a race of beings that had advanced to a level so far ahead of the level we have reached we couldn't even imagine what they were like."

"Spooky. Did they look like us?"

"Not in the least bit. All Anthony would say was that they walked upright like us."

"So what did they look like?"

"That's not important. What is important is that they rendered their planet uninhabitable."

"What did they do? Blow it up?"

"That's what I asked Anthony, but he just said that it wasn't important how they did it. It was enough that they did it. What is important is that when this sort of thing happens in creation, a new place has to be found. But of course, with a new place comes a new physical body. On this planet they found a species of ape which was deemed to be appropriate, and there took place, as he put it, 'an infusion of spirit'."

She smiled. "Sounds like they were making tea."

"Well, I suppose there was a period of 'stewing', but that didn't last long before there was an almighty leap forward in the development of one or two of those apes."

"What caused that?"

"It was the reaction of the apes' bodies to the pressures exerted by an extremely highly developed form of spirit operating within it."

"That means, then, that we're a lot more highly developed than we think."

"Potentially, yes, I suppose."

Anna looked up at the sky and then turned to face David. Drawing him towards her she pressed herself firmly against him so that she could feel every part of him against her body.

"This is all very fascinating," she murmured into his ear, "but I'm now cold and would require some energetic exercise to warm me up. So to coin a phrase, 'Are you up to it'?"

She moved her head back, looked into his eyes and smiled. He bent down, picked her up and carried her over to the bed, where he gently laid her down.

"I think I'll be able to put together a few more movements in this wonderful composition," he said as he lay down beside her and pulled the covers over them.

"I don't mind what you do so long as it's 'allegro con brio'," she whispered.

Chapter Thirty-Three

IT WAS IN THIS way they spent the next ten unbelievably passionate days in that small, very ordinary apartment in Milan, left to themselves by their minders, who did their shopping, unobtrusively, and smiled knowingly when they knocked and received no answer. Later, wrapped in the cold mists of Cornwall, when he looked back at those days, David saw them as amongst the happiest days of his life. For they were truly happy. There was no fear for them, no thought of danger, no future to spoil their joy. They lived in the now, immersed in every delicious moment, oblivious to the danger that was every day growing closer and closer.

It was the eleventh day that changed everything, that brought their happiness to an abrupt, terrible end.

David had had his morning shower and, leaving Anna to wallow for a few more dreamy moments in the warmth of their bed, he went down into the courtyard. The men there, guarding the house, were two of his favourites, Luigi and Mario. They were the most easy going of all the men who had tended to their needs over the past ten days, and it was perhaps this laxness and their indulgence of the 'Inglese' who spoke Italian so well, with so much of the slang that they themselves spoke, that saved David's life.

This morning they all chatted for a few minutes and then David persuaded them to let him walk out onto the street to go to a small supermarket only ten minutes walk away.

"Don't tell the boss," they called after him and laughed as he opened the main door, turned, made a sign that only gangsters used that said, "My lips are sealed," and silently slipped into the street.

Knowing that Anna would perhaps spend another ten to fifteen minutes in the warmth of the bed and then would soak herself in a bath of herbal essences, David strolled easily along the road taking his time, savouring the feel of the energetic Milanese way of life, enjoying the appetising smells from the bread shops and basking in the warm rays of the sun. His whole body tingled with the joy of living.

Reaching Standa, the small supermarket, he sauntered through the shop, hardly seeing any of the merchandise, and just feeling as if he were floating in a bubble of happiness. He realised after some time that he had been smiling at everyone he had met, and that they had been responding also with smiles. "My God, I bet they know," he thought, and then, "Sod it, I couldn't give a damn. If they do, they do," and he continued grinning at all and sundry. After about twenty minutes of aimless wandering he picked up some chicken pieces, a packet of thin spaghetti, a tin of tomatoes, some mushrooms, peppers and garlic, paid for them and, still in a haze of goodwill to all men, made his way dreamily up the staircase to the street.

The realisation that something was not as it should be took quite a time to percolate through to his awareness. First of all, he realised that there were fewer people than usual on the street. Then he noticed a long way down the road a crowd had gathered. The fact that they were outside the apartment block in which he lived came slowly, but when he started to understand, his euphoric state disappeared in a flash to be replaced by a rapidly growing level of alarm. Gradually his pace quickened until he was running faster and faster, breathing heavier and deeper. At the side of his awareness he noticed that he had lost some of his purchases as the bag jumped up and down as he ran, but his concern was now growing stronger and stronger as he saw the flashing lights of several police cars, so it didn't even occur to him to stop to pick them up. It didn't take him long to reach the crowd and he pushed his way through unconcerned by the reactions of those he offended. A policeman tried to stop him but David ducked under his outstretched arm yelling, "I live here! I've got to get in!"

Inside the courtyard David stopped, horrified by the sight of the blood on the cobble stones. By the door lay Luigi, still, his brown eyes staring sightless at the sky. Further in Mario was trying to get up, his face covered in blood from an ugly wound on the side of the head. He staggered and fell. David ran to him crying, "What happened? Who did this?"

Mario, his eyes dull and his mouth slack and bleeding, looked at David and managed to whisper, "I'm sorry. They were too fast for us. Antonio," before he slipped into unconsciousness.

David ran over to the stairwell and looked up in horror as the powerful figure of Antonio, his hands behind his back, his face badly bruised and bleeding, was roughly pushed around the bend in the stairs. He tripped as he came down and would have fallen if the policemen hadn't been holding him firmly. They cursed him and yanked him upright causing him to gasp in pain, but as his head came up he caught sight of David standing at the bottom of stairs. He stopped for a moment and was again pushed on, but David saw a terrible smile of satisfaction pass over his lips, to be replaced immediately by a look of malevolent hatred.

The policemen shouted at David, "Get back! You can't come here!"

"But I live here! What's happened? Where's Anna?"

They hurried down the stairs and pushed past him. One of the policemen savagely knocked him aside, and in a rough voice growled, "Out of the way! You can't stay there!"

Antonio looked back and shouted, "You next, bastardo!"

David moved slowly up the stairs, his muscles tensing, a dreadful fear growing inside of him. On the landing, nearly at the top of the stairs, a body of a man he didn't recognise lay with arms spread wide, mouth wide open as if gasping for air it could no longer breathe. Then, seeing the door of his apartment wide open, he ran to it, realisation finally breaking through into his awareness.

"Anna!" he shouted, and stopped just over the threshold where a policeman appeared from nowhere and painfully thrust a gun into his chest.

"Stop! Hands up! Against the wall!"

Unceremoniously he was pushed with his face against the wall and felt hands swiftly checking his body. Then, he was turned round and roughly thrown face down into the middle of the room.

Another voice, quieter and more educated asked, "Who are you, and what are you doing here?"

David tried to get up but was held firmly in an arm lock. Any slight movement on his part was rewarded with added painful pressure on his elbow. With difficulty, for the side of his face was pressed firmly against the floor, he managed to say, "I live here. I'd just been out to . . ."

He was cut short with a very brusque, "Name?"

"David Henderson. I'm English, here on holiday."

"What's your relationship with the body?"

"The body? What body?" David felt his chest tighten and felt himself gasping for air as he involuntarily tried to get up.

The pain in his arm increased so he immediately sank down into the carpet.

Someone walked towards him, bent down and a sallow, thin, mournful face appeared close to him. David looked at the brown, bloodshot eyes as they keenly inspected his face, then gasped with relief as the pressure on his arm disappeared.

"Please stand," said the quiet voice. "I'm sorry we had to treat you in this manner, but you must understand that we cannot be too careful. In a situation like this we are always ourselves in great danger." He stood aside as David painfully got to his feet. "By the way, you say you are English. Do you understand Italian?"

"Yes, perfectly."

David sat down in an armchair and looked at the man who took a chair from the table and sat facing him.

"What's happened here? Where's Anna? What did that bastard do?"

"One moment, please. Firstly, you must answer my questions."

"You said something about a body."

"And I said that firstly you must answer my questions."

The man stood up and tried to smooth down a well-worn crumpled suit.

"I am Inspector Rosetti. The man we took away, did you know him?"

"Yes, he is Antonio Taverna. I met him in England a couple of times."

"In what capacity?"

"He came looking for his wife who was staying in a cottage opposite mine. He thought I might know of her whereabouts and broke into my cottage one night to interrogate me."

"And did you know where she was?"

"At that time, no, I didn't."

The inspector stared intently at David's face for what seemed to be a long time before saying quietly and sadly, "Well, I'm afraid it looks as though he found her."

David looked up at him, his eyes imploring him to say that it wasn't true.

"Where is she? May I see her?"

"I do not think that that would be advisable."

"Please, I must. I should have been here." He looked imploringly up at the Inspector. "Please."

"Well, perhaps you could be of assistance." He stood up and turned towards the bathroom. "In identifying the bo . . . the lady."

Slowly, hesitatingly, David followed him to the bathroom.

"May I see her alone?"

The inspector hesitated, then pushed open the door and stepped aside to allow David to step into the bathroom.

Anna was lying in the bath, which was still filled with water stained red by her blood. David felt as though all his strength had suddenly left him and only managed to remain upright by holding on to the door frame. He felt a hand on his elbow.

"Are you alright, sir?" asked the inspector.

David took a deep breath and summoning all the strength left to him stood up straight and said, "Yes, alright." Then he turned, went into the sitting room and collapsed into a chair.

"Is that her? Is that his wife?"

"Yes, that's Anna Taverna."

"Thank you."

David sat numbed, staring out of the window he saw nothing, his eyes wide open, his mouth open but rigid with tension. But then he threw himself forward and ran into the kitchen, where he sank his head into the sink and was violently sick. And when his stomach was empty, he retched and retched until his midriff became so painful he cried out. And then he cried out, and cried out, and shouted, and screamed his pain into the universe, until there was no strength left in him to scream any more, when he fell into a heap, quietly sobbing.

The inspector and his sergeant looked away, for they had seen this before, many times.

Chapter Thirty-Four

THE NEXT FEW DAYS passed as in a nightmare for David. The police first of all took a statement from him and then, telling him that they thought he might be still in great danger, moved him to a secret location in Como, where he was lodged at a small hotel in the centre of the town. Beside it was a tiny trattoria, where he took the few meals he ate. For most of the time he aimlessly walked about the streets of the town, not seeing much, not at all concerned about the fat, perspiring police guard who followed his every move, and feeling only the deep sadness that engulfed his every moment.

About a week after his arrival in Como David was sitting in the trattoria having his evening meal when he caught sight of someone he recognised immediately. It was the tall, slim figure of Ugo standing in the doorway. He looked at David, put a finger to his mouth and walked over to the fat policeman. For a few minutes he talked quietly to the man, who seemed immediately to perspire even more. They appeared to argue for a bit and then Ugo passed him a bundle of lira, which the fat man stuffed into his inside pocket, stood up and walked out of the café saying loudly, "I'll be back in five minutes."

Ugo walked across the room and sat in the chair opposite David. His eyes were sad and tired. He licked his lips.

"What can I say?" He spread his hands in a typical Italian gesture. "I'm so sorry, my friend."

David stared hard at him, his mind in a whirl but filled with disbelief that this man, who he blamed most of all for what had happened, should have the nerve to come to see him.

"What the hell happened?" he shouted so loudly that people stopped talking to look at them. "Where were you? I thought you said you would be looking after her!"

He stood up and shouted again, "Where were you, you bastard?" He felt his fists tight against his thighs. His eyes and mouth were wide open as if he had caught sight of some horror.

"You knew he'd come, didn't you?" he screamed. "The whole thing was a set-up, wasn't it? She was just bait, wasn't she? Wasn't she?" In his despair he futilely punched the air and then hung his head as tears of anger and frustration poured down his cheeks. "Just bait," he whispered and sat down heavily.

The customers in the trattoria stared at David, not knowing what to do. Some half stood as if preparing themselves for flight.

Ugo's sad eyes looked across at David and his head shook very slightly from side to side.

"I was away in Rome on business. There was nothing I could have done," he said raising his shoulders and reaching out his arms towards David as if searching for some contact or understanding.

"But you promised!" David pushed his chair back and ran out of the café.

In the street the fat policeman appeared, stood in his way and pushed him against the wall. Holding David firmly he shouted, as Ugo appeared in the café doorway, "I told you it was not advisable, now go."

Ugo turned to go, hesitated for a moment, then said,

"Okay, I'll go. But, David, don't forget, he got two of my men, my friends. You can rest assured that no matter where they take him, wherever he ends up, we'll get him. I promise, on my mother's grave, I promise."

But David didn't hear him. With his face to the wall, he was sobbing too loudly.

*   *   *

It was a dog that finally turned him around and brought him abruptly back to sanity. David had taken to sitting on the banks of the lake, staring out into the distance, acknowledging no-one, unaware of the calm, peaceful beauty surrounding him.

One day, two or three days after Ugo's visit, he had been sitting for about an hour in the late afternoon in his chosen spot, when he felt a smooth warm wetness on the back of his hand. Woken from his reverie he found himself looking down into a pair of soft brown eyes, which then immediately became alive and imploring. It was a small, shaggy dog, which had evidently just taken a swim in the lake, for it was dripping wet. It wagged its tail and skipped away, shook itself, and tucked its tail between its legs. Then it turned towards him, leaned back on its hind legs with its front legs stretched out before it as if to say, "Let's play!" Barking sharply, it rapidly ran in several circles in front of him with its tongue hanging out, stopped, and, hearing a whistle, launched itself away to where a man was standing waiting about a hundred yards away. As the dog reached him the man bent down, attached a lead to the dog's neck, waved at David, smiled and briskly walked away.

The whole incident couldn't have lasted for more than a minute, but it changed David immediately.

It changed him because something happened to him for the first time in his life, something that would happen to him many times in the future.

As he sat there looking out after the dog an idea came into his head, an idea that was more than an idea. It arrived in his brain in the form of a cube, and the cube held within it a concept.

The concept was this: "What you have seen with the dog is one of the main attributes of spirit, and that is, the capacity for a totally uninhibited, loving joy. It is not only yours by right, it is you by nature. To experience it, all you have to do is to find out what it is that is stopping you from experiencing it, from experiencing that which you are."

The ideas didn't arrive in a linear fashion, one after the other. The whole concept arrived in totality, all at once.

David sat for a long time, astonished, whilst the event sank into him. Then, slowly, he started to feel better, more aware. The soul-crushing sadness that had filled him since Anna's death seemed to drain like dirty water out of a sink. He looked at the lake and instead of seeing a vast, dark expanse of murky water, saw a wide panorama of shining, glistening blue, and trees, and boats, and people. People smiling and laughing and shouting. Living. The cold air blowing off the lake, which before had caused him such discomfort, now became bracing, energising. He also experienced once again the feeling of gathering into himself parts of himself that seemed to have been scattered out into the universe, so that he began to feel tighter, more together. The memory of when that had happened once before in the bath at his home in Cornwall flashed into his mind making him smile. The thought of Cornwall and home awoke in him a longing for his dog, Charlie, his friends, his house, his music and above all, Beth. In his mind he could see her smiling, feel her love reaching out for him.

"What the hell am I doing here?" he thought.

Abruptly he stood up and smiled at the fast retreating little shaggy dog, now very small in the distance. Its owner, as if sensing David's gaze on his back, turned and again waved. He then moved away and became lost in the crowd of people standing by a huddle of beached pleasure craft.

With purpose now, for the first time since his arrival from Milan, David strode in the direction of his hotel, aware more than ever of his police 'protector' and the difficulty with which the poor man just managed to keep up with him.

Back in his room David quickly packed his few belongings and lay on his bed, savouring the change that had happened to him.

The thought of the dog and the ideas that had come to him with its appearance continued to fill him with wonder.

"It's so right," he thought. "So simple. So natural."

The following morning avoiding his 'minder' presented no difficulties. Hiring a car he drove down to Milan and in the afternoon boarded a plane bound for London.

It was early evening when he arrived at Heathrow, so he took a room in a small hotel near the airport and booked a seat on the following day's train to Cornwall. After dinner he sat in his room knowing that he should ring Beth, but dreading the thought of having to tell her about Anna.

However, when he finally plucked up the courage and did ring her he was surprised, and somewhat relieved, to find that she already knew of Anna's death.

"It was on the news. Why didn't you ring us? Perhaps we could have helped," she said. But in her heart she knew how he had suffered and secretly she feared that they wouldn't have been able to do anything to help him.

He was silent for such a long time that she finally called out, "Hello, are you still there?" thinking that they had been cut off.

Finally, reluctantly he muttered, "I'm afraid that I went to pieces. I couldn't think. I just didn't know what to do." Again he waited for a while, and then, "Besides, the police whisked me away to Como to a safe house, and they wouldn't let me near a phone."

"You mean, they thought you were in danger too."

"I guess so."

"My God, you poor thing."

"Thanks, Beth, but I'm better now. Thanks to a little dog."

"A what?"

"A dog. I'll tell you all about it when I get in tomorrow."

"Sounds fascinating. Okay. I'll go over to your place and get it heated and aired so it'll be lovely for you to come home to."

"Thanks Beth, I'll see you tomorrow evening at 8.30, Redruth station."

Chapter Thirty-Five
Cornwall

IT HAD BEEN RAINING for days, a light, feathery rain that seemed to permeate everything, even the great granite blocks of the buildings, and drip slowly onto the ground to lie there in shallow puddles, grey mirrors reflecting the occasional car headlight.

Their meeting on the dark, wet station was an awkward moment. The few people that had got off the train quickly disappeared leaving them alone, looking at each other, uncertain and nervous, until Beth, seeing the agony he was still feeling, took him in her arms and held him tightly whilst he sobbed for a long time, both of them ignoring the rain that swept across the deserted platform.

"It's so good to be back," he said at last.

"It's so good to have you back," she replied and smiled. "Come on I'll drive you home."

She drove carefully and quite slowly for the rain was torrential and the headlights of the oncoming cars splashed across her windscreen momentarily blinding her. David sat silent, his eyes heavy. Relief at being home washed over him even though, to his surprise, he found the winding, hedge-lined lanes that led towards the sea and home familiar, but at the same time, quite strange, as if he were seeing them for the first time. Nevertheless, he breathed deeply and found himself relaxing more and more as they neared home. At one point they were forced to stop for a moment to allow a car to pass them and Beth chanced a quick look across at him. His head was hanging forward and his breath was rasping against the back of his nose as he slept. She smiled and drove on, concentrating on the winding, narrow Porthtowan road.

At the cottage, she stopped the car at the foot of the steps, which lead up to the footpath in front of his house and gave him a gentle nudge.

"Wake up, you big lump. There's someone wanting to see you."

The walls of the cottage were four feet thick, but even down where they were in the road, she could hear the excited yelping of Charlie, who had somehow sensed the return of her beloved master.

David woke with a start as Beth leaned across him and pushed his door open.

"What the . . . ?" he started to say and then, feeling Beth's breath on his face and aware of the softness of her breast as she pressed against his arm, he looked into her eyes and wondered for an instant whether she was about to kiss him, when he too heard the faint but insistent sound of Charlie's welcome. "Is that . . . ?" he started to ask, but she answered immediately with, "Well, we couldn't have you return to an empty house, now, could we?"

Beth smiled and David sighed and closed his eyes as tears of relief and joy welled up.

"Beth, you are a treasure," he gasped. "What would I do without you?"

"Well, I hope . . ." she started to say but then, as Charlie's squeals started to become more insistent, she sighed and said, "I think you'd better get in there quick and save your dog from busting a blood vessel, don't you?"

The welcome was noisy and energetic and went on for several minutes, but then, as is normal for dogs, Charlie suddenly decided that she had immediate and urgent business in the garden and left David and Beth still laughing and energised as she rushed outside barking her message to the world, in spite of the rain being driven in sheets by the wind howling in the trees and the bushes.

David walked through into the kitchen and then back into the living room touching everything as if to renew acquaintance with all his possessions. He was amazed at how new and different everything appeared to him, as if he had been away for years instead of just a few weeks.

He sat at the piano and played several chords, improvising melodies and pleasant harmonies whilst Beth sank into the softness of the settee and warmed herself before the fire she had lit earlier.

"God, I've missed this," he said and turned away from the keyboard to look at Beth. "I've missed a lot of things." He looked around the room. "It's amazing how strange everything looks."

"Everything?"

"Yes, everything looks somehow foreign and . . ." He stopped as he caught sight of her looking at him, her head on one side, her right eyebrow arched and her mouth smiling.

"Oh, Christ, no! I didn't mean." He stood and walked over to where she was sitting. As he reached her she held out her hands to him. Her fingers were warm and soft and he gripped them tightly as he looked into her eyes.

"Thank you Beth," he said. "I've felt you with me so many times when I was out there. I don't know how I would have managed without you."

She looked up at him and felt an enormous urge to stand and take him in her arms, but she knew that it was too soon and that she would have to wait. She consoled herself immediately with the knowledge that they would be together for a very long time to come, so she sighed and smiled, "David, my dear," she said, "I think that it's time I put the kettle on and you had a bite to eat. You must be starving. So how about you having a quick wash and taking your case upstairs. I'll call you when it's ready."

She stood, quickly kissed him on the cheek and walked past him into the kitchen, where she busied herself with the ritual of tea making. Five minutes later she called him, and, receiving no acknowledgement, climbed the stairs to his bedroom.

He was lying on his back on the bed, his mouth open, and she could see that he was already in a deep sleep. His case sat on the floor unopened, so she picked it up and laid it on a chair. Then she gently took off his shoes, covered him with a blanket and, as quietly as she could, went downstairs. There she opened the door for Charlie, who came in excited, but muddy and wet, so she rubbed the dog dry with an old towel that she found in the kitchen and persuaded her to lie down in front of the fire. After closing the door that lead to the small hall and the stairs so that the dog would not be tempted to join David on the bed, she curled up on the settee with a cup of tea and a sandwich, and very shortly herself fell into a deep sleep.

Chapter Thirty-Six

THE FOLLOWING MORNING WHEN he awoke David was surprised to find that he was still dressed in the clothes he had travelled in. Dragging himself out of a deep sleep, he immediately forgot the dream that had been his reality up until a few moments ago. His left arm explored the top of the bed in the hopes of finding Charlie there, but he realised that there wasn't even the warmth that there would have been had she spent the night with him. He sat up, forcing his eyes open, suddenly aware of the tantalising smell of fried bacon. Now wide awake, he threw off the blanket, and hurried over to the window. Opening the curtains he lifted the sash window, took a deep breath and looked out on the comforting familiarity of his garden. A light rain was being blown down the valley from the sea and across the roof of Sylvia's cottage. Beads of water clung to the branches of the blackthorn and the tangled knots of weeds in the hedgerows. Directly opposite him a herd of bullocks, young and blissfully unaware of the fate that awaited them, wandered carelessly up the hill. Smiling with delight David stripped off his clothes, quickly wrapped himself in his dressing gown and hurried down the stairs.

The living room was warm and welcoming, brightly lit by a fire burning in the grate. In the kitchen Beth was standing by the cooker turning over slices of bacon in a large frying pan. In another pan several eggs were being gently poached. Charlie was sitting by her feet, the ends of her nose twitching, her head pointing optimistically upwards at the hands she could see moving above her. Quickly she looked at David, briefly wagged her tail, and then, with her tongue hanging out, resumed her vigil.

Beth moved the frying pan away from the heat and said, "Hi. I thought the smell of fried bacon would bring you down."

Her face was clean and bright and her hair was gathered back with a bright blue bandana. Walking to him she took his hands in hers and looking lovingly and full of concern into his eyes said, "My God but you look rough. What the hell were you up to last night?"

"You may well ask," David answered, laughing. "I just wish I could remember."

They embraced, kissed briefly and a little awkwardly looked into each other's eyes.

A short sharp bark from Charlie brought them back to awareness.

"I'm going to have to do something about this bloody dog," David said as they reluctantly moved apart.

"Don't you dare touch her," said Beth. "She's got my best interests at heart. I've been slaving over a hot stove ever since I got up, and I just wouldn't want to see it all ruined."

"Well, for once I reluctantly have to agree with her. It all looks wonderful." He walked over to the stove and looked at the bacon.

Sniffing with appreciation he said, "By the way, where did you sleep last night?"

"On the sofa," Beth replied and covered two plates with sizzling bacon, and tomatoes.

"God, that must have been an uncomfortable night. Did you sleep well?"

"Fine. I was warm, comfortable and I had excellent company," she waved her hand at Charlie who wagged her tail optimistically.

"If you'd care to take your seat, milord, it's all just about ready."

"Okay, but I've got an urgent appointment with the loo which won't wait," David said and hurried into the bathroom.

"Hurry back," Beth said turning back to the stove. "The eggs are just about ready."

When he returned David found his breakfast of eggs, bacon, tomatoes and toast waiting for him on the table. For one moment he was reminded that this was how it used to be when Tina was alive. He sighed and shrugged his shoulders.

"What is it?" Beth asked.

"Nothing. I was just thinking how lovely it looks. Thanks, Beth, for everything."

He gave her cheek a quick kiss in appreciation and sat down at the table.

They ate for a while in silence, hungrily, each acutely aware of the other's nearness.

"What have you got planned for this morning?" David asked as he cleared his plate of the last piece of bacon.

"Well, whilst you're having a nice hot bath, I'm going to sort out your washing and generally tidy up here. Then we'll see what happens with the weather. It's supposed to clear up later on this morning. We'll see, eh?"

Later, the rain had at last stopped, as had been promised, and the wind had dropped to a gentle breeze, so they decided to walk to the café in St. Agnes for lunch. The sun shone and, although it was now November, it was surprisingly warm. As they walked down the hill David found himself suddenly overcome by a memory of the first time he had gone with Anna to St. Agnes. He had been walking along this road and, at the spot where she had stopped to give him a lift, he felt tears well up into his eyes.

"David!" Beth exclaimed, concerned, as he had involuntarily gripped her hand tightly. "David! Are you alright?"

David stopped and took a deep breath.

"Just memories, Beth," he said, and continued walking, but still holding her hand tightly as if for support.

Beth gently pulled on his arm and turned him to face her.

"There'll always be memories, David. Some good, some perhaps painful, but don't, for God's sake, hold back on them. Let it all out."

With that she held him tightly for a moment, and then walked him slowly along with her right arm around his shoulder.

Charlie, who had been totally immersed in the sights and smells of the countryside, sensed that something was not quite right and ran back to them, sniffed at David's legs, barked once and then ran ahead in joyful anticipation.

Watching her apparently limitless optimism David felt the gloom that had filled him lift, and he started to walk straighter and respond to the wild beauty of the hedgerows.

After walking for about a mile, they turned a bend in the road and there on the opposite side stood a house. It stood alone, redbrick, with white plastic window frames and a squat, ugly porch on the side just visible over an unkempt escalonia hedge. The wall of the house facing them, along side the road, had no redeeming features, no windows, no doors. It was just a boring brick wall that someone had painted white. The house was totally out of keeping with the countryside that surrounded it.

"Have I ever told you that that house is supposed to be haunted?" David said smiling.

"No, you haven't," said Beth as she walked over to it and put her hands on a wall, "but I believe you. It feels terrible."

She noticed that Charlie started to walk towards the house, but then abruptly veered away from it and pushed her nose into a tuft of grass on the opposite side of the road.

"I've always felt it to be a sad house, as I've passed it."

"Yes, it certainly is," Beth agreed. "Perhaps one day we'll come and sort it out."

They turned and walked away quickly in order to distance themselves from it.

"Do you know what happened there?" she asked.

"I understand that a chap hanged himself in the cellar a few years ago," David said.

"Then we'll definitely have a go at it and see if we have to help him on his way."

"What do you mean, help him on his way?"

"When people die a violent death," Beth explained quietly, "they pass over sometimes with their consciousness focussed so completely on their grief, their fear, or whatever it is that has brought them to this state, that they can't get away from it. Or, in the case of a suicide, they feel so guilty about having topped themselves that they don't want to get away from it."

"Why not?"

"Perhaps because they feel they deserve it." She said sadly. "There are many, many reasons for someone to get stuck," she added.

"So, what could we do about it?"

"We have a little get-together, you, me and perhaps Anthony, if he's interested, and we try to get the bloke's focus shifted."

"And should we manage to get his focus shifted, what then?"

"Then he becomes open to influence of a more beneficial kind, which he may, or may not respond to positively."

"And what happens if he doesn't?"

She shrugged. "Well then, for the moment there will be nothing that can be done for him, and unfortunately, he'll have to be left until later, when another attempt will be made."

"That doesn't seem very fair to me." David frowned.

"It's nothing to do with fair or unfair. It's to do with what he wants. It's always his decision. No-one forces anyone to do anything."

"But, why wouldn't anyone want to get away from what surely amounts to his private hell? It can't be any fun for the poor bastard being stuck in that."

"There are many reasons, guilt, a desire, or a need, for self punishment. He may even have got so used to the state he's in he feels afraid to move out of it. And don't forget, either, that he has no sense of time. He may be there for years without realising it." She shrugged. "As I said, it's all down to him. There's no terrible God demanding vengeance."

David immediately had a picture of a white haired old man, sitting on a throne, hurling bolts of lightning down on some hapless person squirming in the grip of some ugly red devils.

"I never thought that, even though my parents tried to force it down my throat," he said with a wry smile.

"Thank goodness, at last we seem to be moving away from that concept," Beth said quietly. She took his arm and they slowly moved away from the house.

A little further on they stopped by a field gate to admire some Friesian cows which, on seeing them, slowly moved towards them as if curious, but then stopped as Charlie stuck her nose through the gate.

"Have you done this before, then?" David asked.

"What? Helping those stuck?"

"Yes."

"Yes, a few," she said smiling.

David walked on in complete silence, digesting what Beth had said.

Suddenly he stopped and seized hold of her arms, as a thought occurred to him.

"What do you think, then, happened to Anna?" he cried. "She was murdered, for God's sake. Is she stuck? Is she imprisoned in her own fear?" In his mind's eye he had a terrible picture of Anna held, tortured by her terror.

Beth took hold of both his hands. "David, calm down. It's alright. When we heard what had happened to her, I was at Anthony's and we immediately had a session together. What we found out was that Anna was immediately seized with terror, she was stunned by the violence, but . . ."

David immediately had a vivid recollection of Anna lying in the bathwater reddened by her blood. He stopped, his eyes closed tight.

"Oh God, I'm sorry," Beth exclaimed, seeing how affected he was. "But you must never forget that she's also very aware. She's a very old spirit. After the first shock, she realised what had happened and was able to respond immediately to the help that arrived for her."

David opened his eyes and looked at her. "She didn't suffer, did she? Tell me she didn't suffer!"

"It was all over in a flash. Physically she felt nothing much, just a blow, and then she was out of it. She just had a moment of terror when she saw Antonio bursting in. But, honestly, she was out of the situation so fast and immediately surrounded by love that there was absolutely no suffering at all. Believe me."

She gently pulled David towards her and held him tight for a moment. Then, holding his hands again she smiled and said, "In fact, very soon her main concern was for you, how you would react." Beth released his hands, wrapped her arms around his body and again held him tightly. "You see," she whispered, "you don't have to concern yourself about her. She's fine, believe me."

She felt his body shake as he sobbed, and then she heard him whisper, "I should have been there." Breaking free from her arms and turning away he pounded an old granite post with the side of his clenched fists. "I should have been there!" he cried. "I should have been there!"

They stayed by the post for several minutes, until David had gathered his composure. Beth wondered, at first, whether to try to make him understand the futility of his guilt, but then realised that it would only be healed by love and understanding, and time, so she said nothing.

Ten minutes later they arrived at the café to be met by Anthony's usual warm welcome.

"David! Welcome dear boy! And Beth! So good to see you again, and so soon!"

He stood as tall as his dapper five feet six figure would allow, and led them rapidly to a table in the far corner so as to be as far away as possible from the few customers that were already enjoying their lunch.

"We'll be able to talk here, undisturbed," he said in an exaggerated stage whisper. "Have you walked or come by car?" he asked.

Puzzled, they said they had walked.

"Oh, wonderful, we can celebrate. I'll get some wine." He scurried away to the bar and almost immediately returned with a bottle of Merlot.

"I know you like this, David, so I've had it ready and waiting for when you came in," he said, uncorking it with a flourish.

"Let's let it breathe for a moment or two," he said putting the bottle on the table. "Although," he added, winking, "I really don't believe that makes any difference to it at all."

He smiled his most optimistic smile and said, "It is so good to have you back again, David."

"Thanks Anthony. It's wonderful to be back." He smiled and looked out of the window. "I love Italy and the Italians, but there's nothing to beat Cornwall, even though it has just started to rain again."

They all involuntarily turned to glance out of the window at the street that had already started to glisten.

"I know," cried Anthony, "what you need to really welcome you back is a real proper-job Cornish pasty. We've got a freshly baked batch from the village bakery and they're wonderful." He smiled, turned and hurried into the kitchen, calling over his shoulder, "Don't go away. I'll be right back!"

"After a few weeks of nothing but pasta that will be terrific, thanks!" David called after him. He felt himself relaxing in the familiar, friendly surroundings, so he closed his eyes and breathed deeply allowing the tensions that had gripped him on the walk to flow away smoothly like a wave on the beach making its way back to the strength of the sea. He was vaguely aware of Anthony placing things on the table and of the calm presence of Beth sitting beside him, and then he was abruptly brought back into the present by the delicious smell of the steaming hot pasties as they were placed in the middle of the table.

"Do you know, I think that these are so lovely I think I'm going to join you. I can't resist them." Anthony said as he pulled up a chair to the table.

They ate in silence for a while, a little awkwardly, for neither Beth nor Anthony knew whether David wanted to talk about his time in Italy, and David was still luxuriating in the feelings of relief at being back home among his friends. However, perhaps sensing the lack of ease in his friends as they ate, David suddenly started to tell them all that had happened to him in Milan.

They were fascinated by what he had to say about the night club and the gangster Ugo, but his descriptions of the girls' antics in conning the poor, unsuspecting customers caused them all to burst out laughing so loudly that they became embarrassed as the other diners turned, first to stare at them, and then to join in laughing, even though they had no idea of what they laughing about.

"The way you describe them, some of these gangsters sound quite nice blokes really," said Beth, wiping the tears from her cheeks.

"And so they may seem," said David, "but, believe me, they are quite ruthless in their treatment of anyone who crosses their path that they don't like, or whom they see as a threat to them."

The mention of their habits made David think again of Antonio and the last time he had seen him being led away by the police. Again he felt the hatred the gangster had exuded as he had shouted, "You next, bastardo!" before being bundled out of the courtyard.

He shivered and took a deep breath.

"Are you okay?" It was Beth, concerned by the look of despair that had suddenly appeared on his face.

"Yes," David said abstractedly. "It's just that I've suddenly got this silly feeling that I've not done with that maniac."

Beth and Anthony looked at each other for a moment and then looked down, for they too had the feeling that the affair wasn't over yet.

Chapter Thirty-Seven

A FEW DAYS LATER, following the 'celebration' they had had at the café for his return, David was sitting at the window in his cottage looking out at the dying blossoms of a hydrangea bush whilst he idly stroked Charlie's ears. He had just finished arranging the music for a gig, that Beth had organised for the following week-end, in one of the most prestigious hotels on the Roseland peninsular, and was enjoying a few moments of delicious anticipation of playing again, when he was startled out of his reverie by Charlie rushing, barking to the door. David could hear the faint sound of someone walking quietly up the steps and realised that once more, as his hands began to sweat, that he was experiencing an irrational fear.

"What the hell am I scared of now?" he thought. "That bastard is slammed up in an Italian jail."

The knock at the door, though expected, still made him jump, so he waited a moment, and took a really deep breath.

"Coming," he called out as the knock was repeated.

Charlie had her nose to the bottom of the door, her tail wagging in anticipation.

Carefully, and with some trepidation, he opened the door.

"Denzil!" The thought came that the relief in his voice must have been obvious. "Come in, my friend. I'll put the kettle on."

David turned and left Denzil to close the door and fend off as best he could Charlie's frenzied greeting.

"Is this a friendly visit, or is it official?" he called from the kitchen as he filled the kettle.

Denzil sighed and eased his bulk into a comfortable armchair.

"Bit of both, I'm afraid."

Oh, dear, that doesn't sound too promising." David quickly opened a packet of biscuits. "How many sugars are you taking these days? I've forgotten."

"Two, my 'andsome. I'm cutting down." He smiled wryly to himself.

As the kettle was getting hot, David walked through into the living room, whilst Charlie sat expectantly directly in front of the policeman.

"Where's the girl, then?" Denzil asked. "Where's Beth? Hasn't left you already, has she?" He took out a handkerchief, noisily blew his nose and inspected the result before stuffing the cloth back into his trouser pocket.

David decided to ignore the jibe, and after explaining that Beth had gone into Truro to do some necessary shopping, changed the subject with, "You're looking well, Denzil. Are they keeping you busy?"

"Enough, thanks to you, my friend. Our Italian comrades are not happy. You should have let them know what you were going to do. By the way, my commiserations. I was sorry to hear about Anna. That was very sad. Such a waste. That husband of hers is a bit of a mad dog. When they get him I hope they bang him up and throw away the key."

David put down a plate of biscuits tantalisingly close to Charlie and was on the way back into the kitchen when the full implication of what Denzil had said suddenly hit him. He stopped and slowly turned.

"What did you say?" David stared at Denzil whose mouth was already half open to receive the biscuit he was clutching in his right hand.

"Did you say, 'When they get him'?"

Denzil hurriedly pushed the biscuit into his mouth and nodded, rapidly chewing.

David frowned, perplexed. "I don't understand. I saw them get him. They took him away."

Denzil gulped down the biscuit. "I know, my friend." He hesitated, swallowing once more. "I'm sorry, but I'm afraid he got away."

David stared at Denzil, his mouth wide open in disbelief. He felt a pain start to grow in his abdomen. He took a deep breath. "How? They had him. He was handcuffed. He was caught red-handed! What the hell happened?" He was almost shouting now.

Charlie stared in sudden alarm from David to Denzil and then, sensing no violence, fixed the biscuits with a stare, determined not to let any of them escape.

Denzil, holding on to yet another biscuit just in front of his mouth, shrugged his shoulders and said defensively, "I'm sorry, I don't know the details, just that he got away."

"How do you know? Who told you?" David nervously paced back and forth in front of his friend.

"A mate of mine over there in Milan. We've worked together many times." Finally he managed to hurriedly push the biscuit into his mouth. "Believe me," he said, spluttering crumbs onto the carpet, "It's true. He's done a runner."

David stood motionless, running his right hand through his hair.

"How the heck did that happen?"

216

He could feel sweat coating his scalp and his heart beating strongly in his chest.

"Search me. The Italians are a bit cagey about it. As I said, all that I know is that he's gone, and nobody knows where he is."

"Christ." David walked into the kitchen, a sinking, empty feeling suddenly growing in his stomach, and poured the now boiling water into the tea pot, whilst Denzil morosely broke another biscuit in halves, put one half in his mouth and fed the other to Charlie.

"By the way, don't give any biscuits to Charlie. She's put on some weight at that restaurant. It's a strict diet from now on."

"Don't you worry my 'andsome," he said and swallowed hurriedly. "She won't get any from me. I lost a little weight myself last week and I'm trying to put it back on." He laughed, leaned forward and ignoring Charlie's pleas pushed a complete biscuit into his mouth.

David carried two cups of tea into the room and sat down. They had both been sitting in silence for about a minute, sipping their hot tea, when a strange thing happened to David.

When he had first heard the news, the old familiar fear had flooded into him covering his palms with sweat and churning his stomach, but now, whilst he sat in his favourite chair smoothing Charlie's ears, he felt a wave of warmth and peace wash over him, and all his fear disappeared as if it had never touched him. He felt his stomach relax, the pain leave him, and when he rubbed his thumb and forefinger together he was surprised to feel how dry they were. He looked up at Denzil to see if he had noticed anything at all, but he had his eyes closed as he nibbled on another biscuit.

David closed his eyes and felt as if he were sinking into a soft bed of peace. The emotion was so strong that he felt tears running down his cheeks.

"Are you alright, David?"

"Thanks, I'm fine."

"'Cos you don't have to worry. I'll look after you. You'll be alright."

"Thanks, Denzil, but I'm not worried, honestly. I'm just a little tired after all that I've been through."

"Yes, it must have been tough."

Denzil heaved his huge body out of the chair with a grunt. "Look, there's no real hurry for what I want to know, so I'll be going now and I'll come back another time. You take it easy for a while. Don't overdo it in that garden of yours."

Embarrassed, he stroked Charlie and surreptitiously took another biscuit. "Just in case I can't manage to get lunch today."

He coughed nervously and strode to the door. "Don't bother yourself. I'll let myself out."

"Cheers, Denzil."

David sat quietly for some time with his eyes closed, savouring the feeling that had warmly spread over him, and thought about Anna.

Since leaving Milan he had been torn by guilt. Already the relationship he had with Beth had deepened and become more intense, but in spite of the deep feelings he had for her he had not been able to stop thinking of Anna. Thanks to Beth he had been able to deal to some extent with the guilt he felt, but from time to time he still had a vivid moment of recollection of Anna lying dead in the red waters of her bath, and the deep feelings of sadness and remorse that rushed into him were overpowering. But this morning, it was different. This morning his thoughts were not of the past. He was not remembering her as she had been, as they had been together. This morning he suddenly felt her, her essence, her very being. He felt her more closely than he had ever felt her when she had been 'alive', as if every part of her permeated every part of him.

And as he sat with his eyes closed, he suddenly saw her before him, shining and smiling, as if to say, "I am here. You are safe. Don't be afraid."

She was only there for a moment, and then she was gone, leaving him staring into the blackness. The feeling of her went and he opened his eyes to see Charlie, her tail furiously wagging, staring at him intently, willing him to respond to her demand for another biscuit. He took one, and, wiping the tears from his cheeks, gave it to her. Collapsing back into the chair, he closed his eyes and savoured the sense of peace and strength that the vision had left him with.

In his mind's eye he could still see her, shining and extraordinarily beautiful. But what he was now seeing was a memory, different from what he had experienced a few moments ago. What he had experienced then had been reality! She had been there! Of that he was sure.

Later, he told Beth of what he had seen. "She was there. I know it," he said.

"Yes she was," Beth whispered as she cradled him in her arms. "She really was."

Chapter Thirty-Eight
Naples, Italy

IN A SMALL, SQUALID apartment in the centre of Naples Antonio lounged in an uncomfortable armchair. The youngest of his sisters, Paula, stood by the fireplace looking at him, not daring to say a word, her hands still hot and clammy, a bead of sweat slowly trickling down her ugly pock-marked face.

A quarter of an hour previously, she had answered the knock at her door, and had almost fainted as she felt the waves of terror sweeping over her on seeing again her brother's handsome face. The fear and surprise she felt was also mixed with something else, something she had kept secret from her whole world. Now, on experiencing it again, she had blushed and stammered out a short welcome, hoping that he had not realised what she was feeling. In her shame she was sure the feeling of desire she felt must be blatantly obvious to him. For, as long as she could remember she had secretly lusted after her younger brother, filling her daydreams with erotic adventures in which she surrendered herself to him without restraint, deliciously wanton. She was surprised and somewhat disappointed to see him looking so tired and unkempt, for in her memories he had been always clean and smart and perfectly groomed.

He had walked in without any greeting, and had sat down in one of the two threadbare armchairs.

Paula had waited, nervously picking at the skin of the back of her hand, occasionally glancing across at her husband, Enrico, hoping for support, but he had ignored her and stared, unseeing, up at the ceiling.

"Enrico," she said, "this is Antonio, my brother."

Enrico felt blood rush to his face as the look he gave Antonio was studiously ignored.

"Well, brother-in-law, what the hell are you doing here? What do you wan . . . ?" he started to ask in as insulting a way as he could, but stopped mid sentence as Antonio looked at him. His gaze was unwavering, hostile and threatening.

They all then sat not talking, until Paula, finally, unable to stand the silence any longer, quickly, nervously turned her head and glanced at her husband sitting in the other armchair. Then looking

at her brother she started to stammer, "Well, what do we owe this
. . . ?" She stopped as she saw the expression on his face harden. The
muscles in her neck at the back of her head began to tighten, and she
felt the beginnings of a headache and a pain behind her left eyeball.
Then, for a moment, she relaxed as she saw his face soften and he
smiled at her. However, immediately she felt the fear return, a knot
of it in the centre of her stomach. For his smile became a smile she
remembered from her childhood. A terrible smile, a smile that carried
with it a promise of violent aggression, of shocking pain to come. She
moved closer to her husband, Enrico, a fat, dirty, sweaty lump of
flab, who, when she came near to him, instinctively pushed her away
as if to deny any knowledge of her.

Antonio moved with the speed of a cat leaping onto its prey and
drove his straight fingers into Enrico's soft midriff. He stepped
away and looked triumphantly at his sister's face to see if there was
any reaction in it to her seeing her husband lying on the floor,
groaning, in a pool of his own vomit. The flash of fear in her eyes
came and went fleetingly, and then Antonio felt a surge of
satisfaction as he saw how she looked at the heaving body lying at
her feet with scorn and derision.

He smiled.

"You will tell nobody I'm here. Nobody. Not even your sisters.
Do you understand me?"

Her head nodded quickly and she stared at him, her eyes wide
open. She licked her top lip, her desire for him now stronger,
more obvious, blatant.

Antonio swept aside her unspoken offer with a look of total
indifference. She looked down, her eyes becoming dull with
defeat, the fire of her passion immediately extinguished. She felt
her face suddenly start to burn as her fear of her brother returned
with even greater force.

"When he stops vomiting and gets up you will impress upon him
the need for secrecy. You will tell him what I will do to him if I find
out that he has been indiscreet in even the smallest possible way."

He smiled and as he walked away he called out over his
shoulder, "You may tell him about Vittorio."

Antonio smiled briefly, and nodded his head at the memory of
what he had done to his former enemy, and walked into the bedroom.

"I am going to sleep for an hour or two. Wake me when it's
time to eat. I remember how you used to make a delicious osso
bucco. That would do nicely."

He quietly and carefully closed the bedroom door.

Paula walked to the window and looked out into the sunlit courtyard where some young, dirty, scantily clad children played, shrieking their delight. Behind her, her husband noisily got to his feet, slipped on his own vomit and fell into an armchair.

"What happened? Why did the bastard do that?" He gasped and retched noisily. "God, I feel terrible. He's crazy, a monster. You didn't tell me what a psychopath he was!"

He slowly stood up and started towards the door.

"I'm going to talk to the police. He's not going to get away with this."

Paula ran to him and seized his arm. Her voice low, terrified lest her brother should overhear them, she implored him.

"Don't be stupid! You don't know what you're dealing with."

"Oh yes I do. He's a maniac. He should be put away."

She held onto his arm as he opened the front door.

"Enrico, you don't understand. Believe me, if you do this, he'll get you. Even if he goes to prison he'll send men to get you. No matter where you go to, what you do, he'll find you, and he'll carve you up, like he did to Vittorio."

She spoke as fast as she could as he walked down the stairs leading to the courtyard, and felt relief as he stopped at the bottom.

"Vittorio? Who the hell's Vittorio?"

"I can't talk here. It happened a long time ago. Come back up to the apartment and I'll tell you all about it."

She could feel he still wanted to go out to the police, so she gently pulled his arm and whispered, "Come on up. I'll pour you a cognac. We'll relax for a while and I'll tell you about it, and then you can make your own mind up about whether it's wise to bring the police into this."

He was reluctant, but the thought of a cognac helped to change his mind, and gently Paula managed to steer him up the stairs and back into the apartment.

As he sat in a chair, massaging his aching stomach, Paula poured him a cognac, drew up a chair beside him and very quietly began to explain.

"As you know we lived in a small town in the South."

"Yes, I know, and you were very poor." His voice was heavy with sarcasm. "But weren't we all?"

She ignored his interruption and continued, "Antonio wasn't like the others in his class."

"Yes, I know. He was a bloody psychopath."

Paula slapped the arm of his chair. "Will you shut up and listen!" Nervously she looked at the bedroom door.

Enrico sipped his cognac, and looked away into the corner of the room.

"Well, there was a boy in his class, a big, lumbering animal of a lad, who hated Antonio even more than the rest hated him."

"Sounds like someone I could like a lot."

Ignoring him she continued, "Well, one day, he attacked Antonio from behind, without any warning, completely out of the blue, and gave him a real beating. He really messed him up."

"Good for him."

"Listen, will you." She seized his chin and turned his face to force him to look at her.

"Everybody expected Antonio to get his revenge. We all waited for it. We knew that if they were to meet head on in a fight, when Antonio wasn't taken by surprise, he would take Vittorio, apart easily."

He shook his head free. "And did he?"

"That's just it! No! Antonio behaved as if nothing had happened. He just carried on in his usual quiet way, ignoring Vittorio and in the end everybody forgot it."

"So he is a coward then." His mouth became ugly as he smiled and sneered at the same time.

"Don't even think that. Not for a moment," she pleaded.

Enrico sniggered, "So what did he do then, this big strong brother of yours?"

Paula swallowed nervously. "He waited until about a year after he'd left school, and then he did to Vittorio what Vittorio had done to him."

"He beat him up."

"Worse than that," she said. "He attacked Vittorio from behind, just as Vittorio had done to him. But he didn't just beat him up." She hesitated for a moment.

Enrico laughed nervously "So, what did the great man do then?"

Paula nervously licked her lips as she thought about the terrible day when they had all seen the sickening results of Antonio's vengeance.

"He ripped his ears off." Her voice was quiet as the memories of what had happened rushed into her mind.

They stared at each other, Paula with great intensity, Enrico in horrified disbelief.

222

"What?" His mouth hung open in disbelief.

"I said, 'he ripped Vittorio's ears off'. Off of his head."

"How?" Enrico stared at his wife, the horror in his eyes slowly turning to fear.

"With his bare hands." She pulled her hands down with a rapid energetic movement as if to mimic the action of tearing the ears off someone's head.

Enrico held his stomach as if he were about to be sick again.

"Christ! Didn't the police . . . ? Didn't they get him for it?"

Paula could feel his resolve and bravado dying away, and with even greater urgency explained, "You've seen how fast he moves. He did it one evening, in the dark. It only took an instant. And then he was gone. He picked his time and his place, and nobody saw it happen."

Enrico was silent for a full minute as he digested the horror of what he had heard.

"What happened to Vittorio?" he asked nervously, staring at the cold, empty fireplace.

"He went to hospital and had an ear stitched back on." Enrico was even more disturbed to see a slight satisfied smile appear on Paula's face.

A thought occurred to him. "I thought you said he lost both ears."

"Yes, he did. But they couldn't find one of them. He still walks about without one. Looks a mess." Again the smug smile appeared on her lips.

"My God, but he's frightening." Enrico shivered and looked nervously at the bedroom door. "How long's he going to be here?"

"God only knows," Paula sighed, hurriedly crossed herself and looked at him.

"No more talk of police, eh?" She said, trying not to let him see how terrified she was.

Enrico bent his body and looked at the floor. "I guess not," he whispered, "no." But then he blustered out, "But I'm not putting up with it for long. You see!"

Behind the bedroom door Antonio smiled, and lay down on the bed to sleep properly for the first time for many days.

* * *

Antonio didn't put in another appearance, so Paula and her husband silently ate a frugal supper, withdrawn and separate from each other, crushed by the dread of perhaps upsetting their unwelcome

223

visitor. They both spent that night in the living room, Enrico, having drunk himself into a stupor, slumped on the armchair and Paula, having wiped up her husband's vomit, curled on the hard, dirty floor, beaten and mindless in her fear. She hadn't cleaned for a long time and even she, who had long grown accustomed to dirt and grease and grime was made aware, as she lay, uncomfortable and aching, of how filthy her floor was. Her last thoughts before falling asleep were that perhaps she should do something about it. But then, she shook her head and smiled as she thought of her mother and her sisters and how they used to shout at her for her slovenliness. Her dirt was all she had for her proud defiance.

She woke much earlier than usual, aching and thirsty. Even without a mirror she knew that her eyes were puffy, and her swollen cheeks would be creased through contact with the hardness of the floor. She brushed away some pieces of grit that had stuck to her chin and slowly, painfully, sat up.

The bedroom door was closed, a symbol of her helplessness and rejection. She stared at it trying to imagine her brother lying on the bed, but all she could see in her mind was the cruel mouth of his beautiful face, twisted in a sneer of contempt. Nevertheless, as a wave of fear swept over her, moistening the palms of her hands and drying up her throat, she felt a sudden stab of desire in her loins. Quickly she pushed herself up from the floor and stood with her hands on her hips, her breathing noisy from her efforts and her guilt. Licking her lips she walked to the window, opened the curtains and looked out onto the courtyard below. Normally there was very little to be seen in the early morning, just an occasional figure hurrying out to the local shop for freshly baked bread, or a mother pulling a reluctant child to school, but today Paula was surprised to see several policemen standing in small groups talking and smoking. One of them, a small neat man dressed in civilian clothes, looked up at her window and, seeing her there, waved at her energetically. As she raised her arm hesitantly to wave back the man pointed at her several times and gesticulated, making a movement as if to open a door. Then he pointed to himself, to the stairs and again to her. He then waved to her as if asking her to come down to see them.

Unsure, Paula stepped back away from the window and looked back at her husband's puffed, ugly face. She moved over to him and gave him a tentative shake.

"Enrico," she whispered, not daring to disturb her brother.

"Enrico, there are policemen. In the yard, lots of them. I think they want to talk to us."

Her husband didn't respond in any way, sprawling back in the chair, his eyes closed, his arms hanging loosely, his mouth open, sagging and wet. Suddenly Paula was aware of a dreadful stench coming from him and stepped back in disgust. It was partly her desire to get away from this and partly her curiosity which drove her towards the front door. As she crossed the room she stopped as she heard a very gentle tap at the door. Again she looked at her husband for some support, but finding none once more, she took a deep breath and continued on her way.

As she reached the door she was surprised to see that the key that was normally kept under the mat was in the lock of the door. She frowned because she had a clear impression of locking the door the night before and slipping the key under the mat. Something was wrong, and she was about to go back to shake her husband awake when she heard another quiet tap on the door. As quietly as she could she tried to turn the key, but found that it had already been turned. Hesitantly she opened the door and peered out into the darkness of the landing. After a moment or two she was able to see that there were several men there, among them the man who had waved to her from the courtyard. He put a finger to his lips and waved her to come out onto the landing. As she stepped out from behind the door she felt a hand gently but firmly direct her towards the stairs.

Alarmed she turned to look back at her door, but someone whispered in her ear, "Do not concern yourself with that, signora. We'll take care of it." Then, as she was helped down the stairs the voice continued very softly, "There is nothing to fear. Don't worry. It is just that we think you will be able to help us." Stumbling and unsure in the gloom, she made her way down the stairs.

In the courtyard the air was fresh, but tainted by the cigarettes the policemen had been smoking. Still, she felt it a relief to be out of the smell of her apartment, away from the hateful sight of her ugly husband.

"What's the matter? What do you want? Why are there so many policemen here?" she asked.

Then she gasped as she saw that most of them were holding guns. Her eyes wide with fear she struggled to free herself from the hand that still held her arm.

"Signora, calm yourself. There is nothing to fear. We just want to ask you a couple of questions. That is all."

The voice was deep, masculine and very reassuring.

"Signora, you are safe and nobody is going to harm you in any way. Do you understand?"

Paula nodded and was relieved to feel her arm freed.

"But, why are you here? What do you want with me?"

She looked up at the men surrounding her and shivered, partly from the cold air and partly as a result of standing so close to so many very masculine, powerful figures.

"Signora, we are anxious to talk to your brother, Antonio. I wonder, have you seen him lately?"

"Why?" She felt herself again becoming agitated and apprehensive. She looked around from face to face searching for reassurance. "What has he done? What can you possibly want with him?"

The police inspector could see how nervous she had become, so he spoke as calmly as he could in a deep masculine voice, "It is nothing, Signora. It is just that we think he could help us with a problem we have. You understand?"

Paula found herself pulled in several directions. Although she had a natural, deep suspicion of the police, she found these men to be so reassuring, calming, so wonderfully powerful. And yet she felt that if she helped them she would be somehow betraying her brother to them, something that went against all her upbringing.

Suddenly she jumped in alarm as a loud crash came from inside the building. She turned and looked up at the windows of her apartment and was surprised to see several figures passing across it. Then a moment later one of them appeared at the window and passed the forefinger of his right hand across his throat.

"Porco Dio, he's escaped." It was the officer who had just been talking to her.

Paula turned to speak to him, but was astonished to see him and all his men already purposefully walking to the huge door that led out onto the street.

"What's happening?" she cried out. "Where are you going?"

Nobody spoke to her, or even looked at her.

With her hand in front of her open mouth she ran up the stairs leading to her apartment, pushing past the police as they silently left the building.

The last one, the one whom she had seen pass his hand across his throat, gruffly said to her as she passed him. "Someone will come and fix the door."

"The door?" she screamed at his departing back. "What door?" But he continued down the stairs without saying another word.

Inside the apartment everything was as she had left it, except that the bedroom door was lying flat and broken. Enrico still sat, slumped, asleep in his chair, snoring gently, saliva dripping from his chin onto his chest, totally unaware of anything that had taken place.

Paula slowly sank to her knees and started to sob. Her body gently quivered with her grief that came, not just from the hopelessness of her life, not just from having a drunk, foul, ugly husband, not from the door lying smashed inside the empty bedroom, but from the fact that her brother, the only man she had ever really desired, had abandoned her once more, sneaking out of her life without saying a word to her, and for just a moment she had a terrible, overwhelming, heart-crushing realisation that she would never ever see him again.

Chapter Thirty-Nine
Cornwall

CHRISTMAS CAME AND WENT in a whirl of gigs and parties, garlands, green and red, nostalgic music, piano and forte, swollen stomachs, sore heads, bonhomie, true and false, and cards and gifts and more and more cards. For most of December David and Beth had worked every night, for they were fully aware of the emptiness of the music market that awaited them during the first three months of the following year. For David this was a true blessing, an opportunity to lose himself in the concentrated activity and the abandonment to pleasure that accompanied the holiday season. Thoughts of tragedy and pain, death and bereavement and, above all, guilt gradually faded away as the colour, the lights, the music and the gaiety took hold and worked their magic on him. It is said that darkness is merely an absence of light and day by day David felt the gloom that had accompanied him gradually fading away to be replaced by the brightness of the joy and love that Beth surrounded him with.

* * *

"Have you had any recurrence of the visions you were getting about the lutenist?" Anthony asked one morning just before New Year as they all sat quietly relaxing in his café.

"Gracious me! I haven't thought about that for what seems a long time," David cried out. He was quiet for a moment as he stared into his coffee cup.

"Isn't that amazing," he whispered. "I feel as though all that has finished." He laughed and said, "I suppose it's a bit like tooth-ache. When it goes, as you get on with your life, you know how quickly you forget it ever happened."

"Yes, but the results of the treatment for the toothache are there. The fillings, for example," said Beth.

"So have you noticed any changes in your life, David?" asked Anthony. "Anything you feel different about?"

"Funny you should ask that," said David thoughtfully. "I seem to have lost the rage I used to feel about authority figures. I was watching a program on the telly the other night dealing with the First World War. Now, at one time, you know, I would have exploded at least half a dozen times at the greed, the arrogance, the mind blowing stupidity of the high command and the politicians, of both sides. But this time all I felt was a very deep sadness at the futility of it all." He sighed and then continued, "And then there's the guilt. I've not felt any for weeks now. It's a bit difficult to explain, but it feels as though I've come in a huge circle since the episode with the lutenist. It's as if the deaths of the Roman soldier and the chief's daughter, the torture of Peter Cavanagh in Italy and Anna's murder in Milan were all part of the same huge cycle of experience, and I've come back again to the beginning of it all, but totally changed."

"And you certainly have changed," said Anthony quietly.

"It's weird, really," David said, frowning in thought, "because I feel as though I've grown, but at the same time I've lost something."

"Don't you feel a bit smoother in yourself?" asked Beth smiling.

"That's it!" he exclaimed. "You've got it! I feel as if part of me has smoothed out, got calmer, more understanding."

He looked across the table at Beth and felt a surge of love for her, and as he felt it he realised that there was no guilt in it to spoil it.

* * *

They had decided not to work New Year's Eve in spite of loud, urgent pleas from various agencies and offers of amazing amounts of money.

"This year," Beth had said, "let's have it for us, a quiet secluded celebration at my place."

So they did, with a delicious meal and just enough wine to relax their bodies and loosen any inhibitions that might have been lurking in them.

Charlie wasn't ignored either and was also given a special meal, which she devoured with enthusiasm and great energy.

David and Beth then sat and listened to the radio allowing the last moments of the year to drift past them without any regret.

"It's been a funny old year, hasn't it?" David mused.

Beth looked at him and smiled. "I think you must have upset a Chinaman at some time."

He raised his eyebrows, "How come?" he asked, puzzled.

"You know the old Chinese curse, 'May you live in interesting times'? Well you've just been through what they must mean when they utter it."

David smiled and said, "Interesting is the biggest understatement of the year, but I can't for the life of me remember any outraged Chinamen."

He looked at the clock and saw that there were just five minutes left of the old year. "Well, anyhow, it'll soon all be over, and we can make a new start."

As he spoke Charlie stretched herself and walked out to the front door where she wined to be let out. Beth hurriedly got up and said, "I'll let her out and you fill the glasses ready for the toast."

Dave heard her open the door and go out with the dog. A few minutes later she hurried back in panting, "She's out there and she wouldn't come back in so I've left her."

She flopped with a sigh into her armchair.

Already the sounds of Big Ben were announcing the entrance of the New Year and Dave raised his glass and said, "A Happy New Year, Beth. May it bring you everything you ever wanted."

She smiled and stood without saying anything and met him as he walked over to her, carrying her glass, but to his surprise, instead of taking her wine, she wrapped her arms around him and pressed her lips against his. His mind travelled the length of his body noting the feel of her full breasts against his chest and her thighs moving urgently on his legs.

He felt his body immediately respond and when, eventually, still holding him firmly she moved her head back and looked into his eyes, he knew that this time there would be no fear or guilt to hold him back. In her eyes he could see her desire for him. Her lips were parted and shining, reflecting the light from the fire and the many flickering candles.

"Well?" she asked.

"I think," he said hesitantly, "I think that . . ."

"Yes?"

"I think that, before we go to bed . . ."

"Yes?"

"I think we'd better let the dog in."

They laughed, and both knew that everything was perfect for what was to come as they welcomed Charlie back in, and chased her around the room unsuccessfully trying to catch her before she shook herself and covered everything in her vicinity with a fine spray. When, finally, they caught her, David picked her up and carried her into the kitchen, where they vigorously rubbed her dry with a large towel.

A short while later David and Beth lay side by side in his bed. Charlie had been relegated after a short tussle to the corner of the bedroom where she lay showing her resentment by facing away from them.

Earlier in the day, Beth had prepared the bed with fresh, flannelette sheets, soft and clean. At first they had shivered with the cold of the new bed and clung together until it became warm, and then, facing each other, began to slowly explore each other's body. Tenderly and rather nervously they kissed, hesitantly at first but with growing passion.

Suddenly David drew away and stared at her his eyes wide open.

"Beth, I'm sorry," he said.

"What's the matter?"

"I can't go on."

"Why not, for heaven's sake?"

"There's something I haven't told you." He turned and lay on his stomach staring at the pillow.

"Well?" Her voice was soft.

"Before she was killed, Anna and I . . ." David found he couldn't go on. Beth was gently pressing her forefinger against his lips.

"Hush David, I know. There's no need to say anything."

Gently he moved her finger away from his mouth. "What do you mean, you know? How can you know?"

"We'll talk about it in the morning."

"But . . ."

"I said, we'll talk about it at another time. I know what there was between you and Anna, and I know what happened. I'm psychic. Have you forgotten?"

"But . . ."

Again he felt her finger on his mouth. "Just lie there and look at me," she whispered. "Look at my eyes and see just how much I adore you. And stop thinking, for goodness sake."

She wrapped her arms around his neck and pulled his face down onto her breasts.

"Stop thinking, and just . . ." she murmured.

Chapter Forty

AND THEN JANUARY LEAPT on them, a howl of gales and rain and whirling salt spray, dark clouds and mud–filled boots, cold, wet collars, and dreams of Balearic beaches and Florida skies, as David and Beth sat wrapped in cosy warmth before a hot log fire, sipping mead whilst planning a future, bright with hope.

They shared their life between the two houses. David's had, since Tina's death, been a bachelor pad. His former wife's influence remained in the curtains and furniture, and Beth brought in flowers from time to time. She had left the odd crystal about in an attempt to 'lift the vibes', as she put it, but in spite of her best efforts the atmosphere remained functional and somewhat sad. So they kept his for business, rehearsals, storing the musical gear, and recovery after trips to the Green Man. Beth's they used for relaxation, meditation and togetherness.

It was towards the end of February that their lives changed irrevocably.

They had spent the day at David's cottage preparing for a gig that was due the following evening. They liked to get everything checked and ready well in advance, so that they would have plenty of time to renew any of the many pieces of equipment, essential to the success of their work, that could be in danger of failure.

They had almost finished when Beth looked at David and said, "I don't feel like cooking tonight. Why don't you nip up to the pub and grab a couple of pasties?"

David groaned. He could hear the wind had started to sing through the branches of the hawthorn outside the window of the sitting room, and raindrops were being blown onto the window pane with increasing force.

She smiled, "It's only a couple of minutes trot up to the pub," she said, "and I'll finish up here, and have a nice cup of tea waiting for you when you get back."

"Have you seen what it's like out there?" he asked, his face screwed up.

"Now, don't be theatrical. It's never as bad as it sounds. And the rain's only just starting." She swiftly picked up a couple of sheets of music and put them in a file. "And anyhow Charlie hasn't been out all afternoon. Look at her. The poor bitch is sitting there with her legs crossed."

David looked at Charlie. She sat with her tail wagging, her face excited and expectant, for already she sensed that her hours of boredom were perhaps coming to an end, and she would be released into her world of excitement and wonderful smells.

David shrugged. "I can't fight both of you," he said. "Come on Charlie, let's go."

He put on his thick raincoat, picked up Charlie's lead and gave Beth a quick kiss. "See you," he called out as he closed the back door, and walked out into an evening of cold, wet darkness.

Even Charlie seemed willing to hurry up the hill as if she knew that they were on their way to the pub, for she didn't bother to stop to sniff at the verges and just squatted to relieve herself before running up ahead of David. Half way up the hill, she stopped and looked intently at a gap in the Cornish hedge, where there used to be a gate leading into a pasture. A year ago it had fallen down and the farmer, to whom the field belonged, hadn't bothered to mend it.

By the light of his torch David saw Charlie back away from the opening, her hackles rising and she growled and barked twice. David swiftly caught up with her and, holding her collar, peered into the blackness.

"There's nothing there, Charlie," he said, and, still holding her collar, he pulled the dog up the hill. Charlie continued growling and shaking her head, vainly trying to escape from his grip.

"What's the matter with her, then?" asked Tom as David pulled a reluctant Charlie into the pub.

"I don't know. Half way up the hill she saw something she didn't like in Farmer Chynoweth's field. I had a look, but I couldn't see anything."

"Could be that badger that's been digging up my garden," said Tom morosely. "'Tis a bloody nuisance. Ruined the lawn. I wish Charlie would see it off."

"That's the strange thing," said David. "If it had been a badger, or a fox, she would have been in there like a shot. But she didn't go in. Just stood there and barked with her hackles up."

He lifted himself on to a stool at the bar, and Charlie hurried over to the group of regulars that were crouched around the welcoming flames of a huge log fire.

"There's been talk of someone hanging around," said Tom as he turned to the glasses hanging from a shelf. "Just a half, is it?" he asked.

"Lovely, and can you heat me up a couple of pasties, please, while I drink it? Beth's not in the mood for cooking tonight."

Tom nodded and carefully pulled a half of David's favourite bitter.

"You should organise that woman of yours. Beat her a bit more often."

The voice, deep and rich and Cornish, came from the group sitting around the fire. David turned to look at them and was met by George's big, round face beaming at him.

"You're letting her get away with too much, my 'andsome," he said. "You've got to start the way you mean to carry on. Don't let her mess you about."

"Thanks for the advice, George. I'll make sure I remember it."

"You do that, boy. You won't go wrong." George winked, raised his glass, and turned back to the fire.

"Seems like I've got to start a little gentle wife-beating," David whispered to Tom.

"Not so much of the 'gentle'," shouted George without turning away from the fire. "You can whisper all you like, I'll still hear you, boy."

"He's got the keenest hearing you'll ever meet," cried out Alfred. "He can hear flies fart at two hundred yards, can't you, boy?"

"That I can, my 'andsome. And you'd all better watch out. There's been a couple of 'em in the corner of the bar for the last half hour. Been farting fit to burst. Must have been on the draught bass." George bellowed out a loud self-congratulatory burst of laughter, and was joined by the whole group sitting around the fire.

Tom hurried to the far corner of the bar, swatted the air with a cloth and backed away holding his nose.

"That draught bass does terrible things to the digestive tracts," he growled. "I'm afraid I'm going to have to shut up shop and fumigate the whole place."

"Now, don't you go saying silly things like that," shouted Norman. "You close this place down, we'll have to stage one of they sit-ins."

"That'll be nothing new, Norman," George said through his laughter, bending over and slapping his thigh. "You've been staging a sit-in here for years."

Alfred stood, and cried out to the world in general, "He's not been home for years. It's been such a long time he's no idea his wife's moved in with Andy Trewhella." He sat back in his chair and wiped the tears away from his eyes.

The snug erupted with shrieks of laughter, which redoubled in volume when Norman stood and cried, "You mean she's gone! Thank God for that. I can move back in again!"

As the laughter died down the regulars turned back to face the fire, and poured beer down their parched throats. Tom leaned over the bar and passed a package to David. "Here's your pasties, David. I'll put them on your tab."

Nodding his thanks David called a reluctant Charlie away from the warmth of the fire, and together they stepped out into the cold wet wind, which was now blowing near to gale force. He shone his torch ahead and saw Charlie run to the opening in the hedge that she had been so reluctant to leave on their way to the pub. She stopped and sniffed high in the air, took a tentative step forward, and then turned away as if dismissing the field as not worthy of her attention. She quickly looked back at David and hurried on ahead in an attempt to find shelter from the rain, which had started to fall more heavily.

By the time that David reached the cottage he was soaked and cold drips had started to fall into the collar of his shirt, so instead of going in through the front door he chose to go through the garage, which leads into the kitchen.

"Beth, I'm home," he called and put the pasties into the oven to warm through.

He took off his coat and stepped back into the garage where he hung it up, sodden and dripping.

As he walked back into the kitchen and called out her name again he was surprised to see Charlie standing with her nose low down against the door to the living room, her tail tucked between her legs. She was growling softly.

Alarmed, he pushed the door slowly open. Charlie backed away and turned and ran to the far end of the kitchen, whimpering softly.

"Beth?" David called, hesitating as he stepped into the room.

He had only taken two steps when he felt himself seized by an arm that appeared from behind the door and yanked him forward with great force. Tripping over the mat he fell heavily onto the floor. Stunned and shocked, he lay for a moment unable to move, and then curled up in agony as he was viciously kicked in his side.

The door slammed shut behind him and Charlie howled out her fear and isolation in the darkness of the kitchen.

David lay curled up for a few moments and then tried to lift himself up on his left elbow. Horror and dismay filled him as he caught sight of Beth lying slumped against the wall on the far side of the room. A bruise stood out on her cheek and a tiny spot of blood hung from her lower lip.

"What the hell!" he exclaimed, but a voice, quiet, yet full of menace, interrupted him.

"Stay where you are, bastardo. She is not hurt badly." As the man spoke, David felt himself pressed down onto the ground by what he took to be the heel of a shoe. "Not yet, anyhow," the voice went on. "Later perhaps things could change. We'll see."

The voice was calm, matter-of fact, the voice of one in command, of one enjoying his power.

David shuddered as he recognised it. The memory of when he had last heard it, in Italy, flashed into his mind and with it the horror of what he had experienced there.

"Antonio," he muttered.

"You remember me! I'm honoured." Antonio said quietly. "I said that you would be next. You should have listened." He took his foot away from David's back and moved into the centre of the room.

"You may stand," he said. "But slowly. I do not want to kill you immediately."

David painfully pushed himself away from the floor and stood up. His side ached and his right knee was stinging, but he was more concerned with Beth and how she was. He made a movement as if to go over to her, but Antonio stood in front of him and waved a finger in the air.

"Oh no," Antonio said, and smiled. "If you want to get to her you've got to get past me."

The smile disappeared from his face and he said, "Do you understand?" He took a step back. "You see, it's a little game. We used to play it at school. To get to the other side you have to get round the person in the middle." His head turned a little to the left and an evil smile appeared on his lips. "Or you have to take him out."

David suddenly had a flash back to the time when, as a boy, he was on his way to his first scout meeting and he had been confronted by another boy who had asked him for a fight. Now, as then, he felt all his strength flow out. His legs felt weak and he found he was unable even to clench his fists.

He made a move towards Beth. Not an aggressive move, but just as fast as he felt himself able to do at that moment.

"Oh dear," sighed Antonio as he slammed his fist into David's midriff. "It seems that this game isn't going to be as much fun as I thought it would be."

He had moved with lightning speed, but seemed to expend no effort at all. He bent down and, with apparent ease, picked up David from the floor where he had collapsed clutching his stomach, gasping for air and retching.

"You're going to have to do better than that," whispered Antonio as he pushed David back against the wall. "Much better. If you want her to live, that is."

David felt himself pinned back, so that he was aware of the awkward unevenness of the cob against his spine. His eyes were screwed up with pain so it was with difficulty that he saw before him Antonio's face smiling with arrogant conceit.

"I've had such a long time to think about how I'm going to kill you," Antonio said, without any emotion in his voice. "It's kept me interested all the time I've been slowly working my way here. I thought, maybe I would use the knife, like I did with my puttana of a wife."

This last phrase was delivered with his only show of emotion as he spat the word 'puttana' out with venomous ferocity. For the first time David felt anger beginning to rise up in him and made a futile attempt to move.

"Oh, that's good," cried Antonio. "That's good. So you're not entirely the emotionless, passionless English. Perhaps we'll have some fun after all."

The Italian pulled David away from the wall and just as easily slammed him back against it.

"But I decided that the knife would be too easy. There would be no satisfaction in it for me. You understand?"

He looked at David with the same arrogant, superior smile on his face.

"So," he went on, "I've decided to kill you in the manner that would give me the most pleasure. Capisci?"

Antonio waited for some reaction, but getting none, the smile left his face and he jerked his right knee into David's groin and stepped back. His face was impassive as he watched his enemy fall to the floor, screaming and clutching his agony.

Tears washed down David's face as he writhed in such pain that he was hardly aware of what Antonio said next.

"I've decided that we're going to fight. We're going to fight for this ugly lump of girl."

He turned to the still form of Beth and waited, hoping for the maximum effect of his words, and then quietly, with deadly, vicious deliberation, he continued with, "And I am going to kill you."

He smiled with satisfaction.

"With my bare hands."

He walked over to David, lifted him to his feet and struck him across the face with the flat of his hand.

"Come on, then," he said. "Now try to hit me."

David stood swaying, his whole body shuddering with pain, his eyes not focussing clearly, his fear showing openly in his open mouth and fixed expression.

"You're not even trying," screamed Antonio and hit him several times in the face in rapid succession followed by a sharp punch with rigid fingers in the solar plexus.

David lay on the floor and licked the blood on his lips. His vision was blurred and he drifted in and out of awareness. Time seemed to slow down and he seemed to see Antonio coming towards him in very slow motion.

Suddenly everything changed and he found himself back in the terror of one of his recurring dreams. He was strapped to a table, unable to move and a foul figure was bending over him slapping him slowly across the face, muttering, "I'm going to kill you, now." Present and past seemed to merge and he was then aware of Antonio bending over him, shaking him and slapping his face.

David seemed to have become immune to the pain and was just aware of the concussion of the blows and, distantly, the sound of a voice. He was also suddenly very aware of his fear and how it was stopping him from expressing his true feelings of anger against the indignities and the pain he was experiencing. As he sank into the fear, a realisation blossomed in his mind, one that came as a frightening shock – that what he was experiencing he was allowing to happen because of one thing alone. It was not because he was weaker. It was not because the others were stronger, or faster, or better trained. It was because he thought he deserved it. He wanted it to happen in an attempt to assuage his guilt for what he had done to the girl in Italy. Quickly there flashed before his mind's eye pictures of him going from Scotland to Italy, and once more thrusting himself onto the girl, Francesca Powell. She had been sent there by her father and married to a close friend of the family.

Once more they were discovered together, but this time she also was beaten and broken and forced to watch him as he was tortured.

His guilt shifted to thoughts of Anna and the blame he secretly felt for what had happened to her, and he knew that what he wanted, secretly, had wanted for a long time, was punishment for the wrong he felt he had done.

But then he thought of Beth and the love she had shown him, demanding nothing and accepting him just for what he was, and a feeling grew in him that she did not deserve this. He owed her more than he could ever repay, and with this thought he felt a strength start to grow deep within him, a determination, which fed an anger against all people like Antonio, who use their knowledge and power to bully others.

He lay for a while feeling the blows on his face but now using their energy to build a bubble of rage which he suddenly allowed to erupt in a roar of anger as, with all the power he could muster, he smashed his fist across the bridge of the Italian's nose.

He didn't see the expression of surprise and disbelief that flooded over Antonio's face as he found himself hurtled across the room by the force of the blow. For David sank immediately back on the floor, his strength spent by the energy he had expended.

And he also didn't see the look of satisfaction on the face of Beth as she smashed the heavy base of a mike stand across the head of the Italian.

"Ugly lump of a girl, eh?" she said as he fell unconscious to the floor. She looked at his head and said, "Now, there *is* an ugly lump."

With some difficulty, for she was still feeling a bit groggy from the blow she had suffered from the fist of the Italian, she staggered over to David.

"Come on," she called out to him as she tried to help him up. "He's not going to be out for ever and we've got to get to the pub and ring for help."

David looked at her and the joy he felt in seeing her sent a surge of energy through him.

"What's happened? Where's the scumbag?" he groaned as she tried to lift him.

"I've given him a sore head, but he won't be out forever, so you've got to try to make it out of here."

"Why can't we ring for help from here?" he asked as he struggled to his feet.

240

"He cut the wires before you came back." She gasped as she strained with the effort of helping him to the door.

Charlie barked an excited greeting as they slowly opened the door into the kitchen, and followed them reluctantly out into the rain and wind.

The hill leading to the pub was a struggle for both of them, a battle, not only against the weakness caused by the injuries they had received, but also against the ferocity of the storm that had sprung up since David had arrived back from the pub. The wind howled from the South West, driving the rain into their faces as if it had sided with their enemy and was trying to slow down their flight. However, the massive relief they felt on their escape from the terror of Antonio generated its own energy, and despite the apparent efforts of the elements to hinder them, they managed, muttering words of endearment and encouraged by a buoyant Charlie, dancing in front of them, to reach the pub, finally push the door open and fall in an undignified heap on the stone floor.

An unusual hush fell on the pub as the door flew open and they arrived, wet, dirty and with bruised faces streaked with blood. Even Charlie realised that something was different, for, instead of rushing to the fire, as she normally did, she sat by the two of them with her tail wagging and barked her summons for help.

It arrived swiftly in the form of George, Alfred, and Norman plus two hikers who had arrived a few minutes earlier, escaping from the ferocity of the weather. Together they helped the two bruised figures to stagger to the comforting warmth of the fire, where Tom waited for them with a couple of brandies he had hurriedly poured.

"What the hell happened to you two?" cried George as he helped Beth onto a chair, but before either of them could utter a word, the door again burst open and Antonio strode in confidently, his face a mask of arrogant contempt for all. In his left hand he held a gun, which he pointed at the group around the fire. In his right he had a large dangerous looking knife.

"Well," he said, "what a delightful scene. Our two heroes and all their yokel friends."

He stepped further into the room and smiled.

"Barman, a gin and tonic, if you please," he called out trying to mimic an English gentleman.

He was still smiling when he said with an evil sincerity, "If you do not hurry, I shall blow the brains out of two of your valuable customers." With that he pointed his gun at the two hikers, who now were beginning to wish that they had remained in the comparative safety of the storm.

One of them, a slight, freckled faced lady fell to the ground in a faint.

"Typical English," said Antonio looking down at her with contempt.

"They're German, actually," muttered Tom as he passed to go to the bar.

"Perhaps, then I'll shoot them anyhow," said Antonio with a smile, his eyebrows raised.

The second German opened his mouth in horror and he bent down to cradle his partner in his arms. "Koninchen, koninchen," he whispered tenderly and gently rocked her, tears streaming down his face.

"Don't worry," Antonio said to him, "I've not come for you, or your revolting friend." He turned to the bar, placed the knife on it and took the gin and tonic that Tom had hurriedly poured.

"He knows who I've come for," he said pointing at David. "Don't you, bastardo?" He spat out the epithet with disdain.

David turned to look at him, defeat and despair showing openly on his face. The energy, that had come to him with the thought of escape and freedom, drained away leaving him with a profound feeling of hopelessness.

Antonio quickly drained the glass of its contents.

"Very good," he nodded at Tom. "For an Englishman," he added with a sneer. Then in business-like fashion he picked up his knife and stepped away from the bar into the centre of the room.

"The question is," he said in a matter of fact voice, "do I kill you now, here, in front of your yokel friends, or do I take you elsewhere and really enjoy myself?"

He smiled, "There's no difficulty, really. Is there?"

He levelled the gun at David.

"Stand up, bastardo," he said quietly.

David stood very unsteadily and stared at his would-be executioner. Part of his mind registered that those near him had, with the exception of Beth, moved carefully away from him and he smiled.

"Come here, bastardo." It was clear to all that Antonio was revelling in his power, savouring his moment of triumph.

As David moved towards him, shuffling and obviously still in pain, Antonio stepped to one side and motioned for him to pass by. It was only when David had passed him that he realised that he had made a mistake. For, in order to cover David he would have to turn his back on the rest of the bar, and if he covered the bar he would have to leave David unthreatened. So Antonio compromised and walked sideways his gun wavering between his enemy and the customers of the pub.

As David reached the door and started to open it, a mighty gust of wind snatched it out of his hand and smashed it against the wall. Taking advantage of the surprise caused by the sudden noise George, for he had been in his younger days a cricketer of note, threw a heavy glass ash tray with delightful accuracy at Antonio and struck him a glancing blow on the head.

"Run David!" he shouted. "Run!"

David looked back and saw Antonio had dropped the gun and was clutching his head, so he turned and ran as fast as his tired body could into the darkness and the welcome of the heath.

In the bar there was a roar as everybody took advantage of the reversal of fortunes and hurled everything to hand at the Italian.

He, realising he had, in his pain, staggered too far away from his gun to retrieve it, turned to face the mass of bodies rushing in his direction and waved the knife at them. Quickly but very carefully he moved backwards, and, reaching the door, gripped the handle, stepped out into the night and slammed it shut.

Tom reached the door first, opened it and everybody spilled out onto the road. There they were met by the gale, the driving rain and an impenetrable blackness.

*   *   *

On the heath, David crouched in the middle of a circle of gorse bushes. He had crossed the road as fast as was possible for him, in a mindless panic, running blindly into a world of howling, icy winds, merciless needles of rain beating into his face, mud and impenetrable tangles of brambles and gorse. He knew that there were only a few pathways open to anyone on the heath and realised that it would not be long before Antonio found him, so he had crawled under the bushes as far away from a track as possible, trying as best he could to ignore the painful scratches he received. As he had crossed the road he had managed a glance back at the

243

warmth of the light blazing out of the pub and had seen Antonio stagger out clutching his head. The only pleasurable feeling he experienced came as he wondered who had managed to inflict some damage on the gangster.

There was another advantage to his position, in that the bushes gave him some shelter from the wind and rain, but he realised, nevertheless, that he would not be able to remain out in these conditions for very long without danger of hypothermia.

He had managed to hear Antonio cursing as he crashed through the unfamiliar terrain, and once indeed the gangster came within a very short distance of him, but fortunately turned away before discovering him. After a while there was silence from him and David realised that he too had gone to ground and was waiting to see how long David could last before giving away his hiding place.

Soon, even though he was well sheltered from the wind, David started to become acutely aware of the cold. Beads of icy rain dripped down the inside of his collar and he realised that his feet had started to lose any feeling at all.

To escape his discomfort, for, besides the cold and wet, he was still suffering from the beating he had received from Antonio earlier on, he made a huge effort and turned his thoughts to Beth. He had managed to catch sight of the look of despair and horror on her face as he had been forced to move towards the door of the pub, and he was surprised at how passionately he suddenly longed to be with her.

"At least the bastard didn't manage to get her," he thought, but then immediately there flashed into his mind a picture of Anna, lying in the bath in the apartment in Milan, and he understood clearly how much he had changed since that terrible night. He realised how close he had got to Beth over the past three months, how swiftly the gap had widened between him and Anna.

It was with some surprise that the thought came to him, that he hadn't thought of her since just before Christmas. He had caught the mention of Milan on the news one night, which made him think of her, and he had fleetingly wondered how she was. But then came the holiday rush, and all he could think of was the job, and gradually his need for Beth, professionally and personally, took over everything.

During the day he and Beth had spent a great deal of time at the café in St. Agnes, and a week ago, whilst they were all having coffee, out of the blue Anthony had suddenly turned the conversation to his dreams.

"You said just before New Year that you had stopped having dreams about the torture of the lutenist. Has anything else come up? Have you finished with that torture?" Anthony had asked David as he idly polished a perfectly clean glass.

David remembered his surprise and how he had to think hard, and how he had had to smile as he said, "Do you know, I've not had any problems at all with that for ages. Isn't that strange?"

"Yes isn't it?" said Anthony with an enigmatic smile. "Isn't it, just?"

David remembered how Beth had looked at him and smiled.

*   *   *

Not without some pain and with the greatest of care so as not to make any noise and betray himself, David shifted his position. A moment later, after what had seemed an age, he heard the sirens of the police cars and ambulances as they arrived at the pub and was tempted to run to them, but he knew that he was too weak and too cold to run fast enough to escape a predator as fit and as powerful as Antonio. So he waited in the hopes that someone would come looking for him, and perhaps that tactic would have worked had not he heard a rustling from behind him and a whine telling him that Charlie had found him. Without thinking he exclaimed, "sh, Charlie, hush!" not loudly, but enough for Antonio to hear.

"Eh, bastardo! I know where you are, and I'm coming for you!" the gangster shouted.

It was with a sickening feeling in his stomach that David realised that Antonio was quite near, so he crawled out of his hiding place and started to run towards the lights, shouting as loudly as he could to bring attention to himself. As he raced on he realised that Antonio was running on a course parallel to his and was gaining ground. Suddenly the awful realisation came to him that he wasn't going to make it. Thrusting the thought to the back of his mind he urged himself to run faster.

Run you bugger, run. Think of Beth.

Urging himself on with these thoughts he had the impression that he was faster and lighter. He lost all of the feelings of failure and depression that had surrounded him during his flight and he suddenly felt that he could run forever. The lights of the police vans shone brightly, and, just as the beam of a searchlight cut through the darkness and outlined him, and he was feeling that safety was near, that his friends and the police would save him, he felt a blow in his back that sent him sprawling forward into the mud. Landing heavily he rolled over. As the shock of the fall lessened he looked up and saw Antonio, grinning and triumphant, silhouetted against the blackness of the night sky by the beam of the searchlight. He was holding his knife high in the air and David noticed that there was a bead of blood slowly dripping from the point. It seemed to fall very slowly onto his body and he wondered how it came to be there and wouldn't it make a mess of his coat?

It was then that he heard Antonio cry out, a strange haunting sound, a howl that welled out of the depths of time, an evil cry of triumph that David had had heard many times in his nights of terror, a sound that resonated with others of like kind from down the centuries. It only lasted a couple of seconds but it left him shaking with terror. But then, a strange thing happened, for, as suddenly as it had arrived his terror abruptly vanished, and he sensed himself becoming enveloped by a great blanket of peace. He became weaker and weaker, his eyes started to close, and he quickly felt himself sinking deeper and deeper into a black emptiness. So he didn't hear the police order Antonio to drop the weapon immediately. He didn't see Antonio ignore their commands. He didn't see Antonio start to swing the knife down in an attempt to savagely drive it into his body, and he didn't see his downward movement checked, and his body driven back, with eyes already sightless, by the bullet shot by the police marksman.

Chapter Forty-One
Three Weeks Later

BETH STOOD IN THE middle of the track, which led from opposite the Green Man towards the little bay that had long been David's retreat and Charlie's playground. The place where she stood was the spot upon which David had been lying when the police had found him three weeks ago in a small pool of blood. His tormentor had been to one side of the track where he had been thrown by the force of the policeman's bullet, his arms outstretched and his face washed clean by the force of the driving rain. Tears swelled out of her eyes as her imagination started to take command and she thought of all various possibilities and permutations of what might have been on that awful evening. Vividly she remembered seeing David threatened and humiliated in the pub and her despair as she thought that Antonio was about to kill him. Then came a surge of joy as she saw the gangster struck by the ashtray thrown by George. She recalled screaming as David took his opportunity and fled into the night. She had been at the forefront of those crowding to the door, but so intense had been her emotions that when she had been pushed out into the darkness she had been indifferent to the discomfort of the driving rain, and had stood there calling out her words of encouragement, until one of the men, she couldn't remember who, had gently drawn her back into the warmth of the pub.

Meanwhile, Tom, immediately the ashtray had been thrown, had seized his opportunity, telephoned the police and described the situation, emphasising the fact that they were dealing with an armed and desperate man.

Then they had all waited, silent in their apprehension and fear. Beth and the German lady had clung to each other, shaking with terror, damp and bedraggled. For the most part the men had kept silent, drinking and withdrawn into the shame and frustration of their helplessness.

The police had responded more swiftly than anyone had expected and had arrived with a roar of engines and flashing lights, charging the atmosphere immediately with purpose and energy. Fortunately they had insisted that everybody remain in the safety of the bar, so that none of them had any idea of the drama taking place outside. However when the shouting from the police started and then noise of the shot resounded, Beth could contain herself no longer and she ran headlong out into the night. There she was met by a burly constable who stepped in her way and said, "I'm afraid that you must go back inside, Miss," and gently moved her back into the bar. All she had been able to see had been the light of powerful searchlights flooding the heath and several armed men running along the track.

"What's happening?" she cried, but the policeman had said nothing as he closed the door and stood inside, tall, wide and implacable, obviously making certain that nobody else would be able to make an attempt to get out.

She was abruptly brought out of her reverie about the dreadful events of that terrible night by Charlie, who had perhaps spotted some movement up ahead and barged past her in a futile attempt to capture whatever it was she thought she might have seen.

"Watch it, Charlie," Beth called out, but found that any irritation she felt was quickly driven out by the wonderful feeling of energy and enthusiasm that swelled up in her. So she hurriedly followed the dog along the path, all thoughts of tragedy and what might-have-been disappearing as if swept away by the keen wind that swept over her from the Atlantic. Once on the beach she was rapidly caught up in the wonderful love of life generated by the exhilaration inspired by the boundless vigour of this delightful animal. They played together in much the same way that David used to when he was trying to waste away his negative energy, and finally, when she felt she could no longer continue, she called a halt and they began their trip back along the track.

At the door of the pub she halted for a moment to regain fully her composure, tidied her hair and took a deep breath. Looking down she could see that Charlie had stuck her nose down into the crack of the door and was whimpering in excitement, her tail thrashing the air with the precision of a metronome.

"Okay, Charlie," she said. "Here goes another pint," and lifted the catch on the door.

* * *

As she stood in the porch of the pub she remembered the agony of frustration she had felt when the constable had insisted that she remain in the bar. Pacing back and forth in front of him and staring at him, she had cursed him under her breath. Finally her chance had come when two of the heavily armed police burst in, perhaps looking for a drink to ease their tension, causing the young constable to step hastily to one side as the door flew open behind him. Beth took her chance and slipped out of the open door.

"Hey, Miss!" he called out, but by then Beth had managed to see two stretchers being carried to the ambulances. As she ran towards them she heard someone call out, "No need to rush with that one, eh?" and she had almost collapsed, so great was the swell of fear and anguish that overwhelmed her. On the one the man had pointed to, a figure lay covered from its head down to its feet.

"Oh, God, no!" she cried out, but then she stopped and drew in her breath experiencing a moment when there was a total absence of feeling as, on the other stretcher she caught sight of David's face, deathly pale and wet with the rain. Then, calling out her relief, which rapidly turned to cries of concern as she noticed his mouth made red by the small bubbles that frothed out, she hurried over to him. Of course there were one or two who tried to stop her, but she shook them off and insisted noisily that they allow her to accompany him to the hospital.

The memory of the journey remained a blur, and the wait until a doctor arrived with diagnoses and explanations seemed interminable, but finally one did arrive.

He was small and thin and disconcertingly young-looking. "Are you Mr. Henderson's partner?" he asked, pushing up the spectacles that had slipped down his nose. When she nodded, her ability to speak suddenly frozen by her fear, he first of all motioned her to sit down.

Immediately her mind went into a state of panic.

They always make you sit down when they've got bad news, she thought and immediately had burst into tears.

"Don't cry, Miss. He's alright. He's not going to die. Not yet, at least," he added with a slight smile.

Of course, the sense of relief that overcame her made her cry even more, and it was only after a considerable time that the poor man was able to explain.

"Fortunately the knife avoided the spinal chord and entered the body just below the seventh cervical vertebra," the doctor said, hoping that what he was saying would mean something to the young woman.

Seeing her frown he realised that, unfortunately, it didn't.

He nervously tapped the ends of the fingers of both hands together and with guarded optimism continued, "We've put a drain into his chest." Seeing that this didn't bring about the reaction he was hoping for, he quickly thought of something more positive, "Fortunately, he didn't lose too much blood." He said with a nervous smile.

Beth looked at him and seeing his face looking at her with the same expression she had seen on David's face when he had given her a present and was hoping for a thankful response, she realised that she hadn't treated the poor man as pleasantly as she should have so she smiled at him and thanked him for all that he had done for David. Then timidly, she asked, "Will he be here long, do you think?"

The doctor shrugged his shoulders and said, "Seven to ten days, he should be out." He hesitated, and then continued with, "That is, unless there are complications."

As Beth received his answer with another flood of tears he slowly backed away and left her in the hands of a very capable, no-nonsense nurse. She expertly dealt with Beth's cuts and bruises and at the same time managed to sympathise with her concerns and console and encourage her.

"Actually," the nurse said as she gently dabbed at Beth's face, "they look worse than they are. They'll soon clear up."

Later Beth took a taxi back to the pub where she picked up Charlie and rescued the now crisp pasties from the oven in David's cottage. She then went wearily back to her own cottage where she lit some joss sticks and slid into a relaxing meditation.

"At least," as she said to Anthony a couple of days later, "that's that chapter of our lives definitely finished with."

But, she spoke too soon, for it wasn't quite over yet. Two weeks later, when David had been back from the hospital a couple of days, they had a visit from a very smartly dressed gentleman, a solicitor from London, who informed them that David had been mentioned in the will of Mrs. Taverna. She had in fact left him the bulk of her very considerable fortune.

* * *

And so, here she was, three weeks after Antonio's death, leaner and fitter than she had been for a long, long time, thanks to an energetic and very demanding little dog, and more in love than she could ever have believed possible. She pushed open the door of the pub and walked in shaking her head and pushing her fingers through her hair, made untidy by the wind.

Charlie hurled herself ahead of Beth and raced across the room to where David was lounging before a roaring fire.

Seeing his face light up as Charlie arrived in front of him and immediately sat down in the hope of receiving a small biscuit, brought a lump to Beth's throat and she again whispered her thanks for his recovery.

She strode across to David and pulled over a chair so that she was facing him.

"How long did the doc say it would be before you can manage that scree?" she asked and, before he had a chance to answer, leaned over and kissed him sensuously on the mouth. "Because I can tell you this, my darling," she said when she managed to pull herself away from his arms that had twined themselves around her neck, "you owe me big time for all this walking I've had to do." Her laughing eyes teased him. "Big time, do you understand?"

He was about to give her a placatory answer, when they both noticed Norman, Alfred and George standing behind Beth in a semi-circle.

"One, two, three, four," whispered George.

"Love and marriage, love and marriage," they sang in perfect three-part harmony,

"Go together like a horse and carriage.

This I tell you brother,

Ya can't have one without the other!"

They stood with arms around each others' shoulders, laughing good naturedly

"Oh, come off it lads," David cried. "What are you trying to do to me?"

"Make an honest lad of you, that's what," said George.

"Trying to get me to buy you each a pint, more like it," David said, lifting his eyes to the ceiling.

"I tell you what," Beth said laughing, "If you can sing the whole thing, I'll fork out for a pint for you."

Immediately there were cries of, "Now you're talking, Miss," and "Okay, you're on!"

"But," she added, interrupting the excited shouts, "you've got to let me sing the lead."

"I don't know about that," Norman said, a little petulantly, "that's my line you'll be singing. What the heck can I sing?"

"Oh, belt up, Norman," cried Alfred, "it'll be a nice change hearing it sung in tune for once. You can double up with me."

Norman swung at Alfred with his cap and missed.

"But don't sing too loud, mind," added George and everybody roared laughing.

"Right," said Beth, "off we go. After four," she waited a couple of beats and then cried, "Four!"

"Love and marriage, love and marriage," she began. Fortunately they were all sufficiently experienced to know what it was she was doing and all joined in with her perfectly.

As they arrived at the last line, 'You can't have one, you can't have none, you can't have one without the other,' Beth sat on David's knee and when they had finished, she gave him a quick, but tender kiss.

"That was terrific," he cried, "I think that that deserves a pint from me as well."

George, Alfred and even Norman roared their approval and surged to the bar. "You heard the man," shouted George. "That's six pints to come, Tom!"

But Tom was already pulling the third pint of the six.

Beth, still sitting on David's knee, pulled her head back, as if trying to bring him into focus, and with a questioning smile on her face, said, "Well?"

"Well, what?" he asked feigning ignorance.

She said nothing, but with her eyes laughing and her lips pursed, she moved her head to the right and lifted her eyebrows in an unspoken question.

He turned his head away and looked at Charlie, curled up in front of the fire

"Well, Charlie," he said, "what do you think? Should we, or shouldn't we?"

Charlie looked up and wagged her tail.

David looked into Beth's eyes, smiling at him with love and anticipation.

"Charlie seems to be in favour, so how do you think Anthony's would do for a wedding reception?" he asked.

"Fine," she said, "just fine," and kissed him.

Acknowledgments

Many thanks go to all those friends who helped with ideas, corrections, encouragement and love: Fokkina McDonnell, Jane Osborne-Fellows, Kim Bowyer, Helen McRae, Kate Coughlan, Pat Hall, Jane and Mark Gowan, Frances and Derek Elwell, Lyndsay McKenzie, Shirley Force, Marg and Geoff Sharp, Francis Clarke, Rowena Lamont and of course my dear wife Pat. Should I have missed anybody I ask forgiveness whilst claiming the ravages of senility.

My thanks also go to Les Merton at Palores Publications for his advice and generous help.

About the Author

 Although born in Manchester James now lives in Cornwall having spent many years travelling the world as a musician playing piano, organ and synthesisers. He trained as a healer with the National Federation of Spiritual Healers and now teaches and practices Reiki. He has a diploma in Past Life Regression Therapy and has uncovered memories of over thirty previous lives. He is comfortable in Italian, Russian, French and Spanish. He lives in Mount Hawke with his wife, greyhound and four small ponies.

ALSO AVAILABLE FROM PALORES

KOKOPELLI'S DREAM – by Juliana Geer

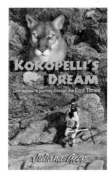

Following a powerful dream, Ana Clair embarks on a search for her destiny. On her journey she encounters books and people that take her beyond her horizon. There is her psychic friend in Cornwall, the Aztec flute player in Canada and the Very Old Man of the Mesa in Arizona. Then there are the children. Together they fulfil the prophesy of the Hopi people and realise Kokopelli's dream – the collective dream of mankind.

ISBN 978-906845-12-4

WHERE SHADOWS LIE – by Katie-Louise Merritt

The rebellious member of a loving family, Kitty feels she is somehow different and apart. As a child, she courts danger and excitement, protected always by a presence only she can sense and hear. When two men vie for her love as a young women, she takes a path that strangely follows a haunting figure from her childhood, leading to a devastating revelation.

ISBN 978-906845-04-9

EDGE OF A LONG SHADOW – by Nigel Milliner

The silence screamed out to be broken.

'Have you ever studied the shags and cormorants from the lookout . . . how they just sit there on the rocks doing damn all for most of the time? They dive around for a while looking for fish and then, when they've got what they need, they go back to the rocks and hang their wings out to dry.'

'What about it? That's the role nature designed for 'em.' Alf did not look up.

'Well, don't you think we're rather like that in Pengarth . . . We old bits of flotsam in the lee of Shag Rock? Just doing what we have to do, then sitting around drying our wings for the rest of the time until the next meal'. ISBN 978-906845-00-1

ALSO AVAILABLE FROM PALORES

TREMANYON - *A Shadow Falls* - by Carol Symons

After a fire destroys the house on the manor of Tremayne, Richard Tremayne and his family return from London to Cornwall where, on the site of the ruins on the beautiful Rhosinnis Peninsular, he undertakes the building of a Georgian Manor House, Tremanyon.

Local young woman, Ginifur Retallick. is employed as a maid for his wife Annabelle and their two young daughters. Annabelle is determined to give Richard a son but, although she has given birth to two healthy children, the third child is 'still born' - casting a 'shadow' over the peninsular.

At the request of William Pitt and Lord Falmouth, Richard sails to the New World at the beginning of the French and Indian War; during the period when the English, Irish and Scots settlers were living with the constant danger of attack and their homesteads burned to the ground.

Meanwhile, in the two years Richard is absent from Cornwall, many things are changing at Tremanyon. But 'Old Betsy', the White Witch who lives on the edge of the village, promises that the shadow will be lifted.

ISBN 978-906845-21-6

EAGLES MANOR - by Terry Barrett

Terry Barrett's novel Eagles Manor provides an insight into the football hooliganism that rampaged throughout the football leagues of the 1970s.

Revolving around four young men from different walks of South London life, who fate has drawn together by their support of a local professional football team. It describes their lives, loves, laughter and sadness.

ISBN 978-906845-17-9